"If Indiana Jones was a kindhearted, progressive Presbyterian minister banished from nineteenth-century Scotland along with his cadre of fellow disciples: the bereaved, the benevolent, the bandit, and the beautiful, you might have an inkling where *Buried Dreamer* will lead you. With imaginative and engaging characters, David Howell points to the Creator's timeless song that calls us to live into the ways of justice, purpose and place, and to never quit the courageous fight for all who have been denied their own."

—Peter Mayer

Lead guitarist of *Jimmy Buffett's Coral Reefer Band*

"A cross-cultural historical novel that crisscrosses several centuries. It's layered with Bible, theology, and plenty of intrigue. Amazingly intricate."

—Peter W. Marty

Editor/publisher of *The Christian Century*

"Whether you come for the story and stay for the inspiration or vice-versa, you will be glad you picked up this book! Engaging characters and a suspenseful plot carry the reader across centuries and oceans, and before you know it, you catch yourself thinking a bit. About war and violence. About friendship. And especially about hope. This is a book that encourages and uplifts while challenging the mind even as it satisfies the heart."

—Jana Childers

Dean, San Francisco Theological Seminary

"In this telling there is a wee thread of life and faith that runs from Scotland to North Carolina, with a detour of duty in Afghanistan. Those who carry that thread of faith and life face many 'trials and snares,' among them racism, rabid nationalism, and regressive fundamentalism. The tracing of this thread is gentle, patient, and compelling. David Howell is a master storyteller."

—Walter Brueggemann

Professor emeritus of Old Testament, Columbia Theological Seminary

"David Howell does it again! *Buried Dreamer* is a compelling, literary voyage you dare to take if you aren't afraid to experience the full-throttled dreams of a buried soldier. Through the many dangers, toils, and snares of life experiences detailed in this novel, readers will discover that although people may be buried, dreams never die. Take and read and dream."

—Luke Powery
Dean, Duke University Chapel

"With a cast of memorable characters for us to walk alongside, David Howell reminds us that when fear dresses itself up as principled violence, it becomes especially dangerous. Howell demonstrates that through time, when the spirit of love is present, hope and true faith both inspires and prevails. This historical novel is an essential book for us today when so many have turned their backs on the lessons of history and tailored their overall perspective, as well as their personal interpretation of sacred Scripture and religion, to their own needs and prejudices."

—Robert J. Wicks
Author of *The Simple Care of a Hopeful Heart: Mentoring Yourself in Difficult Times*

"*Buried Dreamer* opens with a warning, and well it should, for here is no ordinary or comfortable read. David Howell deftly takes us around the world and back again, across centuries, and into the innermost lives of a host of fascinating characters. Be warned: don't read *Buried Dreamer* if you are reluctant to enter a richly imaginative world, if you are timid about hearing some tough truth, or if you are reticent to ponder the mysterious movements of God within the lives of fascinating folk past and present."

—Will Willimon
Author of *Incorporation: A Novel*

"*Buried Dreamer* is a captivating story demonstrating the reverberated effects of divergent choices made by members of the same communities, based on their differing Christian faith interpretations. The radical faith that the main characters exude in this story is anything but neutral, but rather is rooted in social justice, compassion, and love. *Buried Dreamer* is steeped in a theology of praxis, a must-read especially for seminary students engaged in pastoral theological studies."

—Samuel Cruz

Associate professor of religion and society, Union Theological Seminary

"*Buried Dreamer* is a remarkable work of historical fiction. At once elegant, imaginative, and brutally honest, it shares a story of love, faith, and integrity that spans generations and continents in order to illuminate present day crises and opportunities. Following the adventures and commitments of two women connected by family and separated by two centuries, *Buried Dreamer* crosses ethical landmarks stretching from the Underground Railroad to crises of the present day, and will leave its indelible mark on anyone who dares read it."

—David Lose

Pastor, Mt. Olivet Lutheran Church

"*Buried Dreamer* is a testament to what life is all about: care, compassion, peace, perseverance, and generosity, which stem from love and love alone. In the middle of pain and suffering, this story will encourage you to trust the path of the journey and to continue on life's journey, trusting that love will lead you home. *Buried Dreamer* is a testament that even if the world tries to bury you or ship you across the ocean, you are never alone. Love is with you, and new life is always on the horizon."

—Takouhi Demirdjian-Petro

Minister, Grace United Church

"David has done it again: pulling off the intersection of diverse places and people and moments in time, from Scotland in 1847 to Afghanistan in 2020 to the Underground Railroad. I was hooked right away by this rollicking good story, never preachy, with vivid scenes and memorable, lovable characters (well, some of them!), with plenty of fodder to ruminate, from a historical perspective, on the troubles of our own times. Great fiction, that is entirely truth."

—James Howell
Senior pastor, Myers Park United Methodist Church

"In this book, the Reverend Charles Stuart and Samantha Logan take a treacherous and romantic voyage from Scotland to America where they join the struggle to free slaves on the Underground Railroad. Their great-granddaughter then confronts extremism in our day. But *Buried Dreamer* is more than just a good story. It takes us across centuries and continents as one family battles against some of the biggest issues of our day—prejudice, extremism, poverty, corruption. It achieves what many books fail to do—tell a tale that's both interesting and important."

—Jonathan Merritt
Author of *Learning to Speak God from Scratch: Why Sacred Words Are Vanishing and How We Can Revive Them*

"Nineteenth-century Scotland and Virginia; twenty-first century threats to democracy in America; enslavement, injustice, the Underground Railroad, freedom; adventure, terror, life, death; romance and love. The historical novel *Buried Dreamer* has it all and more. Relive a family's struggle for social justice and find inspiration for your own."

—Jacqui Lewis
Author of *Ten Strategies for Becoming a Multiracial Congregation*

BURIED DREAMER

BURIED DREAMER

A Historical Novel

DAVID BROWN HOWELL

Foreword by Michael B. Curry

RESOURCE *Publications* · Eugene, Oregon

BURIED DREAMER
A Historical Novel

Resource Publications
An Imprint of Wipf and Stock Publishers
199 W. 8th Ave., Suite 3
Eugene, OR 97401

www.wipfandstock.com

PAPERBACK ISBN: 978-1-6667-7045-2
HARDCOVER ISBN: 978-1-6667-7046-9
EBOOK ISBN: 978-1-6667-7047-6

VERSION NUMBER 030323

For my parents, Lena and Jack

For siblings, Larry and Carolyn

For cousin, Dennis

For children, Wendy, Shannon, Meredith, Morgan

For grandchildren, Zina, Aidan, Reese, Nolan, Maddox, Abby

For great granddaughter, Capri, Calia

For Mary, Nathan, Jake, John

For my favorite theologian, Mary Ann Howell

The sea is the favorite symbol for the unconscious,
the mother of all that lives.

"ARCHETYPES OF THE COLLECTIVE UNCONSCIOUS"
CARL GUSTAV JUNG

For God does speak—now one way, now another—though no one
perceives it.

> *In a dream, in a vision of the night,*
> *when deep sleep falls on people*
> *as they slumber in their beds,*
> *he may speak in their ears*
> *and terrify them with warnings,*
> *to turn them from wrongdoing*
> *and keep them from pride,*
> *to preserve them from the pit,*
> *their lives from perishing by the sword.*

Job 33:14–18 *NIV*

Contents

Foreword

"We are storytellers. Whether around a burning fire or within a large theater, we have long sought out stories and asked for more. Stories not only inform or entertain, but, if we let them, they tap into the deeper parts of our souls and psyches. Stories inspire us, challenge us, shape us. 'Tell me the old, old story,' the old gospel hymn proclaims, 'of unseen things above . . . tell me the story slowly, that I may take it in.'

The prophets of old often shared wisdom through stories. Jesus told stories, sometimes with explanations, but often just letting them impart meaning on their own. The Bible is an epic story that begins with creation's birth and concludes with 'new heavens and a new earth,' and in between takes on a long journey through God's interactions with the human family. Stories are powerful!

With the words, 'A stream of light shines through a tiny hole,' author David Howell welcomes the reader into a story of another place, another time, introduces us to fascinating characters: Sam, the modern-day soldier buried alive by the Taliban; Samantha, Sam's fearless and compassionate Scottish ancestor; Charles, the principled and down-to-earth minister whom Samantha comes to love; Brody, a young and inquisitive beggar-thief.

We quickly become fellow travelers and follow them along their various journeys, from a nineteenth-century courtroom and jail cell in Scotland to a battlefield in Afghanistan, from an old ship making the arduous trek across the Atlantic to a refugee center today. Along the way, we learn about the harsh realities of slavery and the perilous work of the Underground Railroad, and we discover ways in which our own time is influenced by what has come before.

The story begins with both terror and a dream. It ends with . . . well, you will need to learn that for yourself. For that is what stories are about, drawing us in to their realities and in the process impacting our own. So, as Jesus once told some curious would-be followers, 'Come and see' what awaits in the pages that follow. Embrace the story and perhaps discover more about your own along the way."

The Most Reverend Michael B. Curry is author of *Songs My Grandma Sang* and *Love is the Way.*

Preface

Don't read this book unless you are willing to enter the mind and dreams of a soldier buried alive by the Taliban in Afghanistan.

Dreams carry you back to 1847 in Campbeltown, Scotland. You will relive the hardships and prejudices of a people on the verge of starvation and the journeys of a banished minister, a woman who loves him, a twelve-year old thief, a pregnant teenager, and a widow-woman caught up in it all.

Don't read this book unless you are willing to experience the hardships on an overloaded three-mast sailing ship headed to Carolina and diverted by the storm of the decade.

Don't read this book unless you want to re-experience the horrors of slavery and the Underground Railroad in pre-Civil War America.

And don't read this book unless you want to know how the descendant of the minister in Scotland gets caught up in this nation's greatest crisis since World War II.

The characters in this book are fictitious and products of the author's imagination. Any similarity to real persons, living or dead, is coincidental and not intended by the author.

Acknowledgements

Kristi Anzivino

Darlene M. Davis

Janet Y. Ferrell

Dennis L. Howell

Marilyn Howell

Mary Ann Howell

Linda Cole Reid

Nine Kilometers from Kandahar Airfield, Afghanistan

February 4, 2020

A stream of light shines through a tiny hole.

"Light? Where's it coming from? Must be from the other room . . . did I leave a light on?" Sam emerges from sleep. "Is someone in the house?"

"Wait! I'm not at home! I'm in Afghanistan! What happened? I'm on my back, but this is not a bed!"

Sam squints. A hole, about the size of a #2 pencil, goes straight up about two feet through a mass of old boards and dirt. With just enough room to lift hands and bring them up to the chest, Sam pushes up but cannot move what is above. Dirt and bark fall. The tiny hole stays open. Spitting out dirt and a piece of bark, Sam thinks, "Be careful. Don't want the hole to fill in. Don't suffocate yourself!"

"Where am I?" The last thing Sam remembers the unit was on patrol. Then an explosion. Ears still ring. Hit by debris in the blast, the left leg stings.

Carefully exploring above, more dirt and bark fall.

"I'm buried alive!"

The horror sets in. Buried alive! Sam can hardly move arms and hands a few inches above the chest and feet slightly side to side. It's cold and damp. Thirsty, Sam wonders "will I ever drink again?"

Surely, another patrol looks for them, but how will they know where to look? Did the Taliban leave any signs of the burial pit? Or did they conceal it? What happened to the other soldiers Danny, Sanchez, and Julio? Are they buried alive too or killed in the blast? So many questions flowing through Sam's mind but no way to find answers. Frightening!

Think. That's all Sam can do. Think! Ask questions no one will hear. A maddening helplessness!

Hours go by with the dirt so cold. Sam senses it must be dark outside now. A gnawing itch in the middle of the back, is it an insect? A spider? Oh God, what if this burial pit attracts spiders and insects? Scorpions? Snakes? Deadly carpet-vipers slither around in this barren land, and they love to burrow underground. Never growing much more than two feet, they can maneuver into most any underground area. Their venom brings internal bleeding and most of the time death. Camel spiders can be as much as eight inches long! Their venom not deadly, they use their digestive fluids to liquefy their victim's flesh for days of consumption. Red ants! Sam saw masses of them on corpses in the desert. And deathstalker-scorpions! "Stop it! Got to quit thinking about it! Use training and focus on . . . damn it, on what?" There is nothing Sam can do. But wait and hope.

Sam remembers a breathing technique taught while on assignment with several Navy Seals. They called it Box Breathing. Inhale counting to four. Hold breath. Count again to four. Exhale counting to four and inhale again. Sam does it over and over until slipping into deep sleep.

Light again shines through the tiny hole, day again. Lips are parched and cracked. Mouth feels like sandpaper. Sam must urinate but holds back because of what will happen, bottom side wet and even colder. Not able to hold it longer, relief . . . urine warm as it flows out to the lower thighs and under Sam's butt. But in moments, the spreading liquid turns cold. "Oh God, this is awful."

Wondering how long it'll take to die, Sam remembers about three days without water, but in this hot, arid climate, maybe only hours left. But at least it's February, not the unbearable Afghan summer. Without water and hardly able to move for over twenty-four hours, agony upon agony. A dull throb suggests the brain is dehydrating. Skin dries by the minute. Sam won't have to worry about going to the bathroom again. Kidneys and digestive system shutting down. Joints ache.

How long before the confusion and hallucinations begin? Sam wants to cry but can't make tears.

Eyes open. Dark again. "How long have I been asleep?" Voices! Voices above! Sam pushes air out and screams "Help!" The scream falls back into the grave. Sam's body shakes to make noise. Will they hear? Will they see the tiny hole in the ground? Soon exhausted with the shaking of feet and hands and the screams for help, sleep comes.

Hours pass. Eyes try to open. Without moisture in the eye sockets, eyelids are stuck together. Pulling hands up between the chest and the earth above, Sam's pulls eyelids apart. Light comes through the hole again. Voices earlier! But not now. Waves of sadness sweep through the brain and body. Were there really voices or was the brain playing tricks? Dehydration does that, Sam knows. How much longer will the ability to distinguish reality last? How long before madness? Body temperature soars. "If I could only sweat, I could lick it off my upper lip."

A hand touches something to the right. What is it? It's not a rock, but smooth and round. My God! It's a canteen! Sam pulls and shakes it. It's empty! The Taliban play a cruel trick.

Eyes shut again. Sam wonders how will they remember this disappeared soldier back home? Mother's heart will break. She cried when Sam joined Army Intelligence. Brother and sister will be fine with their very busy lives.

The Tidal Times, the local newspaper in Kilmarnock, Virginia, publishes something like this, Sam thinks: *Missing in Afghanistan and presumed dead. Born in Kilmarnock, Virginia, graduated from Lancaster High School and graduated from the University of Virginia with a Ph.D. in psychology before joining the Army. Captain Stuart leaves behind a mother, one brother and one sister.*

Without spouse or children, life seems so empty. "What would my Stuart ancestors who accomplished so much and helped so many people on two continents think of my pitiful life?" Captain Stuart tries to cry, trembles, and eventually falls into dreamy sleep.

Dreams from a Burial Pit of Campbeltown, Scotland

July 1, 1849

Ten-year-old Brody McCoy lost both parents in a house fire. A neighbor pulled him to safety, but he listened to his parents' dying screams that cold windy night in Campbeltown. Brody's family descended from a long line of working-class peasants. After the fire, no one takes in Brody. Brody, with curly blonde hair that falls on his shoulder in ringlets, ocean-blue eyes, and dressed in his only clothes, loose fitting, torn, dirty, spends his days begging on the streets, usually at the corner of St. Andrew's Street and Killian Road.

Scotland's great potato famine started in 1848. Returning Spanish explorers brought "patatas" to Europe from the New World (South America) starting in 1588. By 1600, potato plants dotted fields across Europe, including Ireland and Scotland. Potatoes were viewed suspiciously at first as products of "heathen Indians" with some people thinking the potatoes might be the product of witches or devils. Slowly, working class people became very dependent on the easily grown crop. The potato blight swept across Europe in the mid-1840s, which became known as "The Hungry Forties." One fourth of Ireland's population died of hunger. Scotland, especially The Highlands, hit almost as hard.

Many of the inhabitants of Campbeltown are close to being beggars themselves. Times are hard and food scarce. Local dairy products kept people alive. Milk, cheese, and eggs are still available but expensive. Strangely one day, Brody has eggs for sale at the corner of St. Andrews and Killian streets.

At the same time, Graham McAlister's hens quit laying, or so he first thought. Suspecting young Brody might have dirty hands, Graham sleeps in his hen barn. About 4:00 a.m., the barn door creaks open, and Brody creeps in. He lights a candle causing some chickens to squawk. Brody shoos a sitting hen off her nest. As he grabs an egg to put into the side bag hanging from his shoulder, Mr. McAlister springs from behind some old barrels. Brody almost jumps out of his skin, drops an egg splattering on the dirt floor, and bolts for the door. Bryan, Mr. McAlister's son, laying behind an old feeding trough, leaps out, and grabs Brody. "Caught! You lil' thief!" Mr. McAlister barks as he points to a wild turkey cage, "Ye'll stay in there 'til morn when we'll take you to da sheriff!" They tie Brody's hands behind his back and squeeze him into the cage made from gnarled juniper branches.

At first light, the McAlisters open the cage and slip a rough seaman's rope around Brody's neck and yank him forward. Pulling Brody down the street, Mr. McAlister stumbles on the uneven cobblestone street and curses, "Lil thief, see what you caused!"

None too pleased at the early hour and in his soiled nightshirt, Sheriff McKendree opens his door after loud knocks by Mr. McAlister. "Ye can't wait til I've had me breakfast?"

"He steals me eggs!" Mr. McAlister declares as he pulls little Brody down on to the planks of the sheriff's porch. Brody cries out as his shoulder and head thud on the hard surface.

Rubbing his eyes, Sheriff McKendree snorts, "Meets me at the jailhouse. The judge is here today. We'll try the lil' thief. But first I'll eat me porridge."

A one room converted feed storage shed serves as a jailhouse with crude bars nailed over one tiny window. A man accused of not paying his taxes and two haggard men accused of raping a young schoolteacher already occupy the cell. The night before screams were heard from the cell. Fortunately for Brody they are escorted out by four armed guards to the courthouse down the street. God-only-knows what those dark, nasty men might have done to young Brody, for they knew this was their last day on earth.

A wavy ocean of heads fill the courtroom in Campbeltown for the afternoon session. The abandoned sanctuary of the United Secession Church serves as the courthouse. Word spread quickly that Brody the Beggar would be on trial. Young Brody can barely walk when he enters the courtroom in heavy, adult shackles. Many in the courtroom gallery boo. A single wooden chair sits in front of the judge. Taking that seat in front of Judge Archibald Ainsley, a tear runs down Brody's right cheek. Judge Ainsley, often weary from traveling his wide circuit of courtrooms spread throughout Scotland, is famously called "Sleepy Ainsley." He once slept through most of his court's testimony, woke at the end, and sentenced a man who was probably innocent to hang.

Judge Ainsley functions as the prosecuting solicitor, the jury, and the sentencing judge. Sometimes, he only makes it to Campbeltown once a month where there are brief testimonies from witnesses and swift judgments. He wears the traditional court dress of black gown and white wig. His small wire rimmed glasses sit on the end of his nose. Some say he has not smiled in forty years. His dark eyes glare down at Brody with judicial contempt.

"You were caught stealing a good man's eggs. What do ye say for yerself?"

"Ther' God's eggs. God sends thems eggs for all of us to eat, not just him and his kin!" Brody snaps.

"Is that yer only defense?" Judge Ainsley asks.

"I don't need no-other, what you call a defense, you grumpy ole sod!" Brody shouts.

"Young man, you're not helping yerself!" the judge declares. "Laddie, I advise you to shut your geggie!"

"Hang all thieves!" a man shouts from the gallery.

"He's just a wee lad," a woman screams.

A chorus from the gallery chants, "Hang all thieves!" "Hang all thieves!" "Hang all thieves!"

"Silence!" the judge demands.

"Is anyone here to speak for this young urchin?" the judge queries.

"I am," a strong voice declares.

A Controversial Minister in Campbeltown, Scotland

July 1, 1849

Along with six-thousand other Scots, Charles Bruce Stuart fought with the British at the Battle of Waterloo in 1815. C.B. Stuart meets a nurse in Edinburgh while he recovers from wounds. Mary Ann came from fisherfolk on the Isle of Iona. In Edinburgh, she learns to be a "healer." She treats C.B. Stuart's wounds in Edinburgh Royal Infirmary. They marry and farm in Campbeltown, Scotland. Charles Rory Stuart's parents conversed with him in both the local Scot-English dialect and in Gaelic. He was bilingual almost from birth.

Charles R. Stuart read avidly as a child. As a young teenager, he consumed John Knox's *History of the Reformation.* Locals said he was "born to be a clergyman." He read David Hume and Adam Smith, Scots who were major figures in the Enlightenment. Villagers were stunned when they saw the young Charles reading Immanuel Kant and Jean-Jacques Rousseau. A local church pastor recommended Charles to Aberdeen University. A fast study, Charles completes his theological education at the age of nineteen.

Campbeltown Kirk ordains Charles Rory Stuart as their pastor in June of 1847. His ordination uneventful but his ministry will be quite different. In Argyll county, Campbeltown has a legion of small churches, some belonging to the Church of Scotland denomination, some to the Reformed Presbyterian Church, and others to various competing denominations. At the time so many denominations and churches come and go in Scotland that Jesus probably had difficulty keeping up with them.

Campbeltown Kirk wrought with controversy, half the membership broke away to form the Argyllshire Free Church. Young pastor Stuart has his work cut out for him for the congregation is in dire need of healing. Competing Scottish clans and their rivalries always simmer in the congregation.

Unappreciated Good Deeds in Campbeltown

July 1, 1849

"What's yer name?" Judge Ainsley demands.

"Reverend Charles Stuart."

"Ye know this lad?"

"I do. May I address ye court, ye honor?"

"Ye may but make it brief and to the point. I must get back to my wife's birthday party in Glasgow this evening."

Reverend Stuart quickly says, "This lad had great misfortune. His parents and sister died in a house fire only months ago. He heard their screams. He has no home. He sleeps in a barn. Look at his tattered clothes. He escaped the fire in only his nightshirt. The clothes he has on were off a beggarman who fell dead in the street. He's never been in trouble before. He deserves another chance . . . "

"Hang all thieves!" comes from the gallery.

"Silence in me court!" Judge Ainsley declares, and then adds as he glares at the reverend, "We don't needs any more thieves in this county. What's you want me to do? Just turn him loose?"

"Your honor," Reverend Stuart carefully and slowly says, "God forbids us to hang a ten-year-old child. Our jails are full. He can stay with Mrs. Connery. She's here today. Leaves more room in the jail."

Judge Ainsley scours the courtroom from left to right. Slowly, Mrs. Connery cautiously raises her right hand until it is just below her ear.

"Mrs. Connery, ye willing to house this young thief?" Ainsley queries.

"I wills. Have lots of room now that the children are grown and married off, and me husband dead," Mrs. Connery drops her head in sadness with those last words.

Judge Ainsley turns his stare and dark beady eyes back on Reverend Stuart, "All right, Reverend, let the court record show that Reverend Stuart . . ." Ainsley pauses realizing he does not know the reverend's full name. "Reverend, state yer full name for this court."

"Reverend Charles Rory Stuart, ye honor."

Judge Ainsley continues, "Let the court records show that Reverend Charles Rory Stuart assumes full responsibility and will receive punishment should this lad steal again or transgress upon any of the laws of this county or of the Crown."

Pausing and glaring at the reverend, the judge wants to make sure the reverend understands the weight and possible consequences of what he has now pledged to do.

Judge Ainsley looks for something on his raised desk which is the church communion table raised up by four pieces of wood under each corner and turned backwards so that "In Remembrance of Me" is turned away from the gallery. He looks for the boy's name.

Finding a small piece of paper with the words "Brody McCoy, thief, steals eggs" written by the sheriff, he declares in a loud voice, "Brody McCoy, you're a fortunate young man! Ye could be hanging by yer neck. Ye will now reside with Mrs. Connery under the supervision of Reverend Stuart. Thar'll be dire consequences for all should ye come before me again! All of ye, do ye understand?"

They nod.

"Mind how you go," the judge warns.

"What a pair! A little thief and a widower woman!" the same heckler cracks from the gallery.

"Sheriff! Remove that man from me courtroom and let him spend a few hours in yer jail!" Judge Ainsley roars.

"Next case!" the judge declares as he motions Reverend Stuart and Mrs. Connery out of the courtroom.

Outside the sanctuary turned courtroom, Reverend Stuart and Mrs. Connery wait for Brody, who is still in the custody of a deputy, to emerge through the main double doors. Minutes pass, and Reverend Stuart says, "I'll check the side door and the back door."

In a few moments, Reverend Stuart and Brody round the corner of the building. Mrs. Connery with a twinkle in her eye says, "Come laddie, I'll show ye yer room. Me thinks ye'll likes it."

Reverend Stuart walks behind them as they quietly stroll down the dusty main street. Brody eyes fresh baked bread in the window of the town bakery. Fresh out of the wood oven, the powerful aroma turns all their heads. Brody's nostrils flare as he inhales the sweet aroma of the crusty loaf.

Seeing the lad's interest, Reverend Stuart says, "Ye wait here, just a minute." He takes even strides and bounds over the one step onto the porch.

The baker is a big, round man with fingers as large as a small child's wrist. Reverend thinks the massive man probably consumes much of what he bakes. Pointing at the bread in the window, he asks, "How much the loaf?"

"Two pence," the burly baker states.

Reverend Stuart raises his eyebrows in astonishment. It's almost as much as his parish pays him for a week.

"How about half-loaf?" Reverend inquires.

"Don't sell half-loaves," the baker firmly replies. "But I do haves a loaf baked last week. Tis still good. Just a harder crust. Ye can haves it for one pence."

Reverend Stuart having ballooned the hopes of young Brody says, "Okay." Digs into his pockets, and then he adds with a big warm grin, "I'll expect ye in Campbeltown Church on Sunday morn with you putting ten percent of this into the offering plate."

"Churches are fer old womens and children, Reverend. I haves too much work to do anyway. Peoples are starving with this potato blight," the baker explains with his hands extended to his sides in a helpless motion.

'How can poor and starving people afford the price of his bread?' Reverend Stuart wonders.

"Well, I hope you can join us some Sunday morn. Be good for your soul. You bake wonderful bread. We offer the Bread of Life," the reverend offers as he turns back into the street, hopping off the small porch.

Mrs. Connery's modest house sits at the corner of Royce and Balfour Streets. Ivy adorns the stone walls, revealing the house's ancient age. The thatched roof needs repair.

"Mrs. Connery, I'll bring a couple of the older lads from the Kirk and repairs the roof before the next rain. It's the least we can do for your kindness and hospitality," Reverend Stuart promises.

"Yer so kind, reverend. Been hard to gets things done since Mr. Connery died," she says as her face droops with sadness.

"Brody, you mind Mrs. Connery and do exactly what she says," the reverend explains. "I'll be round in day or so to checks on things."

Brody shakes his head up and down enthusiastically.

"Could I have a word, Mrs. Connery?" Reverend Stuart asks.

"Mrs. Connery, I have some extra money for you since you have an extra mouth to feed. Some at the Kirk will want to help," Reverend Stuart adds. "Do let me know if you need anything."

Reverend Stuart lives in a house about twenty yards behind Campbeltown Kirk. His primitive straw bed is barely comfortable. The small fireplace keeps him warm although the chimney draws poorly in damp weather, and smoke burns his eyes. A cast iron pot serves as both his only cooking utensil and his only bowl. A rustic iron bar holds the pot by a wire and swings from inside the fireplace for easy access outside the fireplace.

Early the next morning, a loud banging wakes Reverend Stuart. He lifts the wooden latch, and the ill-fitting door squeaks open.

"Reverend Stuart, we losts another good man last night. Mrs. Turner could not stir William this morning. He's cold to the touch, she says. The Barclay boys digging his grave now. Can ye be at the cemetery this afternoon? Mrs. Turner wants to know."

Keltz, the messenger, sleeps in a backroom of the Kirk. Members share table scraps with him as they can. An orphan from birth, the middle-aged Keltz wanders the streets of Campbeltown with his head tilted to one side until it almost touches his shoulder. Children and rude adults laugh at him, but he has been like this since birth. He adopted Campbeltown Kirk as his emotional and physical home. Very protective of the church building, the members, and the pastor, along with huge efforts of patience from Reverend Stuart, Keltz often receives kind glances from the pastor and church members, although they often felt annoyance with the Kirk's self-appointed guardian.

"Thank you, Keltz, I'll make my way to Mrs. Turner's very shortly," Reverend Stuart says as he feels a rush of warmth for this kind and damaged child of God.

"We love you Reverend," Keltz offers as he backs out the door.

"You're a wonderful and caring man," Reverend Stuart says.

Reverend Stuart reads scripture and prayers for the gathered grievers at the afternoon service. Bright sunshine warms the backs of family and friends gathered around the grave. Burlap sacks cut open and unfolded like large towels wrap around the cold body of William Turner. Tears roll down Mrs. Turner's flushed cheeks as Reverend Stuart closes with the benediction. Closing the Bible as it is the closing of the life of William Turner, Reverend Stuart steps toward Mrs. Turner and embraces her. Not to be outdone, Keltz next offers his body of hugging warmth. Mrs. Turner embraces him with as much deep appreciation as she did for Reverend Stuart.

Kandahar, Afghanistan

February 5, 2020

Still in a grave in Afghanistan and soon to die, Sam wakes from a dreamy sleep. "Wow, dreaming about my ancestors. Is that what happens as we die?" Weak and even more exhausted, Sam falls back into deep sleep.

Trouble Brews at the Tavern

August 13, 1849

Reverend Stuart walks down St. Andrews Street that evening, turns right on Bright Street, and steps into Logan's Tavern. Like a faithful puppy but out of sight, Keltz has followed Reverend Stuart to the pub but does not enter. He'll wait outside and follow the reverend home. He is often Reverend Stuart's shadow.

Logan's Tavern, a frequent destination for the reverend, is frequented by most of the men of Campbeltown, those who have extra currency. Reverend Stuart pulls out a rugged stool and sits at the bar that is two simple rows of roughhewn two x twelve's sitting on stacks of empty grog kegs.

"Your usual pint?" asks Myles Logan, the owner.

"Yeh," the reverend replies, a busy, long day behind him, burying the dead.

"Saved a leg for ya, reverend," Myles proudly shares.

"Ye knows me fav," the reverend answers with lifted eyebrows.

Moist bubbles of grog ease the dryness in the reverend's mouth and cool his throat. Each sip brings him deeper pleasure.

Myles' sister pushes through the black drape that hangs over the door opening that separates the tiny kitchen from the dining area. Samantha's wavy red hair bounces as she takes each step. Her eyes are stunning blue like a Highland sky in the spring. Her peasant blouse accentuates the fullness of her breasts. Their eyes meet and quickly glance away.

"Saved the last leg for ye, reverend. We looks after our regulars," she says and wants to wink but holds herself back. Samantha loves Reverend Stuart's voice, just deep enough, smooth, and strong like the wind before a storm.

"I appreciate your kindness, Samantha," Reverend Stuart answers with only half the smile he wants to have.

"Too bad 'bout Mr. Turner," Samantha says.

"Too many funerals," the reverend says. "It's sad. Hard times taking a toll on the people. Suspect I stand over a grave most every two or three days now. The grave diggers and the pastors are the busiest people round now."

"Give the reverend his dinner!" Myles snaps at his baby sister.

Samantha jolts as she realizes she has been standing there holding the reverend's dinner. The pewter plate clanks on the board. The goose leg is golden brown with a few burned marks. On the side sits three large roasted carrots and a warm piece of bread with a slab of fresh butter on top.

"I feel guilty with this fine food whilst so many go to bed hungry, but I only eat bread in the morning to get me through the day, and in the evening, something cooked in my pot or a fine meal here."

"You'll always have a free meal here reverend. Ye do such important work," Samantha says. "Cuppa?"

"Samantha gets back in the kitchen! One more meal to ready," Myles says with a tint of harshness.

Samantha spins instantly, her long red locks lifting off her back and nearly brushes through the reverend's face.

Reverend Stuart loves the food at Logan's Tavern but not as much as he likes Samantha. He feels a warm glow in his chest when she is near.

The reverend's compassion for peasants creates even more trouble. Bernie McDonald, the town "smithy," is well known in the area for discovering the cave where Bonnie Prince Charlie hid on the island of Skye. The British army destroyed the Scottish army at the Battle of Culloden in 1746. Surviving Scottish rebels were hunted down and executed. Bernie's grandfather aided the prince and hid him in the cave. In later years, the location of the cave was unknown except to Bernie, Bernie's father, and grandfather. A group of Scottish historians convinced Bernie to lead them to the cave. A pilgrimage to Prince Charlie's cave is a sacred ritual for many of the descendants of these Scottish heroes slain during and after the Battle of Culloden.

Bernie and Prunella McDonald's sixteen-year-old daughter Myra is pregnant and unmarried. Myra will not tell anyone who the father is, but most suspect Jimmie Joyce who was seen talking to Myra on several occasions. While Myra has a baby growing inside of her, Bernie and Prunella now carry a burden of shame. Neighbors, including some members of Campbeltown Kirk, encourage the McDonalds to banish the sinful young woman to a colony on the Isle of Iona. Thieves, whores, adulterers, and unmarried pregnant women are banished to the colony. Scarce food cause many to die of hunger and disease.

Horses need shoes for early plowing, making spring a busy time for any smithy. Bernie pauses his work when Reverend Stuart pays a visit. After opening pleasantries, Reverend Stuart passionately argues for the McDonalds to show mercy and not give up on their daughter. Reluctantly they agree but face the scorn of some righteous neighbors and church members. Two families leave Campbeltown Kirk saying that Reverend Stuart supports fornication and sinful behavior.

Some of Reverend Stuart's sermons generate controversary as well. He preaches that Christians are to love one another and their enemies, even the Brits. Families who have struggled against the domination of England for generations, with family members giving their lives in clashes with British troops, disagree. Some church members complain. Glasgow Presbytery, the regional governing body for Presbyterian churches, authorizes a council to review Reverend Stuart.

The Skinny Preacher

August 28, 1849

Brewing storms fill the morning sky as Reverend Stuart enters St Giles Kirk. The council of Glasgow Presbytery is comprised of six clergy and six lay people. Half clergy and half lay people make it more difficult to complain that it is clergy dominated. The convener, Reverend Thomas McGrath, is known as the "Skinny Preacher." The pastor of Gloucester Kirk stands at least six feet and five inches tall but weighs only one hundred and thirty pounds. He always stands stiff as a board like he has a rod up his back.

The Skinny Preacher is granted the authority to appoint one additional clergy to be the "Questioner." The Questioner leads the reviewing and questioning of the "Examined." Reverend Stuart takes a deep breath when he sees his soon to be questioner. Hoping it would not be Dr. Leith, Reverend Stuart has an immediate wave of dread sweep over him. Dr. Augustus Leith licks his theological chops. Dr. Leith is nearly seventy and has for over forty years been the protector of the orthodox faith in Glasgow Presbytery. Several young candidates for ministry crumbled under his harsh questioning and abandoned their "calls." Leith, asthmatic and wheezing every few minutes, must draw a deep breath for his next utterance. Leith, a Dutch Calvinist, champions innate human depravity and the stain of original sin while the Skinny Preacher's views are less harsh and rigid.

"Let this meeting come to order," the Skinny Preacher declares, standing erect as a giraffe.

"Fine men of faith, we gather here to re-examine Reverend Charles Rory Stuart as to his theological and moral fitness for ministry. Reverend Stuart was ordained two years ago and began his ministry at Campbeltown

Kirk. Twenty members of the Kirk have signed a petition of complaint. The charges read:

A. Morals not becoming a pastor

B. Involvement in judicial and community affairs outside his parish duties

C. Holding theological positions contrary to our Westminster Confession of Faith and Book of Discipline.

I've asked Dr. Augustus Leith to be the Questioner. He will begin the questioning, and then each of ye will be allowed one question and a follow-up question. We will then vote on his fitness for ministry. Dr. Leith, please begin."

"Thank ye, Reverend McGrath. It is a sad day when we must examine one of our pastors. But it is essential. The required twenty brave souls signed the petition. Our thanks to them for their desire to preserve the purity of our faith." Standing and turning a sharp eye to Reverend Stuart sitting at the other end of the long table, Dr. Leith continues, "I will first examine the defendant on theological issues. That's because weak theological positions lead to immorality and heathenism."

"Reverend Stuart, do ye believe in the inerrancy and infallibility of the Holy Bible?" Dr. Leith asks as he leans his head back so he can glare down more intently upon Reverend Stuart.

Reverend Stuart's plans to share as little of his theological positions and musings as possible. He says, "Aye."

"What about the Catholic Bible which includes the Apocrypha? Do you condemn the papists for this heresy?" asks Dr. Leith, trying to put Reverend Stuart into a theological corner.

"I don't condemn anyone. Only God Almighty can do that," Reverend Stuart responds. Dr. Leith has a look of concern on his face, but Reverend Stuart quickly continues. "The Catholic Church approved the inclusion of I Maccabees and II Maccabees. I respect their doctrinal decision, although I have never preached from any of those books."

Looking not completely pleased, Dr. Leith continues, "So, if ye believe in the inerrancy and infallibility of the Holy Scriptures, why did ye say in a sermon in our Campbeltown Kirk that, 'God's love is for everyone even the heathen savages of Africa?' We know God's salvation and love is promised only to those professing faith in Jesus Christ as Lord and Savior," Dr. Leith's voice gets louder and harsher.

"I don't recall saying 'heathen savages' . . . that is your phrase. I believe the people of Africa and the people of Asia are God's people too," Reverend Stuart calmly responds.

"But they haven't professed faith!" Dr. Leith declares and then leans forward, intently this time.

"The people of Africa and Asia and other parts of the world where Christ has not been proclaimed will be in the hands of God, and I believe God is kind and merciful," Reverend Stuart confidently adds.

"They're not Christian and doomed to Hell!" Dr. Leith roars as he slams his fist on the table.

"How about the Devil, Reverend Stuart? Do you think the Devil exists?" Dr. Leith demands.

"Seems to me there is plenty of evil in the world, but I don't adhere to the dualism like Plato and Aristotle suggested that often creeps into Christian thought. There is but one Sovereign God and not a devil-god that the Sovereign God has to compete against," Reverend Stuart explains.

"So where does this evil come from that's in our world?" Dr. Leith fires back.

"I would be famous if I had the definitive answer to all your questions, but where does evil come from? I think we're all created with freedom for good and evil. People sometimes choose evil over good, and maybe that's because of insecurity, or a life of poverty, or lack of parental guidance, or maybe greed from insecurity," Reverend Stuart carefully explains.

"Ye are a very naive man, but let's move along." Dr. Leith says with a hint of impatience. And adds, "I'm glad ye not my pastor."

"Well, there's at least one thing you can't accuse me of," Reverend Stuart shoots back with a warm glance.

Annoyed by the interruption, but curious, Dr. Leith asks, "What's that?"

"Devil worship," Reverend Stuart says with his lips curved upward. "If I don't believe in it, I can't worship the scoundrel."

Several council members around the table fight to hold back grins. Mr. Mc-Beth holds back a chuckle. Council members are slowly finding Reverend Stuart more likable than the gruff, rigid Dr. Leith.

"What about blood salvation by the sacrificial death of Jesus? Do ye believe Jesus' death on the cross satisfied God's anger over our sin and restores us into a right relation with God?" Dr. Leith asks.

"I'm aware that in ancient religions throughout the Middle East that God was viewed as resentful, angry, and unforgiving. They believed that a sacrifice must be offered to appease the anger of God. But I don't believe the Christian God is that childish and holds a grudge against humans." Reverend Stuart calmly lays out his theological positions.

"So, Jesus didn't die for our sins?" Dr Leith demands.

"I don't believe God killed Jesus," Reverend Stuart responds as several council members turn and look at each other, their faces saying, "the courage this young man exhibits in challenging the formidable Dr. Leith."

"Well," Dr Leith says and then pauses shortly to follow-up with, "That leads me to my next question. Is Jesus the only path to God?"

"That's God's decision, it seems to me. I can't imagine though, that God is so petty that God made the Christian faith only available in the western world and the only path to the eternal," Reverend Stuart answers. He then adds, "I don't know for sure, of course, but I hope God's kingdom is big enough and broad enough, like a big tent, embracing all people," Reverend Stuart explains.

"Ye flirting with heresy and blasphemy, Reverend Stuart and puts me in a state of vexation!" Dr. Leith warns, "but let's go on."

"Predestination. Are we predestined? Are some people predestined to hell and some to heaven?" Dr. Leith asks.

"Sounds like ye are predestined to ask me the most difficult theological questions for sure, Dr. Leith," Reverend Stuart jokes.

Dr. Leith tries to force a warm expression. All the council members grin, with several chuckling.

"Dr. Leith, I have blue eyes and didn't have any choice in that. So, some things ye could say, are predestined. I think I've made it clear that people have freedom to make their own choices about many things. I find it hard to believe that a loving God, and the Christian God is a loving God, would in advance decide the eternal fate of some people randomly or in any other manner," Reverend Stuart lays out.

"The final question regarding theology: Do you believe in the Trinity?" Dr. Leith asks.

"I'll answer the question in three parts." But before Reverend Stuart could continue, Dr. Leith said, "Let's be serious here. Your future in ministry is at stake."

"Well, we have and do experience God in three ways, Creator, Redeemer, and Sustainer. However, there is only one minor reference in the Bible to the Trinity in 2 Corinthian 13. In the fourth century at the Council of Chalcedon, when the church sought to put the Christian faith into written doctrine, there were three competing factions when writing the Doctrine of God. One group of theologians insisted on God as Creator. The Gnostic faction wanted to express God as Spirit, and another group insisted on Jesus as God. That group argued that Jesus was of the same substance or essence, homosousion in Greek, as God. So, they contended we could simply worship Jesus. In the end, the theologians hammered out a compromise: The Trinity." Reverend Stuart impresses the council with his answers, but Dr. Leith looks unsatisfied.

Dr. Leith continues, "There are rumors you want women to serve on Campbeltown Kirk's council?"

"We have some very capable women in our Kirk," Reverend Stuart says.

"Hmm," Dr. Leith moans.

Dr. Leith shifts the questioning slightly. "This is not in the petition presented by the twenty members of Campbeltown Kirk; however, there is a rumor that ye spent time with Celts and dreaded Druids, maybe even witches!" A slight gasp escapes the mouth of Colum McCarthy, the oldest member of the council.

A ripple of anxiety sweeps through Reverend Stuart. This was a serious charge. It had been years since anyone was burned at the stake for witchcraft or association with witchcraft, but superstitions abounded in the rural areas.

"There are no Druids on the mainland now," Reverend Stuart calmly states as he holds his anxiety at bay. "There might be some small sects on the Isle of Man, but I've never been there. But yes, I have some friends who are Celts. I met them at the University of Edinburgh. They're wonderful people and very God loving. They are the opposite of atheists. On the contrary, they believe God is everywhere, immanent or omnipresent as we like to say in theology. Because of that belief, they have deep respect for all people, the earth, the sea, and all creatures, since all are God-filled."

"Well, that's interesting," Dr Leith states with raised eyebrows. "Do ye dance around their fires with them?"

"A couple of times when visiting Celtic friends in the Highlands," Reverend Stuart matter-of-factly states. "But it was all just fun, just dancing, not Devil worshipping, as some assert."

Dr. Leith shifts the questioning again. "Your good friend, Jamie Ross, the luthier, tis he a Celt?"

"He comes from a Celtic family. He doesn't say he is a Celt. Jamie is searching right now. His parents' deaths were so devastating. He's in deep grief," Reverend Stuart quickly answers. "He's hurting. He has no other family. He's very talented musically, so I am glad he has that. I'll always be his friend, and he'll get through this."

"Ye lead a colorful life, Reverend Stuart," Dr. Leith interjects. "Ye have also been seen drinking a grog in Logan's Tavern. Do you get drunk?"

"Never been drunk," Reverend Stuart says. "I do enjoy an occasional grog or mulled wine on a cold winter's night."

It was just a coincidence but not missed by anyone when Reverend Skinny, using his moderator power states, "Let's take a break. If ye need a bit to eat, the food barrows park under the trees just across from the church. Let's come back together in an hour."

Council members file out followed by Reverend Stuart, the Skinny Preacher, and Dr. Leith. Going out the front door, the group fans out. Three council members sit down on the front steps, chat, and soak up the midday sun. The others gather around the barrows, two-wheeled carts pushed around the city streets by food vendors. Apples, nuts, and breads fill the wood-sided carts.

Reverend Stuart purchases an apple and some pieces of dried fruit. He eyes Dr. Leith, crunching on an apple, strolling back toward the church. Taking longer strides, he quickly catches up.

"You've been asking me some great questions. Feels like theology class again and a good review," Reverend says.

Surprised, Dr. Leith turns, pulls his head back, trying to focus his eyes. Stuttering slightly, he blurts out, "Yes, of course, yes, I mean, this is important. We just want to make sure ye still hold the convictions of the Reformed Faith and the Calvinist tradition."

"Of course," Reverend Stuart responds, "You are doing a fine job, the job the Presbytery asked you to do."

They start up the church steps, and Dr. Leith responds, "Be careful ye don't get too far beyond our doctrines and confessions. It could get ugly, and always sad to see a pastor stripped of his ordination and lose his church. Can be truly tragic."

"Indeed, that would be painful for all. I will do my best to avoid that," Reverend Stuart warmly offers.

Back in the conference room, all the members take their seats. All except Colum McCarthy.

"Where's Colum?" William Burns wonders.

"I know he's upset," Josh McClure says.

"Well, that's unfortunate," Skinny Preacher says, "but we must continue. Some of ye have quite a distance to travel."

He nods to Dr. Leith.

Dr. Leith stands just as Colum McCarthy steps through the open door.

"Me apologies for the lateness," Colum says and grimaces as he lowers his arthritic ridden body into his seat.

"Could I speak?" Colum asks.

The Skinny Preacher and Dr. Leith look at each other each hoping the other would speak.

"Go ahead, Colum," Skinny Preacher says.

"This man," pointing at Reverend Stuart with the index finger of his gnarled hand, "tis a simple servant of God. He helps lots of people. My brother, a member of Campbeltown Kirk, says Reverend Stuart helps children and widows, collecting food for them. He goes to court for a young boy, Brody, and saved the wee lad from the gallows. The Reverend studied and thought about religion a lot for his young age. Maybe some of his thinking is new to us, but he has a pastor's heart." A tear rolls down Colum's face.

"I'm long-in-the tooth, eighty-two, and me days are numbered. I figure I've earned my right to say a few things. Thank ye."

Around the table, heads shake in agreement. A rumbling in the mountain of resolve around Dr. Leith causes him to pause. Still, he was determined to get in one more question. "What about the redhead? Let's see . . ." Dr. Leith searches his notes. "At Logan's Tavern, reports are ye are spending time with her?"

"Samantha is her name," Reverend Stuart tries to cautiously state, putting the responsibility of the dialog back on Dr. Leith.

"Rumors of sin!" Dr. Leith blasts loudly, causing members around the table to open eyes wider while some jaws dropped. "And she uses laudanum! Opium!"

"Rumors? Rumors only? No facts, Dr. Leith?" a member asks.

"Well, reliable reports, I can say," Dr. Leith responds as a frown takes control of his face.

"Can ye share the source of these reliable reports?" Colum McCarthy asks.

Before Dr. Leith can respond, John Stafford speaks, "Ye first said rumors, Dr. Leith, and now ye sayin' reliable reports. Which is it?"

"Men of the ministerial council, the sin is fornication!" Dr. Leith barks, trying to regain the upper hand.

"So, ye are not a part of the congregation, but accuse Campbeltown's pastor of fornication?" Colum asks pointedly. "My brother speaks nothing of this!"

A very uncomfortable Skinny Preacher senses a need to intervene. "Men, let's vote on this matter. We'll ask Reverend Stuart and Dr. Leith to leave the room."

"Wait!" Dr. Leith says, "I demand a closing statement!"

The Skinny Preacher bites his two lips together in tense frustration before he speaks. "Dr. Leith, go ahead but please be brief. Some of these fine servants of God have travel before them this day, and we don't want them traveling in darkness."

"Men of Scottish faith and protectors of the purity and morality of the church and ministry," Dr. Leith begins. "Our duty here today is to protect the high standards of our clergy. Reverend Stuart speaks of questionable theology, spends time with Druids and Celts, and is accused of the sin of fornication. He must be stripped of his ordination."

Even, the Skinny Preacher is surprised by the call by Dr. Leith to remove Reverend Stuart from the ordination roll of the Presbytery. Sensing a favoritism among the men for Reverend Stuart, he calls again for a vote. "Reverend Stuart and Dr. Leith, please kindly step outside. I don't think we'll be long."

Reverend Stuart walks to the door, opens it, and steps into the hall. Dr. Leith, with a huff and a puff, follows.

Once again, the two adversaries are occupying the same space. Dr. Leith will not look Reverend Stuart in the eye.

Sensing a favorable outcome on the vote, Reverend Stuart is relaxed and friendly. "Our gathering was interesting. We have good people here," Reverend Stuart offers.

Minutes seemingly go by. Both men are leaning against the wall. "I'm just doing my job to protect the purity of the church," Dr. Leith states as he looks straight ahead.

"I understand," Reverend Stuart says. "We have more in common than I realized. We're both graduates of the School of Theology at the University of Aberdeen. I came along a few years later of course."

Dr. Leith manages to turn his head slightly toward Reverend Stuart. "I know that."

"Maybe when this is over, I'll come back to Aberdeen. We could have tea and talk about our favorite theologians. And my dear friend, Reverend George MacDonald, and I were at the University of Aberdeen together, and we both took courses at Highbury College. He asked me to review *Phantastes*, his novel," Reverend Stuart offers.

Dr. Leith raises his eyebrows, but before Dr. Leith can answer, the door creaks open and the head of the Skinny Preacher pokes out. "Come back in please."

Reverend Stuart and Dr. Leith pull their chairs far enough from the table to slip into their seats. As he slides it, the right rear leg of Dr. Leith's chair slips out of its notch. The odd wobble of the chair leg catches Reverend Stuart's sharp eye. As Dr. Leith's weight bears down on the chair, the wobbling leg gives way, and Dr. Leith starts a serious swoon toward the floor, the color rushing from his face.

"Gotcha," Reverend Stuart assures as he grabs Dr. Leith under both arms. Dr. Leith now has both hands on the table, and Reverend Stuart helps him slowly get to his feet.

The Skinny Preacher rises to bring over another chair sitting in the corner.

"Not necessary. I'll just stand," Dr. Leith says. "Something else has come to my attention. Reverend Stuart is an associate of Reverend George MacDonald, a universalist. He believes all people will be saved, not just the elect. That's heresy. His recent book, *Phantastes*, is about fairies and goblins. It's nonsense and leads people to believe in such stuff. It should be burned."

"It's a novel. It's fiction and clearly states so in the preface," Reverend Stuart says. "Reverend MacDonald believes in universal reconciliation. He believes Jesus came to save people from their sins and not from an angry God. The work of Christ is not to appease a wrathful, vindictive God, but to work against evil itself, the human evil that corrupts and destroys humanity, and to bring God and all people together."

The Skinny Preacher comes back to the table, and rather than sitting back down, he stands as he leans forward with both hands on the back of his chair. "I'll make this quick. This fine committee due to the respect given to Dr. Leith has decided to place Reverend Stuart on one year's probation. He will continue his ministerial duties. I will visit with Reverend Stuart and the church session every month to hear any concerns that might arise. This is a compromise and unanimous decision. I will file a report now and at the end of the year of probation. Thank ye all for coming, and Dr. Leith thank ye for spending time with us. Committee adjourned."

Dr. Leith bows his head toward the committee still seated around the table. "Good day, men of faith," he says.

One by one committee members pass through the door and make their way down the steps outside and into the street, some turning east and some west.

Turning west, Reverend Stuart eyes a familiar figure, Keltz.

"Keltz! Fancy seeing you here!" Reverend Stuart says with his face lit up. "It will be good to have your company on the trip home."

"My pleasure, Reverend," Keltz says. "Me just wants to make sure you okay today."

"I'm fine, Keltz," Reverend Stuart adds.

Reverend Stuart and Keltz arrive back in Campbeltown a few minutes before sundown. "Thank ye for looking after me," Reverend Stuart says as he bids a good evening, or so he thinks, to Keltz.

Reverend Stuart enters the parish house to check on Saint Paul, his cat. He is greeted by a black and white domestic cat, or moggie, who enthusiastically rubs against the reverend's legs, meowing periodically and wonderfully happy. Saint Paul has vomited up his food for the past two days. Scanning the room from side to side, the reverend is relieved not to see any of the cat's stomach contents on the floor. He picks up Saint Paul, and as he stokes him, inquires, "Feeling better, ole' boy?"

Logan's Tavern

August 28, 1849

An hour later, Reverend Stuart opens his front door and makes his way the few blocks to Logan's Tavern. The regulars already seated sip on their grog, Nelliford Viking gin, or scotch. Barrels turned on their ends serve as tables while rustic boxes are their stools. Reverend Stuart recognizes everyone. John McNeil is the town cobbler. Nary a shoe existed in Campbeltown that had not gone through John's hand. Joseph McDonel and his son, Keith, are farriers at the Campbeltown stable. Graham McQuillan is a member of the church and one of the Logan Tavern's best customers. 'Was he the one feeding information to Dr. Leith?' the reverend wonders.

Reverend Stuart recognizes all the customers except the man seated at the other end of the crude bar. The man is well-dressed and wears clean clothes, a rarity among the pub customers. Reverend Stuart notices a fedora on the bench beside him. A fine hat that can only be purchased from the expensive clothiers of Edinburgh or London. Myles and Samantha have a full house and work furiously to heap food and drink before the hungry and thirsty customers.

Samantha emerges from the kitchen. Her face serious, beads of sweat on her forehead from the hot wood-burning stove, but her face beams when she sees the reverend. A large pewter plate in each hand with lamb chops and a few small potatoes and carrots on the side, Samantha, instead of going straight to the table of the two smithies, detours slightly for a flirtatious pass past Reverend Stuart. "Me gets something, a surprise for you this evening," Samantha shares with lifted eyebrows. "Me back in a minute."

A surprise? Reverend Stuart wonders what it could be. Goose? No, he had that last night. Lamb? She takes goose to the smithies and tells them like a caring, attentive nurse, "I'll check on ye in a few minutes."

Before going back to Reverend Stuart, she passes by the grog keg, slides a pewter mug under the tap, and waits patiently until the foam runs over the top. Holding the handle with her right hand, she places her left hand up, turns thumb down and with thumb against her index finger pushes the head of foam off the mug into the pail on the table.

Samantha takes the few steps to Reverend Stuart and gently places the mug in front of him. "I assumed the regular?"

"Of course, ye know me well. Thank ye, Samantha," Reverend Stuart says. "What's the surprise?"

"Gives me a minute. Be right back," Samantha says as she gracefully spins, red locks lifting slightly off her shoulders, and happily steps into the kitchen.

Reverend Stuart sits at the end of the two-board bar. He notices a leg, then another, swing over the board seat. Looking to his left, Reverend Stuart sees Graham Lyndsey from the church. It's not unusual to see Graham and chat a bit with him at the tavern. Graham's wife died from the fever several years ago, and they had no children. Reverend Stuart led the funeral service, and Graham seemed genuinely appreciative of his care and efforts.

"Ye had a meeting in Glasgow today," Graham says. Reverend Stuart told his congregation from the pulpit last Sunday, so it wasn't like Graham had inside information.

"Aye and I be telling the congregation on the Sabbath all about it. The committee was very interested in my ministry here. Nice people," Reverend Stuart says, careful not to disclose too much before he tells his congregation.

Graham lowers his voice so as not to be overheard. "See that well-dressed man at the end of the bar?"

"Aye," Reverend Stuart says shrugging his shoulders slightly.

"He just moved here, moved into the Crane house on Dixon Street. A bookkeeper, he has no wife or family. Ner been married." Then Graham's voice dropped even lower. "Something not right about that." With a slight distortion in his face and a scandalous expression, Graham carefully says, "I hear he be a homosexual." Graham then pulls his head back slightly, and his eyes search Reverend Stuart's for a reaction, an expression of shock, or at least of disapproval.

Reverend Stuart's expression does not change. "Interesting," Reverend Stuart says without any hint of emotion.

"I thinks ye will like this," Samantha asserts, as she steps from the kitchen door, her facial muscles raised in an expression of hopeful excitement.

"I needs to get off. I'll let ye enjoy yer dinner," Graham says as he swings his right leg, shifts his buttocks slightly to the right, and then swings his left leg and finally both feet to the tightly packed dirt floor.

"Thanks for coming over," Reverend Stuart says, still not sure that Graham was not one of the twenty who had signed the petition for his removal. A petition he did not want to see. As their pastor, he did not want to know, as he might be tempted to hold a grudge.

Samantha has no idea about the small drama that just transpired at the bar as she sets the steaming bowl in front of Reverend Stuart, along with a large, thick slice of crusty bread. "Take ye a sip and let me know what ye thinks."

"Fish stew!" the reverend exclaims.

"Fresh trout from the Highlands," Samantha proudly states. "We usually likes to put more potatoes in, but they're scarce."

"Very good! Delicious!" the reverend says as he takes another spoonful and tears off a piece of the crusty bread and dips it into the stew.

"You and Josh playing tonight?" Samantha asks.

"Yeah, he'll be here soon," Reverend says. "We learned a couple of new songs. Josh picks them up quickly. Takes me awhile."

"Ye pretty quick," Samantha says. "We thought about starting a pub contest. Me and brother decided you'd win all the time with all that education. What fun would that be?"

"Ye have a good mind too, Samantha, I've noticed," the reverend says.

"Back in the kitchen, Samantha, another dinner to ready!" her brother shouts.

The reverend takes the last piece of crusty bread, firmly soaks up the last drops from the bottom of the bowl and closes his eyes as he slips the bread past his lips. He moans softly with pleasure.

Turning to his left, the reverend rotates until his legs and his feet touch the floor. He takes the few steps to the other end of the bar. He approaches the well-dressed man at the other end of the bar. Extending his right hand, the reverend says to the stranger, "I'm Reverend Charles Stuart, pastor of Campbeltown Church."

The man forces a small smile. "Reverend, I'm Ben Davidson. I just moved here. I'm a bookkeeper."

"Welcome to Campbeltown," the reverend says. "I think ye will like it here. Nice town. Nice people."

The door of the pub creaks opens and in steps Josh, a violin in his left hand and a guitar on a strap, hanging across his left shoulder. Josh will play the violin while the Reverend plays the guitar.

"My playing partner is here. I guess I need to get ready to play. Nice to meet you. Come join us at Campbeltown Church," the reverend says, smiling.

"Thanks," Ben says.

After filling a mug, Josh tries to get everyone's attention. Swigging back a mouthful of his pint, Josh says, "We're goin' to play some music and have some fun. You know what they say, 'De people of Campbeltown have more fun at a funeral than the people of Edinburgh do at a wedding!'"

Josh and the reverend play for over an hour. The regulars leave one by one until the pub is empty except for Samantha, Myles, the reverend, and Josh.

"One more drink on the house?" Samantha offers and heads to the grog barrels. Four mugs filled, she glides around the room, two mugs in each hand and not spilling a drop. They raise their mugs, and Myles declares, "To Scotland!" The other late night pubbers repeat, "To Scotland!"

An hour later, the reverend says he must go. "Got to write a sermon in the morn, then off to Glasgow to the hospital, William Campbell is near death."

"Yeah, I heard," Myles says. "Give him our best."

"Will do," the reverend says.

"Laters," Samantha says. "Laters," Josh says.

When the reverend stands, Samantha stands and puts her right arm under his left arm. "I'll walk ye to the door."

Josh, carrying his guitar and violin, opens the creaky door and steps into the crisp night air. The reverend and Samantha step through the door together. Samantha reaches back and closes the door. Josh heads down the street, too polite to look back at the pair.

Samantha releases the reverend's arm and turns to face him. "The best part of my day is when ye are in the pub," she says.

"I look forward to seeing you," the reverend says.

Taking both his hands in hers, Samantha says, "Can a pastor have a close friend? What do they say? A girlfriend?"

"I'm not Catholic," the reverend says with a wide grin.

They both start to lean forward. Their arms start to rise when the pub door squeaks open. "Samantha, I need your help cleaning up," Myles says.

Samantha turns and quickly steps into the pub.

Only now does Myles realize he has interrupted a growing intimate moment. "Reverend Stuart, I didn't know." He struggles for words. "I'm sorry, I didn't mean to bust in."

Reverend Stuart doesn't know what to say. If he says nothing was happening, that would not be honest, but he wasn't even sure what just happened.

"There's no problem. We just sayin' goodnight."

"See you tomorrow evening I hope."

"I'll be here," the reverend assures him and turns to walk down the street.

The reverend writes his sermon the next morning and visits the sick in the afternoon.

Up early on the sabbath, the reverend heads to the kirk. He wants to be the first to arrive so he can welcome every person as they enter the door.

Reverend Stuart's sermon is on the woman at the well in The Gospel of John. The preacher explains the geography of Palestine. Jews wanting to go to the northern part of Palestine from the southern part or vice versa usually chose to go out of their way so as not to go through Samaria. The Samaritans were viewed as an unclean people and to be avoided. They were labeled as unclean because they were religiously impure.

Reverend Stuart explains how Jesus goes through Samaria which was remarkable for a Jew. He stops at a well, Jacob's well. Jesus sits down and the disciples go into the village. Jesus asks for a drink. The woman protests, "Jews don't associate with Samaritans."

It comes out in the conversation that the woman had five husbands. Reverend Stuart says in his sermon, "I used to read this story and when it said the woman had five husbands, I thought, 'This must be a bad woman. What must this woman have done to be divorced by five husbands?' I assumed it was her fault. Perhaps she was promiscuous, caught in adultery, or some other bad behavior. But then I realized in reading this story a few days ago that there could be other explanations. Maybe the husbands died, short lifespans then. More likely, husbands wrote her letters of divorce. A husband could simply write on a piece of paper: 'I divorce you.' No explanation was necessary. The now ex-wife had no legal recourse, no legal rights."

Reverend Stuart uses his own new understanding of the text and the woman with five husbands to talk about how easily it is to judge a person prematurely. "Who are the Samaritans in our midst today?" he asks. "Who is the woman with five husbands in our midst? Who are the unfortunate in our community who through no fault of their own, are not like us? Who are the ones we have prejudged as immoral, unacceptable, and perhaps sinful?"

The sermon connects with many in the congregation. Others are distracted by thoughts running through their minds about the week ahead or the lack of money for immediate needs. Thomas McCalway thinks about William McTull's wife sitting to the right on the pew in front of him. Molly Murphy chews on her anger toward her husband who called her "a lazy bitch" earlier in the morning when she burned the biscuits.

Reverend Stuart wonders briefly about Gretchen Callahan sitting to his left on the third pew. She seems to be a very bitter woman with never a kind word for anyone. Will Graham Lyndsey make the connection in his mind to Ross Davidson, the homosexual living on Dixon Street? Is anyone examining their prejudicial thoughts about other people? What other prejudices do I have? Reverend Stuart wonders.

At the conclusion of the sermon, Reverend Stuart prays the pastoral prayer, lifting up several in the church and the community for God's attention. Men in hospital, grieving families, Brody and Mrs. Connery are mentioned. The dutiful repeat the Apostles' Creed and sing the Gloria Patri. "Glory be to the Father and to the Son and to the Holy Ghost. Amen."

At the church door, Reverend Stuart shakes the hand of each attendee. All greet him with warm glances and with hands that are rough and dry from hard manual work, while other hands are weak from illness.

To the left side of the church under shade of the massive oak tree, Reverend Stuart notices what appears to be an impromptu gathering. Graham Lyndsey talks intensely with William Taylor, John Cameron, and Anderson Wilson. Heads shake up and down apparently in agreement on some matter. Reverend Stuart wonders if those congregants are part of the twenty that petitioned the Presbytery for his removal? He wonders. Then, Reverend Stuart tries to put it out of his mind. He is still their pastor even if they do not like him.

Visits pack the afternoon. Pastor Stuart travels to the countryside to visit Mrs. McCant. She is bedridden. Her son, Chester, lives with her. At forty years of age, he doesn't work and has never had a job even before his mother became bedridden. The father was a stone mason and dead for many years. The son's hair, streaked with gray, hangs close to his shoulders. Also untrimmed, his beard descends almost to the middle of his chest. No shoes are on his feet, and his clothes wrinkled and soiled.

Mrs. McCant appreciates Reverend Stuart's visits and tells him so. Chester always nods in approval when Mrs. McCant expresses her gratitude. Reverend Stuart brings them a loaf of Highland Black bread baked by Mrs. Keith of the kirk. The whole-wheat and rye, which gave the bread its black appearance, is baked once a week for the church shut-ins.

Tomorrow, Reverend Stuart will visit Mrs. Connery and Brody.

Buried Insights

February 5, 2020

Sam kicks. Sam screams. "Why?! Why did I join the Army?"

More kicking, more screaming. Nothing changes.

"I'm dying. All because of this damn Army! The Army killed my father, and now it's killing me. I didn't have to do this. I volunteered."

Sam cries empty tears.

Energy spent. Sam calms down. "I knew all along why I volunteered. I'm a psychologist. I knew joining was a sublimated way of connecting with my father, helping other soldiers avoid his fate. But now I am suffering the same fate."

Exhausted, Sam's eyes close, thoughts cease. Blessed dreamy sleep.

Dancing in Logan's Tavern

August 29, 1849

Tonight, it's back to Logan's Tavern. On the way, he walks into the kirk and into the back room where Keltz sleeps. The reverend has not seen Keltz in a couple of days. Usually, Keltz is never far away from the reverend, except for mid-day and evening mealtime when he goes to the Blair's home for their table scraps. Keltz is fortunate to have this as a food source since the area is teetering on the edge of famine.

"Keltz, I haven't seen you all afternoon. You, okay?"

"I haven't eaten in a couple of days. Me's weak," Keltz says.

"I thought the Blairs gave you their leftovers?"

"Mrs. Blair, she sick. Mr. Blair don't cook much. No soup for me," Keltz says.

Surprised, Reverend Stuart had not heard of Mrs. Blair's illness.

"I'll check on Mrs. Blair on the 'morrow. Come on with me. We'll get something to eat," the reverend says.

"Where we going? Logan's Tavern?" Keltz asked.

"Aye!" the reverend says. "They have a great cook. We'll dine like lords!"

"I don't know if I belongs in a fancy place like that," Keltz says.

"Nothing fancy 'bout that place. We sit on boxes and eat on boards resting on large barrels. It will be fine. Let's go. I should eat and be ready to play with Josh," the reverend says.

Down the street they go, the pastor and the very hungry Keltz, following a short distance behind.

"Keltz, come on up here and walk besides me. I don't like having to turn my head to talk to you!" the reverend says.

"It won't be right," Keltz says.

"It'll be fine. You are a man like me. No better, no worse. Come on," the reverend states.

"I'll go but only cause ye the pastor," Keltz humbly responds.

Keltz pulls alongside the reverend. The reverend puts his arm around the hungry man and says, "I don't want you going hungry again. Promise me you'll let me know if you get hungry. God told me to take care of you," the reverend says.

"Really?" Keltz asks.

"God wants me to take care of all the people in the kirk and as many in the town as I can," the reverend says.

"But I'm no member of this kirk," Keltz sheepishly says.

"We can fix that!" the reverend says enthusiastically. "We'll baptize ye on Sunday. I'll get it approved at the session meeting on Wednesday evening."

Like a small child hearing about a first-time trip to see the ocean, Keltz says, "Really?"

"Of course!" the reverend says "You're part of God's family. Baptism is a sign of God's ownership."

The reverend looks over, and Keltz is smiling ear to ear like he had just received a bag of gold.

When they approach the tavern door, Keltz gets cold feet. "Nah, I shouldn't go in there."

"Come on Keltz, they're just people like us," the reverend insists as he steps toward Keltz grabbing his arm and guiding him through the door that, as always, screeches and groans.

The reverend wonders if Keltz has ever been in a tavern before. His life has been on the streets of Campbeltown, and he has survived due to the generosity of kirk members and their leftovers.

"I sit up here. Sit beside me," the reverend says as he points to the end of the row of boards that served as a bar. "I like to sit here as I can see the food coming out of the kitchen," the reverend says as he winks at Keltz. The reverend doesn't say he is especially fond of the cook-server. He knows Keltz is a keen observer of people since that is how he survives on the streets all day. He suspects that Keltz will figure out the romantic tension between the pastor and cook-server soon.

Josh is already seated at the bar as the reverend and Keltz slide in beside him. Josh normally arrives at the tavern just in time to play. He milks cows at the family dairy farm, and the evening milking usually keep him from arriving in time to eat before playing.

"You're early Josh," the reverend says.

"Yea, just got here. Mama was going to help daddy milk so I could get here early. I brought the tavern their milk too. They get two deliveries a week."

"Josh, this is my friend Keltz," the reverend says.

"Keltz, my new friend!" Josh says.

"You're my friend, too?" Keltz says with apprehension and excitement in his voice. "Me gots two friends now, you and the pastor! I'm gettin' baptized too!"

"Really, baptized?" Josh says.

"I'm a child of God. The reverend tells me tonight!" Keltz beams out.

The drape over the door to the kitchen pushes open and through the doorway steps Samantha with a large bowl of steaming stew. "Ah, me sees three wise men!" Samantha says, smiling.

Stunned by the deep blue eyes, smooth face, high cheek bones, and redhaired woman before him and true to his impulsive nature, Keltz blurts out, "You're beautiful!"

Josh and the reverend try to hold back chuckles. Samantha says, "You're sweet to say that. Thanks!"

"Will ye be my friend?" Keltz wonders aloud. "They my friends," pointing to Josh and the reverend.

"Of course, I'll be your friend," Samantha says. "Me be back in a minute. Gots to get Mr. Mann his stew!" Mr. Mann owned the local dry goods store, the only place in town to buy a hammer or a roll of rope.

"She's really alive!" Keltz says.

"She is," the reverend answers.

After sitting down Mr. Mann's stew, Samantha reverses course and stops in front of the three wise men. "Can we have three mugs of water please, Samantha?" the reverend asks. He doubts Keltz has ever had a bar drink, and he didn't know how Keltz would respond. He did not want Keltz to like it too much.

"Of course," Samantha says. "Be right backs."

"What's in the big barrels?" Keltz asks as he points at the grog barrels.

"Oh, that's grog and can make you dizzy," the reverend explains. "We'll just stick with water." Samantha sits three waters in front of them. "What would the three wise men like to eat? Lamb leg stew is very good. Gots a few potatoes in it. Supplier told us today we might not get potatoes again fer awhile. Getting hard to find."

"Lamb stew works for me and Keltz," the reverend says.

"Same here," Josh adds.

"I hopes ye have some of that Highland Black bread?" the reverend says with his eyebrows raised in hopeful expectation.

"Sure do," Samantha responds. "Highland Black bread for all?"

Josh and Keltz both shake their heads up and down.

"Be out soon. Stew and bread for all!" Samantha declares.

As Samantha disappears through the hanging drape, Keltz says, "She's beautiful."

The reverend and Josh say nothing. They don't want Keltz to get too fixated on Samantha.

Changing the subject, the reverend says, "I'm going to present Keltz as a candidate for baptism at the kirk session meeting on Wednesday."

The reverend immediately realizes his mistake. Keltz asks with a wakened voice, "What's this 'candidate'?"

"Oh, a 'candidate' is a person worthy of baptism, that's all," the reverend answers.

Keltz shakes his head that he understands and calms down.

"Me dad says there was another meeting yesterday. The same people are concerned about the man you talked to last week," Josh says.

"I'm not surprised," the reverend says. "It will be okay. They're a small group. Most of our people don't think like they do."

Josh and the reverend talk in such a way that Keltz doesn't hear specifics, as he would become very upset with these people.

The hanging drape pushes open again and out comes Samantha with a huge bowl requiring two hands. "Our largest bowl for our newest customer," she says as she sits the vessel of steaming broth with pieces of carrots, potato, celery, and lamb peeping up at Keltz.

Keltz's eyes are almost as big as the bowl. He looks for a spoon, a fork, anything to scoop out the stew.

"Oops!" Samantha says. "I'll be right back."

Through the hanging drape and before it stops shaking, Samantha comes back with three large spoons.

"Here ye go!" Samantha declares. Quick as a cat, Keltz grabs a spoon and strikes down into the bowl lifting a spoon of broth and lamb. He pushes it into his mouth.

"Enjoy, Keltz," the reverend says.

Wheeling back through the drape, Samantha has two bowls held tightly together by both her hands. First bowl sits in front of Josh, and the second before the reverend.

"One more thing," Samantha says.

Keltz dips his spoon furiously into the broth. "Oh, so good!" he says. He spills a little on the board beside his bowl and immediately wipes it with his fingers and sticks his fingers in his mouth.

Samantha has placed a small basket with three pieces of bread on the table. Josh picks up the basket, puts it in front of Keltz and says, "Bread?"

Keltz's hand strikes the bread like a cobra and just as quickly into his mouth. "Oh, um," Keltz moans.

Josh and the reverend are sitting beside a man truly hungry and enjoying his food like a desert traveler finally finding water and sensing the water's coolness on his lips and tongue.

"This food is as good as a dry bed on a rainy night," Keltz says.

"Glad ye enjoy it," the reverend says.

"Is this heaven?" Keltz asks seriously.

"Might be like this," Josh says, "Good food, good friends."

"The Bible does talk about a Heavenly Banquet," the reverend explains.

"Really?" Keltz asks.

"Aye, and a seat is reserved for you, Keltz," the reverend confirms.

A smile as bright as the mid-day sun spreads across Keltz's face.

"Josh and I goin' to play some music. You can sit here or sits on any barrel you like," the reverend says to Keltz.

Josh and the reverend take their places in the corner of the tavern.

"Play a bit of Irish tonight?" Josh asks the reverend.

"Ye knows more than I do, but I'll try to keep up," the reverend responds.

"I'm sure ye knows *The Banks of the Bann*," Josh says. "And then we'll do *Goodbye Johnny Dear*."

Josh taps his foot and pushes his bow across the strings of his fiddle. The reverend strokes the strings of the guitar but stops when he realizes he is out of beat with Josh. Pausing a few seconds, the reverend rejoins Josh.

Busy, Samantha delivers mugs of grog to the men sitting on barrels. The men, most regulars, sip and sometimes sing along when Josh and the reverend play familiar songs.

The men on the barrels have consumed almost all the grog they can and still find their way home. Samantha pauses at the bar, takes a deep breath of relief, reaches under the board-bar, and pulls out a flute. Josh motions for her to join them.

Josh and the reverend finish *Irish Wind I Love*, and Josh says, "Let's play *I Love a Lassie*."

Feet tap and instruments come alive as tavern customers cheer and applaud. Samantha's flute takes the music to another level. Josh looks at the reverend, and they exchange glances.

The trio plays three songs, and then Samantha plays her flute solo. Putting down the flute, Samantha says to Josh and the reverend, "Play *Dance With Me Love*." Then Samantha does the surprising. She walks across the tavern to a broad smiling Keltz, who is having the time of his life this unexpected evening, takes his hand, and pulls him to his feet.

Shocked, Keltz with a look of sheer terror on his face, tries to find words, "Wait, what's going on?"

Smiling, while trying to hold back laughter, Samantha says, "Let's dance."

"Me? With me?" Keltz says in disbelief.

"Yes!" Samantha reassures.

"I can't dance!" Keltz protests.

"Tis easy." Samantha says, "I'll teach ye."

Samantha pulls a little harder on Keltz's hand, and he takes some awkward steps forward. Amusement sweeps across the faces of the men on the barrels. Josh and the reverend exchange monster smiles.

On the dance floor, Samantha leans toward Keltz, "Just move ye feet back and forth. Feel the music. Relax. And dance likes nobody's watching."

Keltz senses freedom as he moves his feet.

"You're doing great, Keltz!" Samantha insists, leaning forward to be sure Keltz hears her.

Eyes in the tavern are not on Keltz but fixed on Samantha as she moves exotically. Every muscle in her body alive with energy, her hands go over her head as she softly claps in rhythm with the music. Men on barrels clap in unison with her. She dances around the barrels as the men roll their heads trying to catch every move she makes. As she reverses her path, her red locks float above her shoulders. Men's mouths are open as their jaws have dropped. She spins again, and her hair lifts off her shoulders. Every man has a fantasy.

Out of the kitchen her brother steps. He leans against the wall with a disapproving glare. Moments later, the corners of his mouth lift, realizing the joy that is in the room. Samantha knows there is still work ahead of her. She shoots a glance at Josh, and he knows it is time to wind down the music.

Keltz spends the entire time putting right foot forward, right foot back, left foot forward, left foot back, never taking his eyes off Samantha.

"You did great Keltz!" Samantha says.

Breathing heavily, Keltz says, "I loves it."

Samantha's left hand goes to his shoulder, as she leans forward and kisses him on the right cheek.

Keltz, paralyzed with a mixture of excitement and uncertainty, can open his mouth but is too stunned to speak.

Josh and the reverend put their instruments in their cases. Samantha begins cleaning mugs from the barrels and tables. Delighted customers bid Keltz, Samantha, Josh, and the reverend goodnight. Mr. Mann, the local merchant approaches Keltz. "You're going to be a great dancer." Keltz beams so intensely, his face looks like it might break.

Hugs between Samantha and Josh, Samantha and Keltz, and Samantha and the reverend are exchanged. The hug between Samantha and the reverend lasts longer and bodies touch. Something is whispered.

The three men make their exit. "See ye tomorrow evening."

Out on the street, Josh asks, "Keltz, did you have fun?"

"Oh yes! Me heart beat so fast I thought I might die," Keltz says. "She's beautiful. Her eyes are as blue as robin's eggs."

Josh chuckles while the reverend just stares ahead.

"You can preach, and you cans play guitar, reverend," Keltz offers in amazement.

"And you can dance!" the reverend exclaims.

The next morning the reverend visits Mrs. McCurry, another shut in. Mrs. McCurry's husband died last year, and they had no children. She is very lonely and cherishes Reverend Stuart's visits. Often repeating herself, she talks endlessly about her wonderful husband. In his younger days, the husband harpooned on whaling ships, sometimes a year or more at sea in the tropics. In recent years before he died, he worked aboard merchant ships on much shorter voyages to France and Spain.

"Ye have a wife, reverend?" Mrs. McCurry asks.

"No ma'am," the reverend replies. "I've spent all my time in school and serving the church. Maybe someday a wife."

"She'll be a lucky woman. Ye have such a fine heart," Mrs. McCurry says with tear-filled eyes. "I had me a good man. I miss him so." The reverend offers to have a prayer and bids Mrs. McCurry a good day.

A short journey, the reverend is at Campbeltown Harbor where he spends one afternoon a month with "street children." These are the children unable to find a spot in the orphanages. They sleep on the street, walk the streets, and beg for their food.

Many of the children's parents have died. Fathers who were sailors drowned in storms, and others died because of war. Disease takes some parents. Widowed mothers push older children to life on the streets to make scarce food available for the younger children.

The reverend brings bread for the children, although families who usually have extra bread to donate, are now struggling to have enough bread and potatoes for themselves. He has enough for today, although he worries about the children and the cold winter ahead.

After the children eat, Reverend Stuart reads Bible stories to them. They love Daniel and the Lion's Den, Jonah and the Whale, and stories of Jesus and the children.

Reverend Stuart hugs each child and heads back to Campbeltown. He will have dinner with Mrs. Connery and Brody.

Bread Condemns

September 9, 1849

"Comes in! Comes in!" Reverend Stuart hears as he knocks lightly on the door. He always knocks, although Mrs. Connery insists he doesn't have to.

"Ye have a good trip?" Mrs. Connery asks. With a sad face she says, "Such a wonderful thing ye do for the children. I wishes me had more bread to send them."

"The trip was good, the children so thankful and happy. It's amazing given the situation they are in," the reverend responds.

"Maybe you could take Brody with you sometime. He could help cut the bread," Mrs. Connery offers.

"Will do," the reverend says as he hangs his coat on a nail driven into the wood beside the door.

"I've got a kettle on. Ready for some tea?" Mrs. Connery asks.

"Yes, please," the reverend says.

Brody sits on the bench in front of the table, blocking a full view of the dinner table and the food Mrs. Connery has prepared.

"Brody, you like learning to read?" Reverend Stuart asks.

Mrs. Connery taught reading and history at Campbeltown Primary School until her husband fell ill, and she resigned to take care of him.

"I likes reading. I read about pirates today. Blackbeard was a pirate and mean!" Brody says as he shakes his head and growls like a pirate might growl at frightened captives.

"Did ye read about cannibals?" Reverend Stuart asks as he raises his voice and eyebrows.

"No, not yet, but soon I hopes," Brody says, eyes wide.

"Something fills the air," Reverend Stuart says as he lifts back his head and pulls the aroma into his nostrils. "Very nice."

"One of me specialties, vegetables and dumplings. Sorry, no meat." Mrs. Connery says with her face showing her effort not to feel shame.

"Meat is so expensive," Reverend Stuart says, expressing understanding.

" Let's eat!" Mrs. Connery says with a newly found warmth on her face.

"Wait!" A startled Mrs. Connery says, her voice filled with puzzlement. "The bread! Where did the bread come from?" A loaf of Highland black bread sits to the right of the dumplings.

"Where did that come from?" she asks again.

Reverend Stuart looks firmly at Brody, his voice and eyes intense.

"I gots it!" Brody declares. "I hid it 'til dinner ready."

Earlier when Mrs. Connery took an afternoon nap, Brody quietly slipped out the door and made his way around the corner and up the street to the bakery. When the baker goes back into the storage room, Brody slips through the door and quickly scampers out with the dark brown loaf.

"Brody, did you takes the loaf from the bakery?" Reverend Stuart asks.

Brody tries to think of some believable story. His front top teeth bite down on his bottom lip until a drop of blood forms on his lip.

"I tooks it," Brody confirms. "But he didn't sees me. Nobody sees me."

Reverend Stuart and Mrs. Connery look at each other like two people who were just sentenced to the guillotine.

"I know you really likes that bread," Brody protests to Reverend Stuart. "I did it for you."

Reverend Stuart is already weighing the pros and cons of what they should do about Brody's indiscretion. Should they return the bread? Will the baker forgive them or report them to the sheriff anyway? Mrs. Connery cries softly.

"Brody, we must take the bread back first thing in the morning. Thank you for thinking of me, but it is wrong to take bread without paying for it," Reverend Stuart says.

"He'll never miss it," Brody insists.

"It doesn't matter, Brody," Reverend Stuart explains. "If something doesn't belong to you, you can't take it without paying for it."

Mrs. Connery steps toward the table and says, "me takes the loaf to the kitchen 'til morn. Now, let's have some chowder."

Brody, Reverend Stuart, and Mrs. Connery take their seats around the table.

"Brody, hand me ye bowl," Mrs. Connery asks. The bowl slips from her hand and smashes on the table.

Before anyone can react, there's another "bang!" The front door shakes! A second bang! A third bang and the door explodes, flying open, with part of the door jamb falling onto the floor.

"Ye are under arrest!" the sheriff roars, as he steps through the door. As the sheriff moves toward the three shocked diners, Brody jumps out of his chair and steps toward the rear of the house. Just as quickly Reverend Stuart grabs Brody's arm saying, "Wait, Brody."

"We can explain," Reverend Stuart says to the sheriff.

"Where de' baker's bread?" the sheriff demands.

"It's in the kitchen," Mrs. Connery says.

Now standing, Reverend Stuart tries to explain, "We are going to return the bread in the morning."

"Ye are under arrest! All three of ye!" the sheriff bellows out. "Let's go!"

With dinner still sitting on the table, the three are shuffled out the door. Little did they know, they will never see that table or house again.

In the back of the sheriff's wagon, Reverend Stuart sits with his back to the sideboard. Directly opposite sit Brody and Mrs. Connery.

"Where is he taking us?" Brody asks.

"Probably to jail," Reverend Stuart says.

Mrs. Connery, turning white as a sheet, exclaims "To jail? Dear God! What is happening to us?"

"I don't think they can do much to us over one loaf of bread," Reverend Stuart says.

"I'll bake them a hundred loaves if they just let us go," Mrs. Connery says.

The wagon stops in front of the jailhouse, the same jailhouse where Brody was locked up earlier.

"All of ye OUT!" the sheriff barks.

"You're putting us in jail for a loaf of bread?" Reverend Stuart asks.

"Judge Ainsley told me if ye gets in any more trouble to lock you up and send a messenger for him," the sheriff coldly explains.

Reverend Stuart steps through the jailhouse door first. Relieved, there are no other prisoners.

"I only have the one jailhouse, so all ye must stay together and do the best ye can. Thar's water in that bucket," the sheriff points to a bucket under the bench. "That's yer chamber pot. We'll empty it once a day. And we brings you two meals every day, breakfast and dinner. Ain't much, but we'll keep you from starving. But ye won't be here long. Judge probably wants to do this soon. Ye in serious trouble. Judge has no patience for second offenders. Judge believes stealin' is 'bout as bad as killin'," the sheriff says as he turns, closes the creaky door, and drops the large board through the slots on each side of the door, making the door impossible to open from the inside.

Kandahar, Afghanistan

February 6, 2020

Sam separates completely dry lips and very weakly says, "Help."

The one open eyelid falls back over Sam's eyeball.

Losing consciousness, Sam dreams again about ancestors.

In The Jailhouse

September 16, 1849

The jailhouse consists of one room, with a dirt floor, and rough wood walls with shreds of bark from the walls on the floor. The one window has bars and too small for anyone to squeeze through.

The reverend thinks, though, there will be no need to escape. When the truth comes out and that "the crime" is a boy taking a loaf of bread, they'll get to go home after paying a fine of money. When the church people find out it was the mischief of young Brody, they'll gather up the money and get them out. They will have to spend one night in these cramped quarters.

Dinner never arrives. "The sheriff says we gets dinner?" Brody protests.

"I guess it was too short notice," Reverend Stuart says, trying to be understanding.

It is winter, and darkness comes quickly. The cold night air blows through the window. Reverend Stuart sees two blankets in the corner. He gives one to Mrs. Connery and the other to Brody.

"What about ye? Take this blanket," Mrs. Connery says to Reverend Stuart.

"I'll be fine," Reverend Stuart says and with a chuckle adds, "It'll be like the parish house."

Just after first light, a knock on the door and a voice says, "Ye food. I'll opens the door and hands it to ye. Don't try anything. I got a guard with me, ye hear?" Reverend Stuart heads to the door. He reaches out and keeps Brody from getting there first. The door opens, and three bowls of porridge sit on the ground. A short bald man in dirty tattered clothes and a younger man stand at the door. The guard scowls at the prisoners.

"Hands me ye piss pot. Porridge for piss," the guard laughs.

Reverend Stuart, not amused and thinking the man probably uses that line on every prisoner, says to Brody, "Get the pot for the man, please."

Brody and Reverend Stuart eat the porridge with their fingers.

"I'm not hungry," Mrs. Connery says.

"You need to eat," Reverend Stuart insists.

"I'll eat dinner. I promise," Mrs. Connery says.

"I'll eats it," Brody offers, not surprisingly.

The day slowly ticks away. Reverend Stuart suggests they pass the time by sharing where they were born and stories about growing up. Then he realizes he has put Brody in a difficult position due to his parents' recent death.

"Me parents are dead," Brody blurts out, hoping to get his part over with. "Killed in a fire. Ain't much else."

Mrs. Connery surprises Reverend Stuart by relating that her father was also a pastor in neighboring Oran. "Died young, I was just a bairn. I don't remember him," she says.

A knock on the door and Brody's eyes grow big with excitement as he exclaims, "They're letting us out!" Brody dashes to the door, and once again Reverend Stuart holds him back.

"Ye dinner," the man says. "I'm opening the door."

Once again, three bowls of porridge sit on the ground.

"I hear the judge comin' tomorrow," the little man says. "Ye must've done somethin' bad for him to come. Nots his regular routine." The guard laughs and turns away.

Reverend Stuart thinks it best not to say anything now except, "Thank you."

"Me wonders what we did that was so bad?" Mrs. Connery says with a deep worried expression on her face.

"We didn't even eats the bread," Brody holds out his empty hands, palms up.

"Maybe the judge thinks a great injustice has been done by putting us in jail," Reverend Stuart answers but doubts what he is saying is true. Judge Ainsley is up to something, he thinks, but does not want to worry the others.

They face another cold night. Wind howls outside. Even colder air pushes through the window and through the cracks between the logs. Reverend Stuart got cold last night but did not tell his companions.

"Ye'll catch your death if you don't cover with something," Mrs. Connery says. The reverend insists he'll be fine.

First light and the little man with the guard never appear until mid-morning. "I'm late. Had to get the courtroom ready. Ole' judge be here soon," the little man explains. "This bloke," pointing to the guard, "ate your porridge. Sorry." The guard turns his head away and stares out into the distance.

"We'll go to the courtroom, but first bring us the piss bucket," the little man says.

Stepping through the jailhouse door, the prisoners squint when the bright sunlight hits their eyes.

"Follows me," the little man orders. The guard with his big belly full of porridge follows behind the prisoners.

As they walk, Mrs. Connery prays, "Good Lord, be with us. Ye knows, we did not mean to harm anyone. Let the judge look upon us with mercy and lets us return to our homes. In the name of Jesus Christ. Amen."

"That was a beautiful prayer," Reverend Stuart says.

"I hope God intervenes. Ole' Judge Ainsley hard on second offenders. He's cold as a lizard anyway," the little man warns.

"Better hopes the judge in a good mood," the guard laughs.

The sheriff waits for the prisoners at the courthouse door. He motions a group of seven men and women into the courtroom. These are locals, the courtroom spectators. They use the courtroom for entertainment, and they revel in harsh sentences. A half dozen other regulars are already seated in primitive and wobbly wooden benches.

The sheriff leads the prisoners to the front row seats. "Sits down, but ye best stand when the judge comes in."

"I have to pee," Brody says to Reverend Stuart.

"You can't," Reverend Stuart shakes his head. "You're young. You can hold it."

No judge appears. They wait.

"Where's the judge?" Brody asks, showing impatience. No one has an answer.

Minutes go by and then an hour. Several of the spectators walk outside. Their chatter drifts back into the courtroom.

"What ye think the judge will do to them?" one asks the others.

"He might hangs them," a man blurts out.

"No, no, he won't hang 'em," another man responds. "He'll be harsh for sure. He don't likes to see people in his courtroom a second time. It's a long trip for him, and he don't like to travel in his ole days."

"Prison?" another asks.

"Prisons are full. People are hungry, the famine, and alls," the man says.

The sheriff comes outside and looks up the road.

"How long we wait?" a man asks.

"Oh, he be here soon," the confident sheriff says as three more of the spectators come out.

As he turns his head a suddenly excited woman points, "There he is! He's coming!"

The judge's black carriage pulled by an equally black horse comes up the road, a cloud of dust as a caboose.

"If ye staying, gets back in the courtroom," the sheriff commands, and they all scamper back through the door.

The carriage door swings open. The judge grimaces as he steps down. He tries to straighten up, and his face tightens with discomfort. His right hand goes to his lower back as he tries to soften the pain. As his head rises, he clears his throat and launches a light green mass into the air that raises a puff of dust when it hits the ground. His hand then swipes across his mouth to wipe off any lingering green matter.

"Morning, judge," the sheriff says. "Hopes ye had a good trip?"

"Road gets more holes all the time. Dust is awful," he grunts. "The prisoners here?"

"They here. They be before you," the sheriff says. "Just these three, and they says they are guilty," he adds.

"They do, do they?" Judge Ainsley asks, not expecting an answer.

The judge lumbers down the aisle between the benches. His right shoulder dipping as his right knee flinches with every step.

He groans as he lowers his staunch body behind his table. The judge focuses his eyes on the prisoners momentarily and then shifts his eyes to the sheriff approaching his table. The sheriff hands him a one-page handwritten statement. Judge Ainsley exhales a deep breath as he scans down the page.

"All right, the Royal Burgh of Argyll charges Brody McAlister, Charles Rory Stuart, Ruby Connery, with thievery, taking valuable bread from a beloved baker." Then he looks down his nose at the three prisoners. "Ye stole the baker's bread?"

Before Brody can speak, Reverend Stuart politely answers in his softest voice, "Your Honor, we had every intention of returning the bread. It should not have been taken." Reverend Stuart is careful not to put the blame on Brody. He fears what the judge might do to him.

"So ye saying ye stole the bread?" the judge asks in a more demanding voice.

"The bread was taken and not paid for, and we intended to return it, or make sure it was paid for, whatever the baker desired."

The judge, a flush of anger sweeping across his face, interjects, "Reverend Stuart, ye trying to smooth talk this court!" Suddenly Brody interrupts, "I took the bread! The baker should share his bread."

"Young man, ye haves a loud mouth and thieving hands. This county wants to be rid of you and your thieving kind," Judge Ainsley roars. "Reverend Stuart and Mrs. Connery, ye were given charge of this young man. This court holds ye equally responsible for his thievery, and I hereby sentence all three of ye to the penal colony on Norh Rona Island."

The courtroom audience roars in approval.

"Away with the thieves!"

"Hang 'em!"

"Cut off their hands!"

"Silence in me courtroom!" the judge demands.

Mrs. Connery's body starts drooping toward the floor as she moans, "Oh me God."

"Ye ole' bastard!" Brody screams, pointing at Judge Ainsley. The judge loathes Brody with a scowl.

"Sheriff, get these thieves out of my courtroom now!" the judge demands.

"Wait!" Reverend Stuart pleads. "People die on those penal islands ye honor. What we did was not that bad."

The sheriff grabs Reverend Stuart by the left arm when the judge says, "Wait, if ye have money or something to sell, to buy yer tickets, I'll send ye to America."

Mrs. Connery regains her composure and realizes she would die for sure on the penal island and says, "I have a house."

Judge Ainsley's head jerks upright. "I see."

"Sheriff, ye know of this house?" the judge asks.

"Aye, I do," the sheriff quickly answers.

"Will it sell for enough to buy their tickets to Carolina?"

"It wills, I believes," the sheriff adds.

"Mrs. Connery, I am instructing me clerk to prepares a deed of transfer. Are ye in agreement?" the judge asks.

"I've lived in that house for almost forty years. Raised me children. Me husband builds it with his own hands. But if it keeps us out of the penal colony, yes. Yes, I agree," Mrs. Connery reluctantly says.

"Alright then. Sheriff, I am instructing ye to purchase the passages to Carolina. There is a large settlement of Scots there. They'll have a good life if they quits their stealin'," the judge adds.

"Aye, sir," the sheriff says.

"The prisoners will stay in the custody of the sheriff until passage can be purchased for them. Several ships depart the Port of Liverpool weekly," the judge states.

"Ye Honor, I needs to return to me home before I go," Mrs. Connery pleads.

"Mrs. Connery, ye have assigned transfer of ownership of ye house to this court. Sheriff, take them away!" the judge instructs loudly, ignoring Mrs. Connery's desperate request. Mrs. Connery's eyes fill with hot tears. "God help us!"

"Ye Honor, this is a perversion of justice!" Reverend Stuart protests, his eyes darkening with anger.

Brody screams as he points his finger at the judge, "Ye bloody bastard! I'll come back and kill ye!"

The judge, walking toward the door, stops, pauses for a moment, and then takes a stride out the door. The sheriff motions the three prisoners out the same door. They see the judge's black carriage pull away and stir up a small cloud of dust as it heads down the street.

Back to Jail!

September 17, 1849

The prisoners board their wagon, and their sad journey begins. When the wagon pulls up in front of the jailhouse, the sheriff motions them out.

"I'll be taking ye to the harbor soon. Maybe tomorrow or the next day. The Isabelle sails for Carolina soon."

"Me Lord, I can't believe this," Mrs. Connery moans. "I'll never see me house again."

"Will the judge listen to reason? I could get the people from the church to write letters," Reverend Stuart asks.

The sheriff chuckles, "No way. The ole' judge gets his hands on Mrs. Connery's house money he won't let it go. All the money left over from the sale of the house after I buys the tickets, goes into the judge's pocket. How you think he pays for that big mansion he lives in?"

"Oh my God!" Mrs. Connery says hopelessly, her mouth hanging open.

"I told you he's a bloody bastard!" Brody screams. "I'll kill him!"

Reverend Stuart strains his brain, his face expressionless. 'What can I do?' he wonders.

The sheriff interrupts his thoughts, "Gonna gets real cold tonight. I'll try and find another blanket. Ye piss pot, ye put too much in there, and it'll freeze. Splatter on ye and the floor when ye use it again. Keeps that in mind."

They hear the board slide into the holders on the outside door. Their remaining nights in beloved Scotland will be spent in this cold, cramped jailhouse, probably with a frozen chamber pot.

Complete darkness envelopes them. A knock on the door and a voice, "Reverend Stuart? Reverend Stuart, ye in there?"

"Colum McCarthy, that you?" Reverend Stuart asks.

"Aye, are you folks, okay?"

"We are. A little cold and still in some shock but we're okay," Reverend Stuart says.

"William McClure and I are headed to see the judge with a petition signed by over a hundred people asking the judge to reconsider his decision. It not right! It not fair! We want to be there by first light," Colum says.

"Colum, William, thank you!" Reverend Stuart says.

"God's speed! Help us!" Mrs. Connery pleads.

"Just kill the bastard!" Brody screams.

"Brody, we're all upset, but we don't want anyone killed," Reverend Stuart says.

"We hopes to be back soon," Colum says.

"There's hope," Reverend Stuart says in the darkness. "There is hope."

"I'm praying," Mrs. Connery says.

Soon Brody sleeps. Mrs. Connery and Reverend Stuart sit in the darkness with worry and hope swirling within them.

To The Harbor!

September 18, 1849

At first light, knocking booms on the door. "It's time to go."

Reverend Stuart recognizes the sheriff's raspy voice. The board slides off the door holders and swings open. "The Isabella sails this afternoon. You're going to Carolina," the sheriff announces. "Got to get ye to the harbor this morning."

A deep sleeper, Brody must be shaken.

Reverend Stuart approaches the sheriff at the door. "Friends from the kirk are taking a petition to Judge Ainsley this morning, a petition signed by over a hundred people pleading for mercy."

"It's a waste of time," the sheriff says.

"He seems to be a reasonable man sometimes," Reverend Stuart adds.

"Judge ain't there. He and his wife left for London last night. Daughter having a bairn," the sheriff says.

Reverend Stuart feels his jaw drop and mouth open. He blows out a heavy breath. He looks at Mrs. Connery. Her shoulders drop. She bends at the waist, opens her mouth, and gags. Embarrassed, her hand goes over her mouth.

"Let's get her outside," Reverend Stuart says. He takes her by the arm, and as they head toward the door, he reaches down and shakes Brody. "Got to get up!"

The sheriff steps out of the doorway. Reverend Stuart gets Mrs. Connery out the door. Her face is a mass of confusion and fear. She gags as her hand rests against a massive red oak tree. A groggy Brody steps outside and screams at the sheriff, "This is your fault! You and that bastard judge!"

"Get this boy in de wagon!" the sheriff says to his fat companion.

"My pleasure!" the companion says with a sloppy smile. "Come here you lil' runt," the companion orders.

"You can't catch me, you fat bastard!" Brody screams, just as the sheriff plants a heavy hand on Brody's shoulder. "You ain't goin' nowhere 'cept in that wagon," the sheriff says.

The fat companion approaches Brody.

"Damn!" the fat man screams as Brody plants a foot squarely in his testicles.

"God!" The fat man bellows in pain. His knees buckle, and he falls to the ground moaning with a deep dull throbbing in his grown.

"You'll be alright in a few minutes," the sheriff laughs. "Hurt like hell now but won't last long. Me wife kicked me balls last month. Helps keep me in line."

"Let's get in de wagon," the sheriff says as he gives Brody a jerk.

Mrs. Connery stands upright, and Reverend Stuart helps her toward the wagon. "I can't believe this," Mrs. Connery says as she steps up into the wagon. "Never sees me house again."

"Get your sore balls up here," the sheriff says to his fat companion.

"If I gets a chance, little thief, I'll teach ye a lesson," the fat man says to Brody.

"Shut up," the sheriff says to his fat companion. "Or ye gets yer balls kicked again."

The fat man spits a hurling mass on to the road but says nothing.

To The Ship

September 18, 1849

"We'll be in Campbeltown Harbor in about an hour. We put a little water in this jug. Pass it around if ye gets thirsty," the sheriff says.

The horses stir up a cloud of dust as they pull the wagon. Mrs. Connery coughs. Brody goes back to sleep, rousing when a wagon wheel bounces over a hole in the road.

They begin their unwanted and bumpy journey to Campbeltown Harbor. Reverend Stuart sits stoically against the side of the wagon, moving only when the wagon bounces.

A stretch of green farmland lays on each side of the road as their wagon churns toward the harbor. The wagon bounces as it crosses the uneven boards on Bishop's Bridge that stretches over Kintyre Run.

The bouncing wagon wakes Brody. He eyes the water and points, "Bet de water full of big fish! I'll fish soon!"

"Oh dear," Mrs. Connery moans.

"I wonder if the Laird would let me fish?" Brody asks.

"Brody, we will find you a place to fish soon," Reverend Stuart promises.

"We're boarding big ship soon?" Brody asks.

"It appears we are," Reverend Stuart answers.

"Maybe I can fish from the ship," Brody says.

"Maybe," Reverend Stuart answers, and trying to find something positive to say, he adds, "If we must take this wagon ride, it is a clear, cool, gorgeous day. Look at the sky!"

The wagon passes through more fields. Ripe grains sway with the soft winds. Small white clouds dot the brilliant blue sky. They pass by small cottages as they approach Campbeltown Harbor. Dock workers live humbly and modestly in tiny cottages, simple wooden structures with crude shake roofs. Cows with ropes around necks graze on grass around the cottages. The ropes tied to stakes allow the cows to graze in a large circle.

"Look at the cow's teats!" Brody shouts, pointing at the pouch and nipples on a brown and white cow.

"She shares her milk with the family," Reverend Stuart explains.

"My mother, God rest her soul. Milked the cows of the farm next door for many years. She gots up before the sun rose every day so we'd have food on our table," Mrs. Connery says.

Reverend Stuart likes that Mrs. Connery listens and talks. He thinks it is a good sign for her. At least from time to time, she emerges from her sadness.

The cottages soon give way to several small shops. Another wagon goes by them heading north to Campbeltown from the harbor, whipping up another small dust cloud.

"Passengers from the ship. She must not been anchored long," Reverend Stuart says.

"Thar's yer ship!" the sheriff says as he turns his head toward his passengers.

"I see ships! One big one!" Brody exclaims.

They all strain to see. The slender masts of the ship soon came into focus.

"Ship don't have no sails!" Brody says with concern in his voice.

"Sails are down while in harbor. The ship will be steadier. Yer's a three-mast ship," the sheriff turns his head and explains. "Tenders take passengers out to the ship."

"Tenders? What's a tender?" Brody asks.

"A tender is a boat, a rowboat. The little boats take people to the big ships," Reverend Stuart says.

Excited, Brody says, "We gets to ride on two boats? A little boat and a big boat!" Reverend Stuart sees tears running down Mrs. Connery's cheeks. Brody so excited and Mrs. Connery so sad.

One of the wagon wheels falls sharply into a deep hole, and they all grab for something, anything to hold. The wagon levels itself as the wheel rises out of the hole in the road.

"Welcome to Campbeltown Harbor," the sheriff chuckles as he turns his head toward his captives.

A group of people huddle on the little dock. The hapless prisoners strain to make out the faces in the crowd. As the wagon draws closer, familiar faces start to come into focus.

Mrs. Connery identifies a face, "It's Mrs. Clark from church! And Mr. Cunningham and Mrs. Thomson!"

"That's a lot of people!" Brody shouts.

"Don't gets too excited. They here to say goodbye. They can't helps ye now," the sheriff shoots down any hope the ship-bound prisoners might be feeling.

The wagon pulls between the crowd and the dock.

"Alright prisoners get off on that side," the sheriff commands, pointing to the side of the wagon opposite the well-wishing crowd.

"Take a few minutes to say goodbye," the sheriff says.

The first to speak, Mr. Cunningham says, "Reverend Stuart, we have a petition with over one hundred signatures, but the 'ole judge left town."

"I know, we heard," Reverend Stuart says.

"I wishes there was something we could do," Mr. Cunningham says.

"Thank you for trying," Reverend Stuart says.

"It ain't right," Mrs. Clark says as she holds a basket covered with a red cloth. A sad frown forms on her face after the words leave her mouth.

"My companion will take that," the sheriff says as he motions the fat man toward the woman.

Taking the basket from Mrs. Clark, the fat man lifts the red cloth and peeks inside the basket. A big grin lifts his face, "Fresh biscuits! Me likening this trip more and more."

"Alright, let's go. End of the dock with ya," the sheriff commands.

Mrs. Connery and Reverend Stuart wave goodbye to their friends. As the sheriff motions the prisoners by, Brody gets just close enough to kick the sheriff in the right shin. "Damn! Shit!" the sheriff howls in pain and hobbles toward Brody.

"Let's throw him in the water!" the fat man yells. "Come here ye lil' urchin!"

Brody runs down the dock, but, alas, there is no place to go. He stops at the end of the dock where several small tenders are tied up as waves lap at the dock.

As the sheriff and his prisoners approach, the sheriff says, "Sad, ye lost yer basket of biscuits. We'll keep them for the kick. Count yourself lucky. I'm feeling fortunate to never seeing ye again."

"Ye will see me again. I'll come back and cut both yer fat bellies open!" Brody promises.

A round-faced man with a red scarf bound around his forehead and tied in a double knot at the back of his head watches the drama unfold between Brody and the sheriff. The man's eyes are blue like the sea behind him while his skin worn and rough like the bark on a tree. Patches of gray dot his scraggly dark beard. His moustache grown over his lips completely covers his mouth. The moustache pulls up from his lower lip. "Sheriff, you gots you a live one there," pointing at Brody. He chuckles with one dingy yellow tooth hanging from his upper gums.

"Lil bastard, never been so happy to send someone to Carolina!" the sheriff says.

"Me thought there were five of them? Ain't had no schoolin' but looks like thar's three to me," the hard-skinned man says.

"I just has three prisoners," the sheriff says.

"Captain Shanks sent word to me to bring a boy, two men, and two women to the ship. He sails soon," the man says.

"Look!" Brody points. "Another wagon!" A wagon stops at the other end of the dock. Dust settles. Two people hop over the side and reach back into the boarded wagon and pull-out sacks stuffed with clothes and food.

As the newly arrived pair take a few steps down the dock, Reverend Stuart says with astonishment in his voice, "Josh? Samantha?"

"Looks like ye have company for your trip," the sheriff chirps.

"I wonder what …?"

Before Reverend Stuart can find his words, Josh draws near and volunteers an explanation. "We thought we'd join ye. I've wanted to go to Carolina for a long time. My uncle, aunt, and cousins there. Parents say they'll come next year."

"The more, the merrier!" Mrs. Connery says. "And another woman with us, how wonderful!"

"We gots passage for only fifteen shillings. Usually costs two pounds or more. Guess they wanted to fill the ship," Josh says.

Reverend Stuart and Samantha have not spoken to each other. They glance at each other. Eyes meet. Reverend Stuart struggles for words, usually not his problem. "Samantha, surprised to see you here," he says.

Samantha throws her head back slightly. Her red hair, glistening in the sun, falls away from each side of her face.

"My brother told me to go. He says a better life waits me in Carolina," she says.

"Ye wants to be with the Reverend!" Brody blurts out.

"Brody don't ye be sayin' things like that. 'Tis good to have them both," Mrs. Connery says.

"My brother says I'll have more opportunities in Carolina. We have a brother in Wilmington, and another brother in the mountains," Samantha says.

The Isabella!

September 18, 1849

"Gets in the tender!" the hard-skinned man says as seagulls screech overhead. "The Isabella will set sail without ye. Captain Shanks is a stern man, he won't wait."

Brody jumps into the tender. The hard-skinned man helps Mrs. Connery aboard, then Samantha. Josh and Reverend Stuart take their seats.

"You better hopes this is not another fever ship," the hard-skinned man says as he starts rowing toward the Isabella.

"What's a fever ship?" Brody quizzes.

"Five months ago, sailin' to Boston, typhus breaks out on the Ticonderoga. Ship was overloaded, over six-hundred and fifty passengers. Lots of children from the Highlands. Children don't count as passengers," the hard-skinned man shrugs his shoulders, indicating he does not understand.

"Did they die?" Mrs. Connery asks.

"Hundreds," the hard-skinned man says. "Bodies, ten at a time, bundled into sail-cloths, and rolled overboard. The Ticonderoga's a nasty ship. The decks never swabbed and no cleaning below deck. But most of the ships like that. Captains don't care. They have a nice cabin, lots of whiskey, and keep a woman in their cabins."

Pointing with his left hand, the hard-skinned man says, "See the porthole up front. That's the captain's cabin."

"Women? Where the women come from?" Josh asks.

"From the passengers. Food gets scarce on the ship. The captain offers a woman food if she comes to his cabin. A woman by herself in real trouble on these ships." Looking at Mrs. Connery and Samantha, he says, "Ye best stay with these men, and you'll probably be safe."

The tender bounces over the waves. Brody seems to be the only one enjoying the ride. A splash of water slaps Mrs. Connery in the face. Brody laughs. Reverend Stuart offers his scarf, and she wipes the baptism from her face.

"Water's a little rough, so I'll need you men to hold the ropes when the sailors throw them to us. The boy climbs up first, and then the women."

Back on the dock, the sheriff approaches his wagon when two men in black top hats and black coats on chestnut horses ride up.

"Gentlemen, if you are going on that ship . . . ," the sheriff points to the Isabella out in the bay.

Before he can finish, the man with a heavy full mustache says, "Oh no, we don't want to board the ship. We came here looking for a man. His name is Josh Reid. We need him to come with us."

"I puts a woman, a boy, and a man, on the ship," the sheriff says, "but his name wasn't Josh. But another man and a woman got on board with them, and I do recall they called him Josh. The tender be back soon, maybe gets you out before the ship sails. But I see the sails going up now. You probably won't make it in time."

Landstuhl Regional Medical Center

Kirchberg-Kaserne, Germany

February 8, 2020

"Sam! Captain Stuart! Can you hear me?" the nurse asks.

Sam manages to open eyes briefly.

"You're safe now, in a military hospital in Germany."

Sam tries to speak but no words form.

All Aboard!

September 18, 1849

On the tender the hard-skinned man says, "Here come the ropes. We got here just in time, the sails goin' up." Josh and Reverend Stuart grab the falling ropes and pull the tender beside the Isabella.

"You go up first lad," the hard-skinned man says, "Put yer foot here and yer hand here."

"I know how to climb, 'ole man." Brody says as he quickly makes the climb.

"Lady, ye are next." As he grabs her around the hips and pushes her upwards, the hard-skinned man says to Mrs. Connery, "up ye go."

Samantha, Josh, and Reverend Stuart all make the climb and thank the hard-skinned man for the ride.

"Hope ye avoid the typhus and the storms!" he yells back at them.

Two sailors greet them on the Isabella's deck. The much older sailor, his eyes squinting in the bright sunlight, says, "Welcome aboard, you gots here just in time. We'll sail soon. Anchor goin' up now."

The young man's razor-thin face stays locked in a perpetual smile. His beard short and patchy and his uneven brown hair falls almost to his shoulders.

"This is William, William Weldon," the older sailor says. William's green eyes twinkle with the attention.

"He'll take ye below deck where ye'll be staying," the older sailor says, pointing at the smiling, younger man. "My name is John, John Roanoke. William brings yer food twice a day. We'll have a full ship once we pick up people in Liverpool. He'll keep water in the barrels. Otherwise, ye on yer own. Roam

70

about the ship if ye like unless we have a storm or a problem. The captain might then order all passengers below deck. We've had good weather, but it won't last long. William, show them their quarters."

The deck bustles with activity. Sailors going this way and that, climbing masts, and pulling ropes. Deckhands carry crude wooden boxes into storage quarters. Sailors unwind coiled ropes that line the outer edges of the deck. Coils of rigging and bolts of canvas laying on the deck are for new sails if the current ones get damaged.

Chickens squawk from crates.

"We goin' eat chickens?" Brody asks.

"Eggs. We eats their eggs. You wonts get any. They for the sailors," William says. "If the chicken quit laying, the cook holds the chicken over the rail." William points to the outer rail of the deck. "He twists its head off. Blood falls in the ocean and not on the deck. Captain don't want no chicken blood on the deck."

"I hopes I sees that," Brody says.

"Captain tried a cow for milk, but she got seasick, quit giving milk," William says.

"What happened to the cow?" Brody asks.

"It's on an island. Captain traded it to some natives for coconuts and mangos."

"I like that story," Mrs. Connery says.

A flock of seagulls fly overhead, cawing as they swoop and dive. Sailors climb ropes attached to the top of the mast. They start lashing the riggings to the bottom of each sail to hold it steady in the fierce winds they will probably face.

"Be careful on the steps," William says as they approach a square hole on the deck. "They gets slick." The hole is the hatch to the lower deck below.

"I'm going first!" Brody shouts. The new passengers make their way down the steps.

A strong, smelly, stench rises through the opening to greet them. "Oh my!" Samantha says as the rising air hits her nostrils. Her hand goes to her nose.

"You'll get used to it," William says. "We'll all smell like stench by tomorrow."

They all make their way down the creaky steps and begin to look around at their new home.

"Sleep on straw?" Mrs. Connery asks.

"Aye, and this space fills up when we gets to Liverpool," William says. "Gets you a good space now. I hates you have to sleep on the floor. We have hammocks in our quarters. They break sometimes. We heard a 'bam!' two nights ago. Diego's hammock broke. He hits the floor real hard. We think someone cuts his hammock strap, make it easy to break. Some of the sailors don't likes Diego. Not white like most of us. I likes him though. He ain't never messed with nobody."

"I feel the ship moving," Brody says, his eyes big with excitement.

"Is there a deck below this one?" Josh asks.

"Some rum barrels down there. Cargo goes down there, and sometimes passengers if they let too many passengers buy tickets. Rum worth more than passengers now. That's why you got some rum barrels in here," William says. "Me glad you on here now. Gets you a good spot to sleep."

"Sailors been rowdy. Too much rum. We've come from the islands. Ship's full of rum. See the barrels?" William points at the far side of the lower deck. "Captain lets the men have a barrel, but that's a lot of rum. The other barrels will come off tomorrow in Liverpool. Rum barrels off. Empty barrels and people on," William laughs.

"We gets any rum?" Brody asks.

"No! Captain don't allow passengers to get in the rum. Just hope we don't run out of food before we get to Beaufort," William says.

"Beaufort?" Josh asks. "I thought we were going to Wilmington?"

"Oh, we are," William says. "Beaufort is the port across from Wilmington harbor. Beautiful place. Pine trees tall as the ship's mast. Merchants and peddlers everywhere. Goods from the islands, spices from Asia, clothing from New York. Quite a place."

"Good place to land a job?" Josh asks.

"You bet! I've thought about working there me self, but I owes Captain Shanks two more years," William says.

"Why you owe the captain two years?" Mrs. Connery asks.

"I gots in some trouble. Captain knows a judge in Liverpool. If captain needs deck hands, the judge gives them a choice, prison or five years at sea working for Captain Shanks. Judge gets a barrel of rum for every hand," William says.

"William!" A voice booms from above. "You still down there running yer mouth?" John Roanoke yells. "Get up here! You gots work to do."

"Coming, coming, John Roanoke," William says.

"I'll be back with ye dinner. Fresh biscuits. Real good. But won't be fresh after a few days," William says as he scampers up the ladder.

The passengers below hear John Roanoke give William a scolding. "You keep dead beatin', the captain make you wear the hoop."

"What's this hoop, they talks about?" Brody asks Reverend Stuart down below.

"If the sailor don't do his job, Captain puts an iron hoop over the sailor's head. The hoop rests on his shoulders, and he must wear the heavy load all day. Captain also might cut his food in half for a few days," Reverend Stuart explains.

A voice interrupts, "If a man give the captain a hard time, captain hang 'em when he gets to the islands." The figure behind the voice emerges from behind the rum barrels.

"My name's Ross McKenzie. Just getting a little kip. Looks like we're going to be spending some time together. I'm headed back to Carolina. Comes home to gets me parents. Take 'em back to Carolina with me but gots here too late. They dead. Crops failed. Potato fields look like nothing even planted. Starved to death."

"Oh, my!" Mrs. Connery gasps.

"Carolina got jobs, food. It's like heaven compared to Scotland," Ross says.

"How long were you in Carolina?" Josh asks.

"Almost three years. Winters can be rough if you're not prepared, but most people get by," Ross says.

"So, you've sailed with Captain Shanks before?" Reverend Stuart asks.

"No, but I works the ports at Beaufort. Ye cannae work the port without hearing about all the captains. Sailors talk," Ross says.

"What ye do at the docks?" Brody asks.

"Load and unload de ships," Ross explains.

"Pay is okay, but when captains are in a hurry to get back out to sea, they pay good. We loves it when a storm is coming. They sometimes pay double."

"Can me work on the dock?" Brody asks.

"Maybe in a few years. Grows some more. Eat ye biscuits," Ross chuckles.

"Sailors say we gets real crowded down here tomorrow. Lots of passengers boarding in Liverpool. We be packed in here like cattle," Ross adds.

"But all these barrels of rum coming off," Mrs. Connery states.

"They just replaced with empty ones. After dropping us off at Beaufort, this ship heads back to the islands for more rum," Ross says.

"I'm going on deck to tell Scotland goodbye," Ross says.

"Me too!" Brody says and, of course, leads the way and runs to the starboard side.

Sailing Away!

September 19, 1849

"Land's shrinking!" Brody shouts.

"You'll see some beautiful little islands soon, Isle of Man for sure. And the Hilbre Isles are red sandstone," Ross says, "And on the morrow, Liverpool, a beautiful port. The bay filled with tall ships."

"I never dreamed I'd be leaving me home and Scotland," Mrs. Connery moans.

"Why ye leaving?" Ross asks as he eyes small clusters of cotton like clouds in the sky.

"Mean, greedy judge took me home," Mrs. Connery explains.

"Oh," Ross says but stops short of being noisy.

"I'll comes back and kills that judge," Brody says.

"Brody, stop talking like that. Enjoy this beautiful view," Mrs. Connery says.

"You might see a whale," Samantha says.

"Ye won't see a whale in these waters. Maybe when we get south. Close to Carolina if the water warm enough," Ross says.

"Anybody fish from the ship?" Brody asks.

"Naye, naye, Captain don't allow and pretty hard to do cause we're up so high," Ross says.

"Don't try swimming either!" Reverend Stuart says to Brody.

"Maybe the sailors will let me help them," Brody says. "I'd like to climb those ropes."

"You could ask," Ross says.

"Look! Another sail goin' up," Josh says.

"That's the headsail," Ross says. "We are almost at full sail. The sails are fore and aft rigged, so the headsail goes up last. We'll get to Liverpool before sunup. The crew will unload the empty barrels before first light, and the passengers will come on after dawn. This ship has quite a history. She tooks Irish prisoners to Australia and brought slaves from Africa to America."

"What's a slave?" Brody asks.

"Greedy, mean people capture people in Africa and takes them to America and make them work on their plantations," Samantha says.

"Get some good sleep tonight. We'll be crowded down here 'morrow night. Hope too many don't get seasick," Ross says.

"What's seasick?" Brody asks.

"You'll know when it happens," Ross laughs.

"Brody, the movement of the ship out on the waves upsets the tummies of a few people," Mrs. Connery explains. "But they get over it."

"Just wait a few weeks, ye'll think the food is killin' ye. Biscuits hard, salt pork turning green," Ross says.

"I guess the big worry is a storm. Blows the ship off course. Takes longer and the ship runs out of food," Josh says.

"It happens, but we don't want to think about that," Ross says.

"We'll let Brody fish, and I'll cook," Samantha says.

"Lots of mouths to feed!" Ross says.

"I'll just catch more fish!" Brody offers.

"Speaking of food, when does William bring our biscuits?" Josh asks.

"Before the sun goes down. We shouldn't stay out here too long. You ladies shouldna' go anywhere alone on the ship. These sailors have not been with a woman since their last stop in the islands. And some just left prison, their crimes against women," Ross says.

Below deck, they rest on the straw except for Reverend Stuart and Josh. Josh leans against the steps.

"Don't lean too hard. Those old steps could collapse, and we won't get our biscuits," Reverend Stuart says. They both chuckle.

"Sounds like we need to keep the ladies close at hand," Josh says after making sure no one else could hear them.

Reverend Stuart nods his head up and down.

"I'll keep me eye on Mrs. Connery. Your eyes, they be on Samantha. You mind that?" Josh says.

Reverend Stuart says nothing.

Josh lowers his voice even more and whispers, "Is that a wee little smile I see on your face?"

Reverend Stuart's face brightens.

"It's a good thing ye not Catholic," Josh says with a wink.

"Fresh biscuits!" William says as he makes quick work down the steps. William swings the sack from his back and drops its contents on the crude wooden table beside their water barrel. "Ye get salt cod with yer biscuits in the morning, just plain biscuits in the evening. I'll be back with another water barrel. We got lots of people coming in here in the morning."

"What about another ladle?" Reverend Stuart asks. "They're going to be a lot of people down here. "

"I can bring you one more," William says. "Captain don't want too many ladles out. We had a passenger turn one into a knife and stabbed another passenger."

"Oh my!" Mrs. Connery exclaimed as she usually does when she gets excited.

"I'll be back, and a couple of sailors will help me with the barrel. It's heavy," William says.

"We can help," Josh says.

"Maybe comin' down these steps. Be here in case we needs ya," William says. "And you women, especially you," as William points to Samantha, "Don't you be makin' eye contact with Griffin. He has the long dark hair, tied together, and down his back. He's raped before."

"Thank you, William, I'll take heed," Samantha says.

"Enjoy your biscuits!" William says, as he heads above.

Brody darts to the table. "Umm!" he says. "Good biscuits, but not as good as Mrs. Connery's hot biscuits."

"Brody, you are so sweet. Thank you," Mrs. Connery says.

"One other thing," William says as he looks back. "Four buckets. One up against each side of the wall. That's where ya'll go when ya feel the call of nature. You need to empty it at least once a day. Otherwise, it will smell even worse than it does down here now. Oh, and make sure you dump the bucket off the stern," William says.

"What's a stern?" Brody asks.

"He likes to ask questions," Mrs. Connery apologizes.

"That's da way he learns stuff," William says.

Then looking at Brody, William says, "Stern, that's the back of the ship and," but before William can finish, Brody quizzes, "So what's the front called?"

"That's the bow. Captain's up there a lot, but don't bother him."

"What will he do?" Brody asks.

"When we gets to warm water, he'll throw ye to the sharks," William jokes.

"I bets I can swim faster than 'em sharks," Brody boasts.

"You best be a fast swimmer," William warns.

William continues, "Brody, if you are looking at the bow, which way is the bow?"

"That way, the front," Brody proudly declares.

"So, if you are looking at the bow, this side is port side, and that side is starboard," William, obviously enjoying sharing the information with Brody, points to his left and right.

"Back with water barrel soon," William adds as he scampers up the steps.

"Brody, you gonna be a sailor?" Josh asks.

"I'm gonna be captain and throw mean people to the sharks," Brody says.

"Look out below!" A voice warns from above, "coming down with a water barrel."

William and another sailor climb down the steps to receive the bottom of the heavy water barrel from the third sailor who directs the barrel down the steps.

With a wink to Reverend Stuart, William looks up the steps and says, "Griffin, you stay up there, these strong men will help us with the barrel." And whispers to Reverend Stuart, "He has the morals of a great white shark."

Reverend Stuart and Josh help the two sailors with the barrel.

"This thing is heavy!" Josh says with a hint of surprise.

"We needs at least two good rains to replenish our drinking water on this voyage. We hope for rain once a week or so," William says.

With the barrel in place, they turn around and see Griffin coming down the steps.

"Me thought I would just check things out down here," Griffin says as his eyes turn toward the women.

Josh and Reverend Stuart notice that Samantha stares straight at Griffin, like she is not intimidated by him.

"I like red hair," Griffin says.

"I like my hair, too," Samantha says without batting an eye.

"I will look out for you, Miss Red," Griffin says.

"That will not be necessary. My brother taught me how to take care of myself," Samantha says.

"All right, Griffin, let's go," William says as he motions Griffin toward the steps.

When they are up the steps, Mrs. Connery says, "Samantha, you best stay close. I don't likes the way that man looked at you."

"You don't worry, Mrs. Connery. I'lls be fine," Samantha says.

"De sun setting soon. Let's go see," Ross says.

Once again, they make their way up the rickety ladder steps.

"Where did the land go?" Brody asks as he steps out on the deck.

"We won't see land until morning when we see the tall ships docked in Liverpool," Ross says.

"Look at that sunset," Josh says. "Looks like the sky is on fire. Red, orange. Magnificent."

"This will be our view every morn and evening, unless we gets clouds," Ross says. "Makes it almost worth the voyage."

"The creator made a magnificent world," Josh says. They all shake their heads in agreement.

"I like listening to the ship cutting through the waves," Reverend Stuart says.

They all stand silent for a time and enjoy the rhythms of each wave hitting the ship's bow as the sky darkens.

"Look! That star is flying through the air," Brody shouts.

"Meteorite," Reverend Stuart says. "It is a piece of rock, big piece of rock hurtling through space. I had to take a science course at the university. They think there are lots of these out there. Floating around. When they get close to earth, they catch on fire and usually burn up before hitting the ground."

"I wanna take that course!" Brody says nearly shouting with excitement.

"We'll get you in a course, in a school, when we get to Carolina," Reverend Stuart says.

"Really?" Brody asks.

"Everybody should go to school," Josh says. "There's so much to learn."

"Go to school and fish. I'm going to like this, Carolina."

"Let's get down that ladder before it gets dark and gets some kip," Ross says.

Below deck, they each find a place on the straw. Josh volunteers to sleep near the steps. Reverend Stuart beds down beside Josh.

"Brody, you cans sleep between me and Samantha," Mrs. Connery says. Mrs. Connery and Samantha leave space between them for Brody. This puts Samantha beside Reverend Stuart.

"I've been sleeping over there by the post. But I'll join ye if you don't mind. Okay if I makes me bed beside you, Mrs. Connery?" Ross asks.

"Be good to haves a familiar face nearby," Mrs. Connery says in a soft voice. "Brody is already asleep. He puts his head down, and he's asleep."

"Good thing we goin' to sleep now," Ross says. "They'll be in for those rum barrels a long time before sun comes up."

"They wonts wake up Brody," Mrs. Connery says. "He sleeps like a rock, maybe like one of them meteorites out there." She says slowly, "Did I say that the way it supposed to be said?"

"Perfect," Reverend Stuart says as he feels his eyelids getting heavy. "Good night, everybody."

"Same right back at you," Ross says.

Light wakes up Reverend Stuart. It is a moving light, not the sun's light, he realizes.

"These people still sleep," William says as he coming down the steps, lantern in hand. Four more sailors including Griffin make their way down the steps.

In a soft voice, William says, "Griffin, you go back up the steps. Me, Diego, and O'Brien will push the barrel up the steps."

"I can help too," Reverend Stuart says, rubbing his eyes.

"We gots it," William says.

"Ain't nobody helps me up here," Griffin says.

"I can help," Reverend Stuart offers in a voice just above a whisper.

"He'll be fine. Just has to steady the barrel. We'll go up and helps him after we push up three or four. Gots twenty-seven in here," William says.

"Christ! They filled these bastards completely full," O'Brien says as he struggles to roll the barrel.

"Don't tries to do that by yourself. We going to help. Just remembers this is a reverend here, watch what you say," William says.

"It's okay," Reverend Stuart says.

"You sound like my kind of Reverend," O'Brien says. "And gots you a good-looking woman sleeping there. That red hair and all."

Reverend Stuart chooses not to respond.

"Up we go," William says as they struggle with the first barrel. "You got it, Griffin? Just let is lay on its side. We'll be up after a few more."

Liverpool!

September 20, 1849

"Must be coming into Liverpool," Ross says. "Waves not hitting us as hard. Musts be out of the main channel."

"You got it. Crew will be throwing anchor soon," William says. "We drop anchor at the King's Dock. The lil' ships go up the River Mersey to the Queen's Dock."

Ross, Josh, Mrs. Connery, and Samantha start to stir. The top two buttons of Samantha's blouse have come undone during the night. The sailors see the abundant cleavage and quickly look away.

"The buttons," Mrs. Connery whispers, and Samantha quickly ends the excitement for the sailors.

"We be finished soon," William says. "Then, I'll bring ye biscuits and salt pork."

More barrels go up with heavy grunting. The sailors scurry up the ladder steps and help Griffin.

"Just rolls them up against the small mast," William says.

Back down the ladder with the others, William says to Reverend Stuart, "This is hardest part. After we get 'em up there, we just rolls 'em across the deck and down the ramp. We gets 'em on the dock, and we done. Merchant man takes 'em from there."

Lots of grunts and strained muscles later, the final barrel is through the hole.

The hungry passengers below hear William say to the other sailors, "Roll de barrels up to the gangplank side. I'll get der biscuits. Later at dinnertime, all of you will have to help. A lot more biscuits to take down there."

A short time later, William lowers himself with biscuits in a large wooden bucket down the ladder steps.

"Better wake that boy up. His biscuits are here," William says.

"Brody, wake up, your biscuits!" Mrs. Connery says as she gently shakes Brody.

"Leave me be," Brody protests.

"Brody gets up, or I'm going to eat your biscuits," Josh says.

Brody sits up and rubs his eyes. "I smell 'em." He jumps to his feet and heads to their little table and the pile of biscuits.

"I like 'em. Good! Better than yesterday," Brody says.

"It's the salt pork," Ross who has joined them says and then adds, "I'm going up top soon and watch us dock at Liverpool."

"Me goin'," Brody says.

"I think we'll all probably go," Mrs. Connery says.

Biscuits devoured, Ross heads up the ladder-steps.

"I'll help the ladies," he says.

Mrs. Connery, then Samantha, climb the steps. Brody tries to butt in, but Reverend Stuart intervenes, "Ladies, always go first, Brody."

"Oh, all right," Brody says as he steps back.

Josh is the next to last one up the steps, and from below Reverend Stuart says, "I'll take first turn and empty the buckets."

"Oh dear," Mrs. Connery says. "We'll have to take turns."

The wooden buckets have a wooden lid and a rope handle. Reverend Stuart only has to empty two of them. He turns his head to the side as he pours the smelly mess over the stern.

Joining the others near the gangplank, Reverend Stuart, hoping no one mentions the buckets, says, "Looking like that is the last of the rum barrels they're rolling down."

"They'll bring the empty barrels on board before they let the passengers on," Ross says.

"Good heavens," Josh says as he points to a mass of people coming toward the gangplank. "Must be hundreds . . . men, women, and lots of children. I remember John Randolph said children don't count in the passenger totals."

The mass of humanity, most with eyes drawn and cheeks hollow, turns into a single line at the first checkpoint. Two sailors check off their names from the manifest.

William says as loudly as he can to the new passengers, "De sailors lets twenty-five people through at a time, and we'll take ye to yer quarters. My name's William. This's O'Brien." O'Brien raises his arm slightly. "He'll take the first group up the gangplank."

"I guess you can call that 'quarters,'" Josh whispers to Reverend Stuart, and then says to Ross, "Thanks for the tip . . . putting an article of clothing where we slept last night. I hope the new passengers respect that?"

"The sailors makes sure they know dat when they takes the new passengers down," Ross says.

On the dock, William addresses the new passengers, "Before the first group goes up, lets me tell you something for your own good. The captain is a good and fair man, but he don'ts like no stealing. You needs to follow his rules. No stealing, no fightin', no gettin' in the sailors' ways. And stay away from the bow. That's this end of the ship," William says as he points to his right. "We'll be bringing you foods in the morning and in the evening. Take turns emptying the chamber buckets over the stern," he says pointing to his left. "And if the captain gives orders, follow them. If we hits a storm, he might order passengers to stay below deck. Oh, and don't complains about the food. Captain don't like no complaining. If you gets seasick, come up to the main deck and go to one side, port or starboard, and looks straight ahead. But don't go on the bow. Captain don't likes that. Any questions?"

A few of the passengers look at each other and shrug their shoulders.

"Okay, no questions, good. If you have any later, any of the sailors will try to answer thems for you," William says. "O'Brien takes the first group up."

Reverend Stuart and friends watch as the passengers file by them after they reach the main deck. They are the desperate, without jobs, and the poor, hunger written on most of their faces, sunken eyes surrounded by dark circles. With haggard, soiled clothes, torn, and mostly baggy, all of them look like they have lost lots of weight.

"Look!" Mrs. Connery blurts. "It's Bernie and Prunella McDonald's daughter. Good Lord, she is by herself and so pregnant. Oh my!"

"The smithy's daughter," Josh says.

Myra marches up the gangplank with the second group.

Reverend Stuart says what they all realize, "Mr. and Mrs. McDonald couldn't handle the shame. They are sending her to Carolina."

"Strange, she is boarding here in Liverpool," Josh wonders aloud.

"They found out Reverend Stuart put on this ship. He's been the only friend the poor girl had," Mrs. Connery says.

As the second group nears the top of the gangplank, Reverend Stuart waves his right hand over his head and shouts, "Myra's over here!"

Warmth spreads on Myra's face when her eyes meet Reverend Stuart's.

Mrs. Connery darts ahead and greets Myra first. "You poor child, going to Carolina by yourself in your condition. You can join us."

"I would like that," Myra sighs with relief.

"You know Reverend Stuart. This is Samantha from Logan's Tavern," Mrs. Connery explains.

"I know Samantha. When I could get out, I use to go to the pub. She served me some great Irish stew."

Samantha steps forward and gives Myra a big hug.

"This is Josh, and Ross, we just meet yesterday, and little Brody," she says.

"I ain't little!" Brody protests.

"If you aren't little, the captain might put you to work," Reverend Stuart says.

"I woulds like that!" Brody says.

"Come on, we'll show you our quarters," Reverend Stuart says.

"Quarters? I don't know about that. It's like a floating barn down there. We sleep on hay," Josh says.

"I'm just so glad I ran into you. I was really scared. I didn't know what to expect," Myra says

"Your parents know about this?" Reverend Stuart asks.

"Aye, they know all about this. They got Ben Malley to bring me down here. They ashamed of me," Myra says

"We're not ashamed of you," Mrs. Connery says.

All the others nod in agreement, but Brody blurts out, "What are they shamed of?"

"Myra goin' to have a bairn, and her parents don't like that," Reverend Stuart says.

"We all were bairns," Brody says. "That mean."

"Brody, I like that!" Mrs. Connery proudly snaps.

Sailors strain and grunt as they bring on cargo, not only empty rum barrels but crude wooden boxes, obviously very heavy.

"Goods for America. Things that are hard to find there. Spices, china, silverware, and even perfumes," Ross says.

"Brody come back here. You don't want to be in the way!" Reverend Stuart shouts as Brody darts ahead.

A bearded sailor waiting his turn to take a box into a cargo hold says, "I'll put him to work!"

"Yea!" Brody says with excitement.

"You best wait until you get a little older, Brody," Reverend Stuart says.

"You never lets me have any fun," Brody complains.

"You gots a lively one there, mister. And some good-looking women. The red-headed one turns a sailor's head," the sailor nods.

They ignore the sailor and walk toward their quarters. A long line of people, the first two groups of twenty-five, wait to go down the ladder-steps. The sailors are still loading the empty rum barrels, barely squeezing them through the quarters-cargo hatch.

"This one is heavy!" an old sailor gruffly complains.

"The' all gettin' heavy for you, old man," a young sailor shouts, and all the sailors laugh.

"Let's get in line before the next group arrives," Ross says.

Going down the ladder a bit later, they hear cursing below from the new passengers. "No beds! Must sleep on bloody straw! Bullocks!"

"One cursed water barrel!" another roars.

"It is a bit of a shock," Ross whispers.

Reverend Stuart and the others sigh with relief that no one has taken their "beds."

Looking at the complaining man, Ross says, "William said they would be bringing more water barrels."

"He best. We starts a bloody mutiny down here." The others laugh.

A man who appears to be his companion quips, "The only mutiny you'll start will be in your own bowels!" Laughter roars across the quarters.

"You best watch your words about mutiny," Ross says. "These captains fear a mutiny and wills come down hard on anyone talkin' bout it."

The complaining man begrudgingly says, "At least, I'm headed to Carolina, a land filled with milk and honey."

"That's Palestine! You old fool! Carolina filled with sweat and toil," another man laughs.

The complaining man shakes his head but does not say another word.

"Nots even a 'donkey's breakfast!'" a man says from across the room.

"What's a donkey's breakfast?" Brody asks Ross.

"It's a bed, well, kind-of. On some ships they take big sacks and stuff 'em with straw, 'bout enough straw for a donkey's breakfast, and the sailors use 'em for beds," Ross says.

The women among the new passengers busy themselves with what little they can be busy about: fluffing the straw, arranging their bags of clothes into pillows, and greeting their fellow passengers.

"Just a big bedroom," one says. "But better than what the Vikings had . . . they had to sleep on the open deck."

"Some things to be thankful fer," another says.

"How's de foods?"

"Tis' wonderful if you like biscuits. Lots of biscuits," Ross says.

"I ready for some biscuits," a man says.

"They be awhile. Sailors must gets all the cargo on first," Ross says. "John Randolph's crew brings our food, William and some other sailors. We are lucky. William's a good man. Some of the sailors steal biscuits from the passengers."

"I say cut off the hand of anyone who steals me biscuits," a large man says.

"You probably eat the hand too!" a man cackles.

"Ewww . . . ," a woman moans.

Meanwhile, Mrs. Connery and Samantha try to make Myra comfortable. "You cans sleep between us. Samantha on that side, and I'll be on this side."

'Everybody trying to keep Samantha and Reverend Stuart together,' Josh thinks to himself since they will still be sleeping side by side.

"Comin' down," a voice says from above.

William, Griffin, and O'Brien come down the steps. O'Brien and William come down first while Griffin lowers the water barrel. Carefully, they lower the barrel to the floor. Josh and Reverend Stuart walk toward the steps just in case they are needed.

After the barrel is rolled to the wall opposite the first water barrel, William announces, "Here your other water barrel and a ladle. Don't be wasting water. We only gots so much, and if it don't rain, we could runs short. That's no fun goin' without water even a day. And the ladle, it stays with the barrel. Captain won't let me give you any more ladles. So always leave it right here."

"What about a wash?" a woman asks. "We goin' to be on this ship for weeks. Where's do we bath?"

"No wash on this ship. You'll have to wait until you get to Beaufort, that's the port at Wilmington," William says. "We sailors we'll have to wait until we gets to the first island, probably Bermuda, go ashore, and jump in. Count yourselves lucky."

"Don't matter bout ole Joseph here," a man says pointing to a grey bearded, hunched-back man who has nodded off to sleep. "He ain't had no bath in five years."

Several men cackle with laughter while Joseph sleeps through it all.

"A lot of these people know each other," Josh whispers to Reverend Stuart.

"Lots of them from the same villages. When one farmer's potatoes get the fungus every farm 'round gets it," Reverend Stuart says. "And the English efforts have not helped in Ireland and Scotland. English take grains from our people and give them to their soldiers. To make things worse, the peasants who rent land have no crops to sell, and then they have no money for rent. The wealthy landowners kick them off the land. All they care about is their money, it seems."

"They're a desperate looking lot, but they haven't forgotten how to laugh," Josh says.

"Yea, they are remarkable people. Strong willed and determined," Reverend Stuart observes.

"Make ye-selves comfortable. Goes up on the deck if ye like. Goin' be a lil' while fer we bring yer biscuits. We gots lots of cargo to put away," O'Brien says as he and William climb up the steps.

"Let's go up and watch us sail away," Ross says to his group.

Never outdone, Brody scampers up the ladder, soon followed by the rest of the group.

On the deck, they see a scurry of activity. "It's as busy as an ant hill up here!" Mrs. Connery says.

Deckhands and sailors bring on board the last of the provisions for the long voyage. Boxes and barrels, big and small, sit on shoulders of fast-walking sailors.

A tall, muscled man wearing a black knit cap, with a missing right arm and a giant brown birthmark on his left cheek, directs the traffic. "No, no, those boxes go to the galley!" he bellows out at a young sailor. "Ye keeps making me correct you and captain send you back to the judge and prison," he warns.

"How'd he lose his arm?" Brody asks Ross.

"I heard he losts it on a whaling ship," Ross says. "He was a harpoon thrower. Throw a harpoon farther than any man. He leaned over the hunt-boat to pull his harpoon out of a whale, and a shark leaped through the air and tore his arm off."

Brody's eyes flash as large as the sun. "Did it hurts?"

"I'm sure it did. You best not get too close to the railings. One'll jump up and bites you," Josh teases Brody.

"Nay, can't jumps this high? Can they?" Brody wonders aloud.

"Never happen," Samantha reassures Brody.

"You try to scare me!" Brody says to Josh. "You shouldnae do it."

"What's in all the boxes?" Brody says to anyone who will answer.

"Everything," Ross says. "Supplies for the crew and passengers. Maybe bread, salt pork, jerky, dried cod. But we won't gets much of that. It's for the crew. We gets biscuits."

"They're taking goods to the Carolinas," Reverend Stuart adds.

"Cloth, quills, rugs, you names it," Ross says.

"What are those?" Brody asks as sailors go by with a bundle of boards.

"Staves for an emergency, boards to repair the sides of the ship if it's gets damaged by big waves," Ross says.

"Really?" Brody says. "Waves that big?"

"Oh yeah," Ross says. "It can get really rough out there during the big storms."

Two sailors, one on each end, carry a large chest into the captain's quarters.

"That's the best provisions on the ship," Ross says. "No tellings what's in it. Fine English sweets, scotch, the bests Liverpool has to offer."

Sparse, Grueling, Boring Life on the Biscuit Ship

September 20, 1849

"Look! They're pulling up the gangplank," Samantha says.

Two sailors on each side of the gangplank pull on massive ropes. "Pull like ye pulling a pirate off ye mother," a sailor says. Creaking and moaning, the gangplank reaches its apex and then falls into place on the side of the ship with a loud thud.

"Anchor up!" a sailor screams as he and three other deckhands on the bow pull up the heavy beast.

"They like to drop the anchor from the bow," Ross says. "Cause they don't wants to take a chance of hitting the rudder. But in some harbors, they must go off the stern."

At the bow, several sailors strain on ropes as they lift a white mass from the deck, and a sail comes to life, flapping in the wind.

"Brody, that's the foresail. They puts it up first," Ross says and adds, "See that sailor goin' up the riggings?"

"Yea!" Brody says.

"He's going' up to the fore-top-castle. See it up there? Looks like a big basket," Ross says. Brody nods his head.

"That sailor will scan the sea in fronts of us. He'll look through his eyeglass some of the time," Ross makes little circles with his thumbs and forefingers and puts his hands to his eyes like an eyeglass. Brody does the same thing, and a big grin sweeps across Ross' face. "You'd makes a good look-out, Brody."

A grin spreads on Brody's face as he points at the stern. "Look, more sails going ups!"

"That's yer bonaventure sail," Ross explains.

"You sure know lots about ships," Josh says to Ross.

"Been on a few voyages," Ross explains.

"Top-sails going up now," Ross points straight up.

"Lil' baskets up there too," Brody says.

"Yeah, they yer main top castles at the top of the main masts. Captain might send a sailor up if he needs to see as far as he can," Ross says. "When we gets out a little more, the main sails will go up on the two main masts. Those sails really drive the ship forward. The lil' sails help with steering and direction."

With anchor up and sails set, the Isabella glides toward deeper water.

"I loves it!" a wide-eyed Brody exclaims. "I wants to be a sailor!"

"In a few hours, we might gets a glimpse of the point at Holyhead, pass through Saint George's channel, leaves the Irish Sea, and head west on endless, wide waters," Ross says.

"It's glorious!" Brody says, nearly shouting.

"I didn't know you knew that word," Reverend Stuart says to Brody.

"I heards you say that in a sermon," Brody proudly says.

"I'm glad you were listening, Brody," Mrs. Connery interjects.

"All ye cargo hatches locked?" the tall, one-armed man bellows. "Any sailor leaves his hatch unlocked will have the morning watch for the first week."

"What's a watch?" Brody wonders aloud.

"Each sailor must take a turn on a watch. It's usually four hours. One sailor on the bow and another on the stern. The sailors don't wants the last night or morning watch. Haves to stay awake fer four hours, after midnight until dawn." Ross says.

"We lucky to wake you by mid-morning, Brody. Ye wouldn't be a good night watchman," Mrs. Connery laughs. Brody for once says nothing.

"Our biscuits comin' soon, I hopes," Josh says. "Let's go to our quarters."

"Biscuits and water, but sometimes for a change we gets water and biscuits," Ross chuckles.

"De biscuits are soft now. Later, they'll be hard. That'll be a variety," Josh offers.

"Ye fellows funny," Mrs. Connery says.

Reverend Stuart thinks to himself that it's good Mrs. Connery talks and jokes. He worries about her the most. The others are young and adaptable, he thinks.

They aren't down below very long until William and O'Brien come down the steps with buckets of biscuits.

"Do it however ye wants," William says. "But maybe lets the women and children come first. One biscuit per person. There should be enough for every person when we get all the biscuits down here."

"Go up and hand down the other two buckets," William says to O'Brien.

"Could I have a volunteer to puts the buckets up on the deck when they empty so we don'ts have to come back down here?" William asks. Josh raises his hand, and William thanks him.

"It should be a clear night. You might wanna to go up on deck and enjoy the sky," William offers. "It looks like everyone has found them a good bed of straw. Should be a good night for sleeps. Sea calm but we just enough wind for a good stout sail."

After William reaches the deck, Josh says to the others, "We're not going to gain any weight on this voyage."

"When we gets biscuits and salt pork in the morn' it'll be like a feast," Samantha says.

"Until they run out," Ross says.

"Really?" an astonished Mrs. Connery says.

"Could happen," Ross says. "Some of the sailors steal somes of our biscuits. Or the big rats get in 'em."

"Big rats!" Mrs. Connery shrieks.

"They on all the ships," Ross says. "But those big rats keep many a sailor alive when the ship runs out of food. They hard to catch, but a hungry sailor does what he has to."

"I never had any mice, let alone rats in me house in Campbeltown," Mrs. Connery laments.

"You miss your home. It saddens all of us what has happened," Reverend Stuart empathizes.

"I'll just have to get used to it," Mrs. Connery says.

"You'll be with us," Samantha offers comfort.

"Let's go see the sea," Brody says.

"Everybody want to go?" Reverend Stuart asks.

"Me legs tired. I thinks I will stay here and rest," Mrs. Connery says.

"I'll stay with her," Myra says.

"I'll stay too," Josh joins in.

The others scamper up in the steps.

"Let's go to the starboard side," Brody says.

Impressed, Reverend Stuart says, "Brody, you are really catching on. You might be a captain some day!"

Brody beams.

Ross, Brody, Samantha, and Reverend Stuart position themselves along the railing and listen to the waves softly batter the side of the ship.

"I know why you wanted to come to the starboard side, Brody. You wanted to see the sunset," Samantha says. "Good choice." Pride spreads on Brody's face.

The tip of the sun dips into the water on the horizon. A span of orange and red glows to the right and to the left across the vast horizon.

"Red sky at night, sailors delight," Ross says. "I've found that to be true and always wondered why?"

"Most storms move west to east. So, if the sky is red in the west at sundown, that probably means the sky is clear to the west and probably means it will still be clear in the morning," Reverend Stuart says.

"That doesn't sound like bollocks. That makes a lot of sense. You a smart man, Reverend Stuart," Ross congratulates Reverend Stuart.

"I took some science courses at the university, that's all," a modest Reverend Stuart says.

"Look!" Brody says.

High above, crossing over the ship from east to west moves a massive black cloud. The mass swirls to the right, then down, then to the left, then back up again.

"It looks like a teardrop!" Samantha says. "A moving teardrop!"

"Maybe Mrs. Connery's teardrop?" Reverend Stuart says. Samantha and Ross nod at the symbolism.

"Looks like a ball now," Brody exclaims. "Now, a bucket. What is it?"

"I'll answer before Reverend Stuart does." Ross says. "I've seen this several times off the coast. That's a flock of starlings, crossing the Irish Sea."

"How do they stick together and take all those shapes?" Brody asks.

"I don't know. Maybe Reverend Stuart does?" Ross suggests.

"I don't know for sure, but maybe they are like two dancers that move together. Their minds and bodies in sync. When one goes in one direction, the other follows. Just a theory. I really don't know," Reverend Stuart says.

"Makes sense to me," Ross says.

They all stare at the ballet in the sky.

"So much beauty on this earth," Samantha says.

"I must remind myself most of the time to slow down and appreciate it. Aye, it's all around us," Reverend Stuart says. "I have been a bit sad about something today. It just occurred to me earlier today that I'm going to miss Reverend George MacDonald's wedding next year. He has been such a good friend, and he is marrying Louisa Powell, a lovely and wonderful young woman from near Aberdeen."

"George MacDonald, he's the writer?" Samantha asks.

"Aye, *Phantastes* is his first novel, but there will be more. Brilliant man, writer, and theologian. He has some theological ideas that are very interesting and quite controversial. He believes all people will be saved. He doesn't believe a loving God would send some people to an eternal punishment just because they don't believe the proper doctrines or don't even believe in God at all. What loving parent would send their child to eternal punishment? He thinks God is at least as forgiving as a parent. But it's getting late. Maybe we should think about going in."

"Brody, let's go down and check on the others. Okay?" Ross says.

"Oh, all right," Brody says and with head hung down begrudgingly joins Ross in the walk back to the hatch steps.

Samantha and Reverend Stuart stand in silence. They have not planned this, but it feels like the others want them together.

After several minutes of pleasurable silence and watching the moonlight dancing on the waves, Samantha says with a sweet glance, "Is it okay if I call you Charles, Reverend Stuart?"

"Of course, I wish everyone did, but most insist on the reverend thing," Charles says.

"Well, you're so reverend-like," Samantha says half-serious and half-joking.

"Sometimes, I don't feel so reverendly. You know the whole turn the other cheek thing and all. Sometimes, I get really angry with some people, with mean people, but I have to keep the reverend image going. People can be so cruel to each other, oftentimes, for material things that don't last long any way. Vanity, vanity, all is vanity . . . Ecclesiastes. Damn, there I go, getting preachy. Sorry," Charles says, somewhat disgusted with himself.

"It's probably hard to switch out of your role. You are a wonderful minister. I think it just comes natural to ye. Ye really love people, try to understand them, and ye help people," Samantha says with deep admiration in her voice.

"Thanks. I . . . just want to be a . . . regular person sometimes," Charles bemoans.

"Ye are a regular person and a wonderful minister at the same time," Samantha comforts him.

"Coming from you that means a lot," Charles says.

"It's true," Samantha says.

"Look!" she says. "A star flying across the sky!"

"Wow!" Charles says. "So . . . what did Brody say . . . glorious?"

"Glorious! Yeah, that's what he said," Samantha laughs.

For the first time, their heads turn toward each other. They stare. Minutes, it seems, go by as they search each other's eyes. They hardly blink.

"I guess we better go down with the others," Reverend Stuart says.

"Yea, I guess so. It's wonderful out here. What more could a girl want? Gorgeous night sky . . . streaking, brilliant stars . . . a wonderful man . . ."

Before Samantha can finish, Reverend Stuart says, "a wonderful woman."

As he turns, Samantha reaches for Reverend Stuart's right arm and with her left arm extended wraps her left hand around his arm just above the elbow. They pause, looking deeply into each other's eyes, and then walk together to the steps.

Down below, sleeping bodies cover the straw, a few already snoring. Brody is fast asleep beside Mrs. Connery.

From his straw-bed, Josh says in a hushed voice, "Beautiful night out there."

Samantha and Reverend Stuart nod in agreement, trying not to say a word lest they bother the sleeping multitude or so it seems.

The soft straw welcomes them. It's been another long day. Reverend Stuart thinks about all that has happened in the last few days. Surreal, he thinks. Life turning on a shilling. Lost in his thoughts, he feels a hand, the same hand as on the deck, come around his elbow. It is a hand of comfort and . . . he stops the thought and closes his eyes. The hand soon goes limp. Samantha sleeps.

Reverend Stuart usually goes quickly into a deep sleep. His body and mind need the rest and regeneration from his pastoral duties that require lots of travel, much of it on foot. He feels a numbness coming over him. "Blessed sleep," he thinks to himself. How welcome it is.

"Tap, tap, tap, tap." Reverend Stuart near sleep still has enough awareness to hear it.

"Tap, tap, tap, tap." The tapping stops briefly, and then it's back again. He listens more intensely. The tapping seems to be coming from the empty rum barrels stacks just beyond where they are sleeping.

"Reverend Stuart, do you hear that?" Josh asks.

"Aye," Reverend Stuart says in a soft voice. "Seems to be coming from the empty rum barrels. Let's check it out."

Careful not to awaken the others, they creep over to the empty rum barrels in the dim light. They carefully place their steps around the sleeping passengers.

"Tap, tap, tap." They get closer.

"Reverend Stuart, I think it is coming from that barrel over there on the bottom. Let's set the top two off," Josh whispers.

They hear a moan inside the barrel. After the top barrels are off, Josh pulls a knife out of his pocket, flips the blade open, and puts the blade under the edge of the barrel top. He wiggles the blade, then moves the blade over, and wiggles the blade again. They take off the loose top. It looks like dark hair in the barrel. The hair raises up slightly.

"It's a head!" Josh whispers.

In the dim light, they reach down and grab the torso under the armpits and slowly pull. It's a person too weak to move his arms or legs. Josh and Reverend Stuart keep pulling. Head, shoulders, then arms come out of the barrel. Stuffed in the barrel, the person's arms and legs are limp.

So far, they have only seen the back of the head. Now, they can tell it is a man. Reverend Stuart leans over and peers closely at the face.

"Keltz!" Reverend Stuart gasps.

"Reverend," Keltz mutters.

"Josh, let's get him over to our straw," Reverend Stuart whispers.

"What be going on?" Another passenger is awake.

"Tis nothing. Just go back to sleep," Reverend Stuart says softly.

Each hold an arm as they get the very weak Keltz over to the straw between Reverend Stuart and Josh's beds.

"Josh, get him some water," Reverend Stuart says.

Reverend Stuart holds up the weak man, and Josh holds the ladle to Keltz's lips. He is strong enough to take a few sips, and then they slowly let him back down on the straw.

Reverend Stuart starts whispering to Josh. "The others will wake soon. We can tell our people, but we must be careful about telling the other passengers. He is a stow-away, and I don't know what the captain will do to him if he finds out. We'll have to hide him down here until we decide what to do."

"Makes sense to me," Josh says.

"Let's let him sleep if we can. Let's pile our coats on top of him so no one, especially William and his crew, sees him," Reverend Stuart says.

"Let's get our people up, well, everyone except Brody, and tell them," Josh says.

"Good idea, and we'll just gather here in front of him, so no one really notices until we figure out what to do," Reverend Stuart says.

Mouths fly open with amazement as Reverend Stuart tells the others who is under the coats and how they found him.

"I bets he just couldn't bear the thought of being separated from you," Samantha says to Reverend Stuart.

"He risks his life to be with us," Mrs. Connery says.

"I remember seeing him following Reverend Stuart around. It was so cute," Myra adds.

"If ye wants to see the morn' sun, I'll stay here with Keltz," Mrs. Connery says. Keltz has moaned a few times but packing himself in a rum barrel has left him exhausted.

"I bet he be very sore when he wakes up," Mrs. Connery adds.

With biscuits and salt-pork in their bellies, Reverend Stuart and the others make their way to the deck. A misty morning greets them.

"Aye, the English fog follows us," Josh says as he looks out on the blanket of mist that meets the sea.

"It probably won't last long. Early morning mist is common in this part of the sea. We are approaching where the Irish Sea meets the North Atlantic Ocean. Some peoples calls the water in front of us the Celtic Sea, but I just say the North Atlantic," Ross says.

"Where'd the land go?" Brody asks.

"Ye wonts see any land for weeks," Ross says.

"This ocean sure is big!" Brody exclaims.

"The sun is burning through the mist, vanishing before our eyes," Josh says.

"Goin' be a beautiful day at sea," Ross says.

"Just enough wind to push up those beautiful white caps," Samantha says.

"And da water so blue," Myra adds.

"I do so wanna be a sailor!" Brody screams.

"We'll be lucky to have this perfect weather all the way to Carolina," Ross says.

"I can't wait to see Carolina. Have me bairn there," Myra says.

"Tis a beautiful land. I've only seen the coast, but I hear there are long plains and then towering mountains," Ross says.

"I wanna see mountains," Brody says.

"Let's get to the coast first! Quite a journey in front of us," Ross says.

"I must warn you. If the slave ships are docked at Wilmington, it can be upsetting," Ross says.

Quick to pick up on things and quick to ask a question, Brody says, "What a slave ship?"

"A slave ship brings Africans to Carolina. Then they sell the slaves at auction. It's a terrible thing to see. We might see 'em with chains on their legs being taken off the ships, chained together so they can't run away," Ross says. "Awful sight, they come up on the deck . . . been below deck for weeks . . . with little food or water. They're not use to bright sun now and must shield their eyes. Their clothes are torn probably from trying to run through the bushes to get away from the slave catchers back in Africa. But that might not be the worst part. They sell the slaves oftentimes on the dock, especially if the big plantation owners have crops coming in and need workers. Families are torn apart. One plantation owner only needs men to work the fields. So, he buys the husband. Another plantation owner buys the woman. I don't know what happens to the children. The Africans are all crying, but they are pulled away, never to see each other again," Ross says.

"That's awful," Samantha says. "How can they do that? These plantation owners . . . aren't they Christian?" Samantha asks.

"Yea, they go to their churches, but they must think the Africans are like animals," Ross says.

"Animals? Aren't they people, like us?" Brody asks.

"They just have a different color skin from us, but, aye, they are people like us. Created by God," Reverend Stuart says. "The plantation owners can make more money if they have slaves and don't have to pay wages. The plantation owners are insecure and worry about not having enough. When they get enough, then they want more. Human greed might be the evilest thing on earth. Most of our problems come from greed . . . rich people who don't want to share with poor folk . . . most wars arise out of greed . . . one country wants another country's land and resources."

"Don't the preachers in their churches tell the plantation owners it's wrong to make people into slaves?" Myra asks.

"Unfortunately, they don't," Reverend Stuart says. "The preachers tell them there were slaves in the Bible, so it must be okay."

"Them preachers white people too?" Brody asks.

"Aye, they are," Reverend Stuart says. "Brody, you pick up on things quickly."

"Why don't the slaves just run away?" Brody asks.

"Some do, but most of them get caught. They hang them," Ross says.

"Hang 'em by the neck?" Brody puts his hands around his neck.

"Aye, I've seen them do it. Sometimes they bring the runaways to the docks and hang them in front of the other slaves as they leave with their new masters. It's a way of showing them what will happen if they runs away," Ross said.

"I'm goin' help them runaway," Brody says.

"I'll help you," Samantha says.

"That would be very dangerous," Ross says. "They might hang you, too."

"Myra and I will go check on Mrs. Connery and Keltz. Maybe he's awake," Samantha says. "Brody, go with us."

"No, I wanna to stay with the men," Brody says.

"Charles, I means, Reverend Stuart, that's okay?" Samantha asks.

"Aye, we'd love to have Brody," Reverend Stuart says.

Death at Sea!

October 20, 1849

"Help! Help! She's in the water!" They hear shouts from the stern.

"Josh let's go. See what's happening," Reverend Stuart says. "Brody, you best go with Samantha."

As they near the starboard side of the stern, they see deckhands and passengers who have come in response to the cries for help.

"What's going on?" Reverend Stuart asks.

An older woman leaning over the deck screams, "It's me daughter! She jumped!"

"Oh, me God!" Josh says. "She jumped with a rope around her neck!"

"I wonder why no one saw her do this?" Reverend Stuart asks.

"The morn's a busy time for these sailors. Decks to clean. Some are helping in the galley, cleaning the captain's and mates' quarters. Guess she picked a time, an unfortunate time, and she was successful," Ross says.

"Probably just grabbed a spare rigging rope, like the one over there," Josh says as he points. "Tied two quick knots, one around the railing and one around her neck, and jumped. Wouldn't take long."

Reverend Stuart approaches the hysterical mother and puts his arm around her shoulders.

Before he can speak, she wails at the sky, "Why, God, why? Why did ye let this happen? My baby girl, it can't be. No! No!"

"I think it best you come with us," Reverend Stuart says to the wailing woman. "Josh, get on her other side."

Together they help the woman down the deck and behind a storage area so she cannot see the sailors pull the body up.

Weeping and sobbing, the woman says, "She did not want to come. I did not want to come, but we had no choice. The crops failed. Mr. McCoy threw us off the farm. He said he had no way to feed us. He told us to go to America. If me husband here, he would not let all this happen."

"What happened to ye husband?" Josh asks.

"Died, last winter," she says. "We lived on that farm and helped Mr. McCoy since we were married, over thirty years."

"Me daughter did not want to come. I made her. It's my fault," she screams.

"Don't blame yourself. Sounds like ye had no choice," Reverend Stuart says.

The grieving woman just shakes her head. "She had a boyfriend. They were going to marry. He went to London to look for work and never came back. She was so sad, crying for days, sit and stare at the floor. And then we had to leave the farm. Just too much for her, I guess. I should've . . ."

"Don't blame yourself . . ." Reverend Stuart says and then two approaching figures get their attention.

"What's happened here?" a strong voice demands.

Reverend Stuart realizes the captain of the ship stands before him. A tall man who might have been quite distinguished looking if in different clothes and on a London sidewalk. As he was, a salt and pepper moustache and beard cover the lower part of a ruddy face worn by harsh sea winds and salty air, a reddish-brown appearance that partially hides a scar alongside his right eye. Beside him stands, Reverend Stuart figures, his first mate. An equally weather-worn man in white, brown-stained, baggy pants, a tight shirt revealing very muscular arms and chest. His dark hair bound by a dirty red bandana. Dark eyes peer out from under bushy eyebrows.

"I'm your captain, Captain Shanks."

"Sir, an awful tragedy has happened."

Reverend Stuart realizes he does not know the woman's name. "This woman's daughter drowned. She went off the side of the ship."

"I see," Captain Shanks says. "Where's the girl?"

"She's down there," Reverend Stuart says, pointing toward the stern.

"How did . . . ?"

But before Captain Shanks could finish, Reverend Stuart stands and says, "Let's walk down this way." He didn't want the mother to hear him describe what happened.

"Josh, stay with her until we get back."

As they walk toward the stern, Reverend Stuart explains what he knows about the daughter and her death.

"I've had that happen several times over the years, but they just jump overboard. We never find their bodies. Never had one to tie a rope around their neck. Strange," Shanks says.

"My guess is that she didn't want the sharks to eat her body, or something like that. But I really don't know. Strange things go through peoples' minds when they want to die," Reverend Stuart says.

"What's your name?" Shanks asks.

"Charles. Reverend Charles Stuart."

"Always like to have the reverends on board. Maybe a little extra protection and good fortune? But it did not help this young lass. Reverend, can you give her a little service? Probably should do that soon. We don't want any more spectacle than necessary."

"Aye, of course. Allow me to talk to the mother. See if that is okay with her."

"Sounds like you are a good man, reverend. Please offer my sympathy to the mother."

"I will and thank you for having us on board."

Captain Shanks nods quickly, turns, and heads toward the bow with first mate beside him.

Reverend Stuart goes back to the woman and Josh. "That was the captain. He sends his sympathy."

"I don't want no sympathy. I wants my daughter, alive!"

"We are all very sorry, and sad with you, and wish we could change what has happened. It is so tragic. Losing a child is a terrible kind of pain," Reverend Stuart says.

"What will I do now?" the woman says.

"We'll help you. We'll be with you," Reverend Stuart says. "Josh, would you go get Mrs. Connery, Samantha, and Myra, if she feels like it? And stay with Keltz and Brody until I get there."

Josh departs, and Reverend Stuart says to the woman, "I'm a pastor."

But before he can say more, the woman screams, "Why didn't you do something? Why didn't God help her? Why does God always do nothing!"

"I'm so sorry. Things happen that we just can't explain. The captain has asked me to comfort to you," Reverend Stuart says.

"Some comfort!" the woman cries.

"I know. I know. This's an agonizing time," Reverend Stuart says. The woman weeps and puts her head against Reverend Stuart. He puts his arm around her.

When Reverend Stuart sees her wiping tears off her face, he thinks it might be a good time to speak again. "I must ask you about this. It's not a good time. You're still trying to get your mind around this unbelievable and terribly distressing thing that has just happened, but the captain has asked me to lead a service, on deck, for your daughter this afternoon. Would that be, okay?"

Shaking her head side to side, the woman says, "I guess it has to be." She continues to weep.

Reverend Stuart continues to hold her. In a few minutes he says, "I'll read some scripture, offer a prayer, and we'll sing a hymn. Will that be, okay?"

She nods and whispers, "Okay."

Reverend Stuart realizes once again that he doesn't know her name or her daughter's name. So, he begins asking questions hoping to find out more about this deeply sad and grieving woman.

"What was your husband's name?"

"Graham."

"And his last name?"

"That is our last name."

"And his first name?

"Andrew."

"Was your daughter named after anyone in the family?"

"After me, I'm Elizabeth. We called her Liz."

Mrs. Connery, Samantha, and Myra arrive and introduce themselves.

"You goin' to have your bairn! My bairn is dead! Gone! Forever! I can't believe it!" Elizabeth wails in anger upon seeing Myra. She puts her head in her hands and weeps deeply.

Mrs. Connery and Samantha get on each side of her and put their arms around her, not saying anything for several minutes while Elizabeth wails.

After about five minutes, Elizabeth takes her hands away from her face and says, "Reverend, I guesses we have to have that service."

"Aye, we do, Elizabeth," Reverend Stuart says. "The ladies will stay with you a few minutes while I go check on things."

Reverend Stuart walks toward the stern and sees two sailors (an older man and a young man) sewing a hammock together. He sees the body of Liz Graham inside the hammock, her casket.

"I'm Reverend Stuart. I'll be leading a brief service for Liz when you have finished your work."

"Won't be much longer," the older man says. "We heard the mother wailing around there." Reverend Stuart realizes that it must be the captain's practice to match up a young sailor with an older one, like William and John Roanoke.

"Thank you very much," Reverend Stuart says.

As he leans up against the storage room wall, Reverend Stuart thinks how hard this must be on Elizabeth Graham. Not even a half day has passed since her daughter died, and now she has to say her final goodbye.

"I assume the body will be dropped into the sea?" Reverend Stuart asks.

"Aye, we'll do that. You just give us a nod when you ready in your service," the older man says.

"She's so pretty. Such a shame," the young sailor says. "Why would she jump?"

"She had a broken heart. Her love disappeared to London and never returned. She didn't want to take this voyage. I guess she just got to feeling she had nothing to live for," Reverend Stuart said.

"Awful. Just awful," the older sailor says. "We've had 'em jump on other voyages, but never with a rope round their neck. We've had many to die on this ship . . . sickness . . . some go to sleep and never wake up . . . murder . . . chokings, but never one as young and beautiful as this one."

Funeral at Sea!

October 20, 1849

When the last stitch goes into the hammock-casket, the sailor grabs the nose of the young woman and looks up at Reverend Stuart. "Just so you know what I am about to do. The last stitch goes through the nose. That way we know they dead."

"I see," Reverend Stuart says, turns, and walks around the storage building where he asks the group to follow him. When they turn the corner, they see the sailors have placed the body near the railing. Reverend Stuart walks over to the body, and the others stand on the other side of the body. Several sailors not on watch or detail join the gathering. Reverend Stuart looks to his right and sees the captain and his first mate coming toward them. They stand behind the little congregation.

"Friends, we gather here today to call upon God Almighty to watch over us and guide us as we pay our last respects to Liz Graham. Let us pray."

Reverend Stuart prays and then quotes from memory Psalm 23 and a section from Revelations 21:

> *Then I saw a new heaven and a new earth, for the first heaven and the first earth had passed away, and there was no longer any sea.*
>
> *I saw the Holy City, the new Jerusalem, coming down out of heaven from God, prepared as a bride beautifully dressed for her husband.*
>
> *And I heard a loud voice from the throne saying, "Look! God's dwelling place is now among the people, and he will dwell with them. They will be his people, and God himself will be with them and be their God. He will wipe every tear from their eyes. There*

will be no more death or mourning or crying or pain, for the old order of things has passed away."

Mrs. Graham slumps but does not faint as she is steadied by Mrs. Connery on one side and Samantha on the other. Reverend Stuart asked Samantha in advance to start singing *Amazing Grace* after the final scripture. Most of the others join in. Only one sailor sings, but others including the captain and the first mate don't know the words.

When they finish the next to last verse, Mrs. Graham, who has now steadied herself, unexpectedly raises her hand, and the singers pause. A small burst of anxiety sweeps over Reverend Stuart, what will she do? Then in an incredibly angelic voice, Mrs. Graham sings,

> *When we've been there ten thousand years*
> *Bright shining as the sun,*
> *We've no less days to sing God's praise*
> *Than when we've first begun.*

Heads jerk to attention. Most never heard such a voice. Reverend Stuart, stunned, motions to the two sailors. Each takes an end of the hammock-casket and lifts. They look to Reverend Stuart. He holds both hands above his head.

"Almighty God, we commit to the depths the body of Liz Graham and her soul to your loving care, to be with you forever and to be united one glorious day with her mother and family. And now the blessing of God Almighty, be upon all those gathered here. Amen."

The two sailors swing the body slightly toward the group and then send the body over the railing. Liz Graham's body splashes into the water, floats momentarily, and then disappears into the deep.

After the burial, the two sailors slip away, but the others all hug Mrs. Graham and speak softly to her. The captain makes his way to Mrs. Graham and offers his hand.

"I'm sorry for your loss," he says. "Ye in good hands with Reverend Stuart and these fine people." Turning abruptly, he heads to the bow with his first mate.

"Your voice is so beautiful," Samantha says to Mrs. Graham.

"When young I sang in church. When I got married, me husband didnae want to go to church. Ner went back," Mrs. Graham pauses and looks at Reverend Stuart. "Reverend, maybe that's why God took Liz away from me. God's punishing me for not goin' to church!" she says in a heightened voice and suddenly starts to weep.

"God's not like that, Mrs. Graham," Reverend Stuart says. "God did not take Liz or punish you."

"Then why did she jump?!" Mrs. Graham demands.

"Sounds like she got so sad. Her boyfriend does not return. The two of you must leave the farm and go off to a strange land. And that's all she could think about, was all that she had lost. It happens to good people. They get trapped in their own thoughts and get overwhelmed. During this kind of time, they don't think like they usually do. All they can think about is their pain, and they want an escape from the pain."

Mrs. Graham embraces Reverend Stuart. "Ye such a wonderful man."

Reverend Stuart motions with his head for the others to step closer, and they surround Mrs. Graham with loving arms.

Reverend Stuart looks at Samantha. "Why don't you and Mrs. Connery take Mrs. Graham down below and show her where she can sleep. Tell Brody he can come up here with us."

As they walk away, Josh says to Reverend Stuart, "Looks like your congregation is growing."

"Aye, but it's so good that Mrs. Graham can be with Mrs. Connery and Samantha. This might help Mrs. Connery. Give her a purpose and maybe not think about her sadness so much."

"Mrs. Graham didnea take to well to Myra," Ross says.

"Aye, but I think she'll get over that," Reverend Stuart says.

"Speaking of Myra, we have a gibbous moon but comin' up on a full moon soon," Ross says. "Lots of babies born under the full moon. Seems like the full moon pulls the babies out."

"We'll see," Reverend Stuart says. "She looks about ready."

In a few moments, a bouncing Brody joins them on the deck.

"That man, Keltz, start'n to wake up."

"Brody, you stay with Josh and Ross. I'll go check on Keltz. Show Brody where the rudder is," Reverend Stuart says.

"I doubts we see the rudder. It's under water," Ross says.

"Shows how much I know about ships!" Reverend Stuart laughs.

Down below, Keltz sits up with the women standing around him, so the other passengers don't see him.

Reverend Stuart, his face full of warmth, sits beside him. "Keltz, you're amazing."

"I hopes I don't cause you no trouble," Keltz says.

"I'm glad you're okay. You sore? Anything hurt?" Reverend Stuart says.

"'Tis' nothing. Me life always hard," Keltz says with his unique smile that appears on one side of his face. "Everybody in Campbeltown talking about you on da ship docked in Liverpool. Hides in a wagon taking empty rum barrels to Liverpool. Figure I justs crawl in one of those rum barrels since I gots no ticket or money."

"You're very clever, Keltz," Reverend Stuart says. "But you're a stow-away now. Captains don't like stow-aways and can be very harsh."

Reverend Stuart does not tell Keltz he might even be thrown overboard.

"Keltz, you must stay right here and don't talk to the other passengers. Best they don't even see you until we figure something out. The sailors will bring down biscuits tonight, but we'll stay in front of you, so they don't see you. You stay out of sight and quiet. Okay?" Reverend Stuart says. "If you need water, let us know. We'll get you a dipper."

"I'll do it. I'll do it," Keltz repeats himself making sure Reverend Stuart understands.

The night is uneventful, and they all sleep until Mrs. Connery screams. "All over me! Get 'em off!"

"What is it?" Ross, the first one to his feet, says.

"They crawlin' on me!"

"Where?" Ross asks since the light is so dim.

"One's on my neck!"

Ross grabs something off Mrs. Connery's neck and heads to the steps for more light.

In a moment, he is back over. "It's just a cockroach. Lots of 'em on the ship." Then he turns to the others raised up from their straw beds, "Go back to sleep. Just roaches. They won't hurt you."

At first light, while the others rub eyes and stretch limbs, Ross and Reverend Stuart check on Mrs. Connery. She apologizes.

"Don't worry. No bother," Ross says. "Could have been so much worse. Vermin on ships can be bad. Fleas, ifs it get warm enough, will come out of the wool cargoes that came on board in Liverpool. And lice, rats, they here. Ole' cockroaches not so bad. Won't take but a week or so but ole' weevils gets in our Liverpool pantiles . . . Sailors use to 'em. Call 'em fresh meat."

Interrupting, Josh asks, "What's this Liverpool pantile?"

"That's what the sailors calls the biscuits," Ross says. "Somes call 'em sea biscuits."

Josh chuckles, "Yea, a pantile, a roof shingle. Hard as a roof shingle, I guess."

"Ye right, but ole weevils still gets even in the hard biscuits. They come runnin' out if ye gives the biscuit a hard lick on the side of a table or beam. Still good biscuit. We has nothing else," Ross says. "The weevils eat the inside of the biscuit and lay their eggs."

"Ye mean the inside of our biscuits can be filled with maggots?" Josh asks.

"Sometimes, no doubts. One times a ship comes into Wilmington, dock for two days before sailing on to the rum islands and had biscuits left over from the voyage from Liverpool. The captain sent the left-over biscuits to a baker not far from the port. He baked the biscuits again with the maggots inside and sent the biscuits back to the ship," Ross says.

"Oh, me God!" Mrs. Graham says.

"Is it true that de rats all jump off a sinking ship?" Mrs. Connery asks.

"Dat's what the sailors say. Thank the Lord, I never been on a sinking ship," Ross says.

Birth at Sea!

October 22, 1849

They soon hear William and the other sailors talking as they approach the steps.

"Ladies, we need to be sure and stand in front of Keltz," Reverend Stuart says.

Brody and Myra continue to sleep. Myra begins to moan.

"Myra, you alright?" Mrs. Connery asks.

"I don't know. I think something's happening," Myra grimaces in pain. "I'm all wet down there."

"Oh, ye water breaking. You goin' to have a bairn soon," Mrs. Graham smiles, shaking her head up and down.

Reverend Stuart sees the pleasure on Mrs. Graham's face and feels a swell of relief. Mrs. Graham can step outside her sadness at least for a while.

Myra moans and holds her breath after sucking in a big breath. As she breaths out, she cries out, "Oh! Sharp pains!"

"Don'ts ye worry, honey. I've helped bring a lot of bairns into this world. Ye goin' to hurts some, but it'll be over soon, and ye will have a little one to love," Mrs. Connery says.

"Brody, got to get up. Ye biscuits are here and with the salt pork you like," Reverend Stuart says.

Brody rubs his eyes, looks at the moaning Myra, and says, "What's wrong with her?"

"Goin' to have a bairn," Mrs. Connery says. "Eat your biscuits."

Brody attacks the two biscuits they have saved for him, goes to the water barrel, and washes down the last of the biscuit with a dipper of water. "I don't want to see a bairn born. I wanna go up," he says as he points to the steps.

Keltz sits up behind the others and swallows a mouth full of biscuit. Reverend Stuart says, "Keltz, you'll have to stay down here with the ladies. Just go back to sleep. You must be exhausted." Keltz rolls over on his side, away from the moaning Myra.

The other men make their way up the steps, but only after Reverend Stuart goes over to the other stirring passengers and informs them about the birth about to happen.

"A bairn, how wonderful!" a woman exclaims.

On deck, Reverend Stuart says to Brody, "I'll ask the captain if William or one of the sailors can show us around the ship. Maybe see the sailors' quarters."

"Can I climb up to one of the nests?" Brody asks.

"We'll see," Reverend Stuart says.

A couple of hours go by as the men enjoy the fully risen sun and the bright blue waters. Small white caps surround them. They listen to the sound of the bow cutting through the water.

William and a sailor approach. "Reverend, the sailors said you led a lovely service for the young woman. I couldn't come. It was my turn to be on watch."

"I understand. And thanks. It was a real shock, especially for Mrs. Graham, but she seems to be doing okay. Our ladies are taking good care of her," Reverend Stuart says.

After William walks away, Reverend Stuart says, "I'm going down to check on Myra, but I'll be back soon."

As Reverend Stuart backs his way down the steps, Keltz starts to come up. "Keltz, just stay down there."

Reverend Stuart takes Keltz behind the steps where he hopes they won't be seen. "Keltz, you have to stay down here until I talk to the captain."

"But Reverend," Keltz says in a low voice. "I heards the women talk . . . they saids it might be a bitch bairn. I don't know what that is, but I don't want to be down here if it a bitch bairn."

"Keltz, it's breech. Breech bairn. It's when the bairn gets stuck. Can be very painful to the mother," Reverend Stuart says, not wanting to tell Keltz how dangerous that could be for Myra. "Let's go back below before the captain spots you."

Below, Reverend Stuart asks, "How's Myra?"

"I thinks I can turn this bairn. I've done it before," Mrs. Connery says as she stays on her knees attending to Myra.

Captain's Quarters

October 23, 1849

"Reverend Stuart?" a voice calls out from the top of the steps.

Reverend Stuart starts up the steps and sees the face of William.

"The captain says to tell you to come for dinner in his cabin."

"When?" Reverend Stuart asks.

"He usually eats at the end of the afternoon watch. When you hear the next bell ring, you should go," William says.

"I'll go for sure," Reverend Stuart says. "Thank you."

"What's a watch?" Keltz asks.

"When the captain sees the sun at its highest point, a sailor rings the bell," Reverend Stuart says.

"I heard a bell not long ago," Keltz says.

"That's the start of the afternoon watch," Reverend Stuart says. Reverend Stuart starts to tell Keltz about the thirty-minute hourglass that one of the senior sailors or the captain will start, flipping eight times, until it is time to ring the bell for the second watch, but the reverend thinks better of it, as it might be too difficult for Keltz to understand.

Still recovering from his barrel ordeal, Keltz sleeps. Reverend Stuart tries to comfort Myra. Her moans turn to screams. The passengers who have not gone on deck seem bothered by the screams. Reverend Stuart makes his way over and explains the birth that will soon take place.

"Just takes her on deck, so I can gets some kip," a crusty old man says in a harsh voice.

A woman near him says, "Hush, how do ye thinks ye came into the world? If ye don't likes it, ye go on deck, ye bugger!" The old man rolls over on his straw, facing the opposite direction, saying nothing.

"Why did you do this to me? Bailey, you bastard! You don't have to go through this. You just walk away. Bastard!" Myra continues to moan and scream.

"Who's Bailey?" Keltz asks.

"Her boyfriend," Reverend Stuart says.

"Reverend, your bell rings," Keltz says.

Hearing the bell as well, Reverend Stuart says to Keltz in his firmest voice, "Thank you. Keltz, you stay here and be quiet as a snowflake falling from the sky."

A stiff wind greets Reverend Stuart as he emerges on the deck. Thunderheads form on the horizon. Several passengers head his way to get out of the wind. Moments later he knocks on the captain's door. A deep voice from inside rings out, "Come in. Just push on the door. It's not locked." The door creaks and swings open.

The smells of old leather and sweaty clothes greet Reverend Stuart. A hard looking, wooden, single bunk with a couple of unfolded blankets occupies the far end of the cabin. In another corner, a barrel-like table holds an uneven stack of maps and charts. Shelves house an assortment of hourglasses, a brass nautical telescope, a Gunter's scale, a sextant, and various nautical instruments. In the center of the cabin sits a table with a top of four thick, wide boards held aloft by curved, wide wooden legs, one on each end. The yellow tint to the wood suggests to Reverend Stuart that the table is made of pine. A much smaller board runs just above the floor and holds the two supporting sides of the table stable. Large pine pegs hold it all together. The four chairs look like oak while the seats are a woven mat of thin wood strips.

In a long black coat over a ruffled white shirt, the tall Captain Shanks stands at the far-end of the table. His hair black as a crow's back, deep blue eyes, salt and pepper beard give him a distinguished air. The scar along the left side of his weathered face suggests a rugged life.

In an equally rugged voice, the captain says, "Welcome, Reverend Stuart, and thanks for joining me for dinner."

"Thank you for the invitation," Reverend Stuart says smiling.

"Dariel has brought our rum," the captain points at the table. "He'll be back shortly with our dinner."

On the table sits a ceramic flask with a large body and a small neck. Jagged brown at the bottom gives way to blue toward the neck. Two chalice like pewter mugs sit near the rum bearing flask.

"Aye, please, rum sounds wonderful," Reverend Stuart says.

Captain Shanks pours the rum into each mug, splashing a few drops on the table. He takes two fingers, swipes up the drops, and sticks the fingers in his mouth. "Can't waste a drop," he says as he hands a mug to Reverend Stuart.

Shanks raises his glass saying, "Cheers!" Reverend Stuart responds, "Cheers."

"I have to know how to say, 'cheers' in several different languages," Shanks says. "Docked in Ireland, I say, 'Slante.' Italy, I say, 'Chin, chin.' Holland, it's 'Proost.' It's the cost of being worldly." They both laugh.

"Where's the rum from?" Reverend Stuart asks.

"Oh, 'dis my personal rum. Barbados, West Indies. The locals save me a barrel, sometimes two, from their best batch. Barbados in the Caribbean, you been there Reverend?"

"No. No. My first time on a ship," Reverend Stuart chuckles.

"Well, I think you are a fine minister. That service for the young girl who jumped, well done, well done," Shanks says.

"Tragic," Reverend Stuart says. "From what her mother says, sounds like she was so down in spirits. Her boyfriend had left and not returned. They lost their place to live. She didn't want to go to Carolina but had no choice. I guess she showed she had a choice."

Shanks puts his mug to his mouth and takes a massive swallow. "Now that hits the spot, Reverend. And what takes you to Carolina?"

"The lad with us had no parents, lived on the street, and got into some trouble. The judge allowed me to take responsibility for him and allowed him to stay with Mrs. Connery. One day, Brody took some bread from a baker. The judge took Mrs. Connery's house and sent us all to Carolina."

"That sounds harsh. What the judge's name?" Shanks asks.

"Ainsley, Judge Ainsley," Reverend Stuart says.

"I don't know him," Shanks says. "I know some of the judges in the ports. They give some of their criminals the choice of prison or sailing with me. A lot of them want to sail with me, and I can take some, only a few gives me trouble."

"This judge had it in for us after he found out Mrs. Connery had a house," Reverend Stuart says. "He took the house and put us on this ship."

"But you're a Stuart. You should have very good standing with the Scottish judges. Are you of the Royal House of Stuart?" Shanks asks.

"Aye, but that doesn't matter anymore. Not since Bonnie Prince Charlie's army was routed at Culloden," Reverend Stuart says. "Scots have been reluctant English citizens since then."

"Lest I forget. I want to tell you how helpful William's been," Reverend Stuart says. "All your sailors been pleasant." Reverend Stuart did not want to tell the captain about Griffin's inappropriate remarks, thinking he did not want that to get back to Griffin.

"Your wife, the redhead, you should keep her close to you. She's a lovely lass, a store-bought lady. All your women should have men with them all the time," the captain says. "Women need to stay close to men. Some of these sailors have not been with a woman for a long time. They lose their minds sometimes. Even the pregnant one tell her husband to stay close."

"I will," Reverend Stuart says as it dawns on him that the captain thinks he and Samantha are married and Josh to Myra as well. He quickly thinks to himself that it's probably best to let the captain and the sailors keep on believing that.

The door swings open.

"Dariel. Always good to see Dariel. Put the food on the table," Shanks says. "Dariel, this's Reverend Stuart. His wife is the beautiful redhead."

Dariel nods his head.

"Dariel don't talk. That's why I like him so much. He justs does his job. Right, Dariel?"

Dariel nods.

"I've been captain of three ships, and Dariel been with me on every one. We saw the white continent together," Shanks says.

"The white continent? Antarctica?" Reverend Stuart asks but thinks he knows the answer.

"It won't our plan. We trying to get around the horn," Shanks says.

"Cape Horn?" Reverend Stuart asks.

"Aye, we sailing to Valparaiso, near Santiago, but a terrible storm, out of nowhere, hit us, just west of the Falklands. Pushed us far south, and there it was, white as a Christmas snow, the white continent. We didn't have any charts for that part of the world, but most sailing charts are half wrong. Best follow ye instruments," Shanks says.

"It was beautiful. Right, Dariel?"

Dariel shakes his head as he places the plates on the table.

"Ah, pie of fowls!" Shanks says with a pleased look on his face. "Snipes? Woodcocks?"

Dariel shakes his head.

"Me favorite. Pie of fowls with snipes and woodcocks. The food's good for the first half of the trip. Then the galley runs out of caged fowl. And the last of the pigs are gone," Shanks says. "More rum, Reverend?"

Shanks pours more rum for himself and his guest before Reverend Stuart can answer. Dariel leaves the room.

"Dis' stuff powerful," Shank says as he raises his mug. "Drink too much and in the morn' our heads feel like squeezed between two bricks."

"I'm curious. Who owns this ship?" Reverend Stuart asks.

"London Shipping," Shanks says. "Most of 'em require captains to buy a one eighth share now. So, I own an eighth. It's a way of making us take care of the ship and cargo. Something bad happens, they lose, but the captain loses too. My friend Captain Austin Craven lost everything when his ship went down in a storm a few years ago. He and most of the crew were rescued from the lifeboats, but he was ruined."

"How long will it take us to get to Carolina?" Reverend Stuart asks.

"With good weather 'bout 34 days," Shanks says. "We get close to storm season though. Really big storms usually send signs a day or so in advance, dark clouds and winds. We try to steer around but hard to tell where the worse be."

"So, you like being captain?" Reverend Stuart asks.

"Yea, I love the salty blue, always have," Shanks says. "Just don't feel at home standing on dirt."

"Where did you grow up?" Reverend Stuart asks.

"London, hard east side. Me father, a sail maker at the docks. They didn't pays him much. Times, we almost starved. I swore I be a captain someday. I joined the royal navy when I was fifteen. That was when the sun never set on the British Empire. Much has changed now."

"Reverend, I've done some bad things. I hopes I don't have to do more."

"Bad things?" Reverend Stuart asks. "Making sailors wear iron hoop?"

"Worse. Much worse. I caught a sailor stealing. We cut off both his little fingers. Whipped many sailors with a cat-o'-nine-tails. Their backs dripped blood on the deck."

"Cat-o'-nine-tails. That's a whip?" Reverend Stuart asks.

"Rope whip with nine knotted cords at the end. It's like being hit with nine whips at the same time," Shanks says. "That's not the worse though."

"What was that?" Reverend Stuart asks.

"I hung two men on Little Corn Island. They were talkin' to some of the other sailors about throwing me overboard and taking over the ship. A captain can't have that kind of talk. So, we grabbed them, tied their hands, rowed 'em ashore, and hung 'em from a big tree. Hard way to die. Necks didn't break, just choked to death."

Reverend Stuart shakes his head, showing he understands.

"Reverend, as I get older, I wonder if the Lord will send me to hell for all these bad things?"

Reverend Stuart senses this man has a conscience heavier than a ball and chain and says, "I know God loves a repentant heart and a penitent man. You might want to consider that."

"I try to be good to the men now. I don't let my sailors get in debt to me, like most of the captains. I don't deduct from their wages what I must pay the judges to let them sail with me. Most of the captains loan the sailors money to spend in port knowing they'll have a hard time paying it back. In debt to them, these sailors are stuck on their ships. It's just another way to crimp sailors," Shanks says.

"Crimp is that the same thing as shanghaiing?" Reverend Stuart asks.

"Aye, same thing. I don't like it. Gives captains a bad name," Shanks says.

"I'm impressed with how you do things," Reverend Stuart says.

"But I don't know what I'd do if I hear of another mutiny brewing," Shanks says.

"Could you just lock 'em up, somewhere on board?" Reverend Stuart asks.

"I could, but a sailor would have to guard them. Then I'm down the mutinous sailors and the guard."

"Being the captain a hard job," Reverend Stuart says.

"Aye, it is," Shanks pours more rum.

"Just a wee little for me," Reverend Stuart says. "I can't handle much more."

"Ye are a Reverend," Shanks laughs.

"I do have a problem, captain. We have an extra passenger. At my church, a man slept in the church and pretty much followed me wherever I went. He's a good man and always wants to do the right thing and help as much as he can. But he's limited in his ability to think and reason. He tries so hard. He got pretty upset when I was forced to leave. He made his way to Liverpool and climbed into one of the empty rum barrels at the port. In our quarters, we heard knocking in a rum barrel. We took off the top, and there was Keltz. I had no idea he was on board. We can try to scrap together enough to pay his fare."

Shanks face turns stern, and his dark eyes bear down on Reverend Stuart. "I guess we throw him overboard."

"What! You can't do that!" Reverend Stuart has feared severe consequences.

"Aye, I cans," slowly Shank's face begins to lighten. "I'm just joking. I guess it's the rum," he cackles.

Reverend Stuart blows out his held breath and laughs as well.

"Tell me more about this man. Sounds like he has less than a whole shilling for a brain but what can he do? I'm down two sailors. I lost a good sailor in Liverpool. Messing with a woman in a bar, her boyfriend cut my sailor's throat. Another sailor took to the laudanum. I left him in Liverpool," Shanks says.

"I suppose he could scrub the deck, carry cargo on and off board like the other sailors. I don't know if I would let him keep watch or go up into the crow's nest, but he could do some things."

"Bring this man to me tomorrow," Shanks says. "What's his name?"

"Keltz. I don't know his last name. I don't know if he knows. Poor guy never knew his parents or family."

"We have a deal then, Reverend Stuart, but this means you must have more rum!"

"Just a little," Reverend Stuart says. "Much more and I might fall overboard."

"Awh, but ye gets to curl up with that beautiful wife tonight," Shanks says raising his eyebrows.

"She's a wonderful woman, heart of gold," Reverend Stuart says.

"Do make sure you or some of the other men in your group stay with her all the time. This ship never seen a beauty like her," Shanks says.

"Been a wonderful evening, captain. Thank you so much," Reverend Stuart says.

"You must come again for dinner and next time bring your lovely wife."

"Just let us know," Reverend Stuart says. "One other thing, I've asked William to show young Brody the sailors' quarters. That be, okay?"

"Of course, I'll get word to him. He can do it after breakfast tomorrow. Go with him though. I don't want anything happening to the lad," Shanks says.

Through the captain's door, Reverend Stuart heads down the deck, lowers himself through the hatch, and down the steps into the quarters.

Mrs. Connery greets him. "We have a boy!"

Myra holds her baby and beams proudly. "Reverend, we must have a baptism soon."

"Of course," Reverend Stuart says. "What's his name?"

"I think I'll name him after my grandfather, Joshua."

"So, we'll have Joshua and Josh. Wonderful," Mrs. Connery says.

Reverend Stuart quietly motions Josh to join him by the steps and explains how the captain thinks they are married to Myra and Samantha and explains they probably should go along with it for the safety of the young women. Josh agrees.

"Josh is going to take Brody and Keltz up to the deck. Full moon. Could see stuff in the ocean," Reverend Stuart adds.

"Yeah, let's go," Brody says as he quickly climbs the steps, with Keltz and Josh close behind.

Reverend Stuart shares his dinner experience with the remainder of the group and how he did not correct the captain about his or Josh's marital status. The group agrees with the idea.

"I think Josh best move over there and sleep beside you, Myra," Reverend Stuart says.

"I don't mind if you get a little closer to me," Samantha says. They all laugh.

In a short time, Josh, Brody, and Keltz climb back down the steps.

"Best get some kip while the bairn sleeps," Ross says. All agree.

Ship Tour

October 24, 1849

The next morning, Reverend Stuart wakes Brody when William descends the steps with biscuits. "Brody, when you finish your biscuits, William is going to take you and show you around the ship."

Brody jumps to his feet. "Can't wait. Hand me a biscuit."

Reverend Stuart explains to Josh it might be best if he stays with the women. Ross says he would like to take the tour. "Always something to learn about on a ship," he says.

William leads the tour group up the steps. "Let's see the sailors' quarters first, but we must be quiet. The sailors just off the last watch sleep."

They climb down the steps to the sailors' quarters. A stench greets them. At least a different stench from their quarters, Reverend Stuart thinks, more like urine than dusty straw. Hammocks, everywhere, hang from the floor beams above.

"When we have extra sailors, they have to sleep on 'donkey breakfast'," William says. "Sweet Jose sleeps on that one over there."

William whispers to the Reverend, "Sweet Jose likes for the other sailors to fool around with him. Some of the other sailors say they don't want that stuff going on around them. They make Jose sleep over there."

"What's a donkey breakfast?" Brody asks. "I forgot."

"Just a big sack stuffed with straw like the straw you sleep on," William says. "Sorry we didnae have any extra sacks for you."

"We has it better than the passengers. Buts we haves a long, long voyage. We gets vermin here too. Roaches, rats, you name it. The British Board of Trade say we suppose to have nine feet of space per sailor, including the hammock. We might have that. Smells really bad when we get in bad weather and must close that hatch and don't have any fresh air," William laughs softly as he continues to show his visitors his quarters. "Sailors eat off their sea chests there by their hammocks. The Board says we suppose to get seven pounds of food like the passengers, but none of us gets it. You don't either. Each sailor get that tin plate, a spoon, and the pannikin."

"What's pannikin?" Brody asks.

"It's that tin cup, the sailor's drinking cup. One's hanging from the bottom of the hammock," William points out.

"You sailors, get anything besides biscuits to eat? All we gets is biscuits," Brody asks.

"We eats a little better," William says with a little embarrassment on his face. "We have lots of biscuits, good ole salt horse, molasses, but nutin to find a big ole cockroach in 'em molasses."

"What's salt horse?" Brody asks.

"Beef, pork, or horse. Heavily salted to make it last for weeks. Most of the time mixed with potatoes, beans, or rice. When we get to Wilmington, we usually stock up on pemmican. That's dried deer meat mixed with dried cranberries, cherries, and blueberries. When we gets to the warm islands, food gets much better. At ports we get fruit, vegetables, fresh water. Around the islands, we gets fish, sea turtles, wild birds, whatever comes along. We met some sailors at a port. They been to Africa. Off the coast, their ship found a hippopotamus swimming in the sea. They had a harpoon on board and ate hippo for weeks. You just never know," William says.

"Well, at least, most of the sailors have extra clothes," Ross points to the pants and shirts hanging from most of the hammocks.

"Wet clothes are one of the worse enemies of sailors," William says. "When clothes drenched in salt water dry, the pants, especially, are stiff and dry. Sailors get boils on their skin. Hurts bad."

"Sailors get sick a lot?" Reverend Stuart asks.

"All the time, but most captains don't care. They say, 'take ten minutes, that's how long it takes to die, if you don't die, come back to work.' Our captain's a little better, but when we get in bad weather, it's all hands on deck. If you can stand up, captain wants you on deck."

"Looks like the chests are made from cedar wood and bound with brass," Reverend Stuart says.

"Yep," William says.

"What kind of wood are the floor beams made of?" Reverend Stuart asks as he looks overhead.

"That's teakwood, prized teakwood. Best wood to build a ship out of. It's strong and flexible to withstand the battering the ship gets from wind and waves," William says. "Let's go up, and I'll show you around the deck."

On deck, Reverend Stuart asks, "Who's in charge after the captain?"

"The captain has three mates: First, Second, and Third. First mate's in charge of navigation. That's Slippery John. The sailors named him that after he fell down several times on the wet deck. Second mate has responsibility for the cooks, carpenters, and stewards. Third mate supervises all the sailors and decides who's on watch. Rest of us justs hands, sailors, whatever you want to call us," William says.

"If I can't be a captain, I wanna be a first mate," Brody says proudly.

"You be young to be a captain. Better grow some more," William laughs and then adds, "I best gets back to me duties."

"Thank you, William," Reverend Stuart says.

Boring No More!

October 25, 1849

Days go by. Ship life becomes boring except for when baby Joshua wakes everyone up in the middle of the night. Same routines every day. Walks on the deck and looking at the same ocean, small white caps, or larger white caps, not much changes for the passengers.

Biscuits, always biscuits, the only suspense is how hard they might become and when would they find weevils in their biscuits. Reverend Stuart remembers how the Hebrew people wander in the wilderness of Palestine before they enter the Promised Land and became so tired of manna, the food miraculously provided by Yahweh. Manna in the morning, manna in the evening, always manna. The Hebrew people longed to return to the fleshpots of Egypt for something different. Reverend Stuart doesn't think his group wants to return to Scotland. Nothing is there for them. Hopefully, new opportunities wait for them in Carolina. They just want to get there and get off this ship.

That night about an hour into his sleep, a muffled sound awakens Reverend Stuart. He's not sure what it is. Dim light flickers down the steps. He thinks it's nothing. But then he notices a figure standing in front of Samantha. He dismisses the thought, but then in the bare light, he makes out the figure of a man. He's staring at the sleeping Samantha and unbuttoning his pants. Reverend Stuart's mind still doesn't want to believe it. Is it a dream? A crazy dream?

It's no dream, he realizes. He realizes this man means Samantha harm. He reaches to his left and shakes Josh. Josh moans but opens his eyes.

In a low voice, Reverend Stuart says, "Josh, we have a problem. Get up." As he says that, Reverend Stuart jumps to his feet and in the same motion pushes the man backwards. His push so hard, the man falls on his back. Josh and Reverend Stuart both stand over him. The fall awakes several others including Samantha, her long red hair glistening in the dim light.

"I don't know where you are sleeping, but you better get back there. And don't ever come back over here again," Reverend Stuart barks.

"Take your perversion someplace else," Josh demands.

The man scrambles to his feet. He looks about forty years old. His beard has not greyed much. His clothes like most of the passengers are torn and soiled. His hair well over his ears.

"Find me a knife, I'll come back and gut both of you," the man says.

"We got you outnumbered, old chap," Josh says. "Sod off! You nutter!"

Mumbling the man walks away and disappears into the near darkness on the other side of the quarters.

"Oh, my gosh," Samantha mumbles.

"Filthy men," Mrs. Connery says as the disturbance stirs her from sleep.

"Several like him on every ship, I'm afraid," Ross, now awake, says.

Brody has slept through the entire event. 'Good thing,' Reverend Stuart thinks to himself.

Both back on the straw, Samantha turns on her side and quietly says to Reverend Stuart, "Thanks."

"That was awful. Sorry some men are like that," Reverend Stuart offers.

"From what I could see, it didn't look like he had anything to brag about anyway," Samantha quips.

A soft chuckle comes out of Reverend Stuart's mouth before he can realize it.

"Samantha, you are amazing. Most women would be terrified," Reverend Stuart says.

"Now remember, I grew up with older brothers. I've seen everything." Samantha laughs softly.

"Okay. There's something to be said for that," Reverend Stuart admits.

More light begins to peek down the steps. Reverend Stuart opens his eyes and feels them adjust themselves to the increasing light. Another boring day dawns.

Reverend Stuart realizes he should tell Keltz about his new opportunity.

"Keltz, I talked to Captain Shanks about you."

"What'd he say?"

"He wants to make a sailor out of you."

A huge grin spreads across Keltz's face. "Really? Me? A sailor?"

"Looks like you like the idea."

"Oh, I do. When I start?"

"Soon, I'll take you to meet him, or he'll send for you."

"I wanna start now."

"You'll probably have to move to the sailors' quarters, but you'll probably get a hammock and better food."

Keltz's face glows like a Christmas morning, Easter, and every other joyous holiday rolled into one.

"You gonna have to work hard. Scrub the decks. Carry cargo. Maybe, you'll get to help pull up the sails and you'll get paid."

"Ner had a job before and get paid too! Thank you, Reverend! Thank you!" Keltz embraces Reverend Stuart. "I so happy."

"You're a good man, Keltz. I know you will work hard."

"I will. I will. And I'll keep thinking about that sad-eyed lady."

It takes a second, but Reverend Stuart realizes Keltz talks about Mrs. Graham and the loss of her daughter.

That afternoon William comes for Keltz. Keltz announces to all in the quarters within the sound of his voice, "I'm goin' be a sailor!" He then proceeds to hug Reverend Stuart, Samantha, Ross, Josh, Myra, Mrs. Connery, and Mrs. Graham and kisses little Joshua.

Keltz follows William up the ladder to begin a new life. Faces around the room show how happy they are for Keltz.

"Let's continue the celebrations," Reverend Stuart says. "Let's baptize Joshua tomorrow."

"I would like that," Myra says.

"The captain and the sailors think Josh is the father and your husband. It's probably best to let them keep believing that. Josh will need to stand with you, and the baby will have to be named Joshua Reid," Reverend Stuart says.

"That's fine with me," Myra says.

"I'm okay with that," Josh says.

The next day they gather on the portside deck for the baptism. Reverend Stuart sent word by William to Captain Shanks. Shanks and Dariel stand behind the small congregation. Bright sunshine warms Reverend Stuart's back but glares in the faces of the attendees. A southerly wind blows across their faces.

Reverend Stuart reads scripture and prays. He takes the baby from Myra.

"Joshua Reid, I baptize you in the name of God, the Father; God, the Son; and God, the Holy Spirit. May God's grace descend upon you now and forevermore!"

Tears run down Myra's face as Mrs. Graham leads them in a hymn.

Reverend Stuart raises his hands and announces the benediction:

"Joshua Reid, go with God. All of you gathered here, go with God in your minds and in your hearts."

Still behind the group, Captain Shanks raises his hand.

"Captain Shanks. You would like to speak?" Reverend Stuart asks.

The group turns around to see a smiling captain as he says, "Come to my quarters. Rum for all. Let us celebrate this joyous occasion. Dariel been instructed to have the rum ready."

The group migrates down the deck to the captain's quarters.

"This is my finest rum, served in honor of Joshua Reid and his parents, Myra and Josh," the captain says and adds, "I don't have enough mugs for everyone. So, some of you will have to share." In unison, the group nods in agreement.

Captain Shanks makes his way over and says to Samantha, "Your husband is such a good man and fine minister."

"I like him too," Samantha says.

"We did drink like camels when he came for dinner. Before we get to Wilmington, I want you and your husband to join me in my quarters for dinner," Shanks says.

"We would love to," Samantha says.

"And so it will be," Shanks says.

"How long before we reach port?" Samantha says.

"We've made really good time," Shanks says. "Probably within the week."

"That's wonderful," Samantha says.

"The trades have been kind to us," Shanks says.

"Trades?" Samantha asks.

"Winds. Trade winds," Shanks says. "There are two trade winds in the Atlantic. Northern winds usually blow west, and sometimes we call them westerlies. In the south Atlantic, trades blow from the southeast. We've been fortunate to catch the 'variables.' They're the winds between the north trades and the south trades and have been blowing west. Been easy sailing for us. Must be because we have a reverend on board. Having a reverend on the ship is much better than having a Jonah," Shanks says.

"What's a Jonah?" Samantha asks.

"A Jonah is bad luck. Ship gets in storms and gets tossed all about. Goes off course. Can be a terrible time. On this voyage we must not have a Jonah," Shanks laughs. Samantha is not sure Shanks really believes the Jonah curse.

"Well, Reverend Stuart tells me you are a good man who wants to do the right thing," Samantha says.

"I thinks me and the Reverend could be good friends, but I guess we'll have to go our separate ways soon," Shanks says.

"So thoughtful of you to have us here at your quarters after little Joshua's baptism," Samantha says.

"I ner kissed a beautiful woman like you before. May I kiss you on the cheek?" Shanks asks.

"I've never been kissed by a captain. So, aye, you may," Samantha says.

The captain takes a step toward Samantha and with his hands still at his side he leans over and lightly kisses Samantha on her left cheek.

"If I die soon, I'll die a happy man," Shanks says.

"Oh, I'm sure you'll have many more years," Samantha says.

The group stays together as they make their way back toward their meager quarters.

"Look! It's Keltz!" Ross says. Up on the forecastle, Keltz on his knees scrubs the deck. He sees the group as they all turn to see him, his face as bright as a glowing candle. They all wave to him, but he doesn't stop working, except to nod his head and beam with happiness.

"He's whistling!" Samantha says.

"So happy," Mrs. Connery says.

"He's happier than a dog with two tails," Ross says.

Close the Hatches!

October 31, 1849

Out on the deck for their evening stretch, Ross notes, "Winds are picking up. Dark clouds rolling in like mountains over the sea."

"Waves gettin' higher," Josh adds.

As night falls, they hit the straw, hoping little Joshua will let them have a good night on the hay.

Still dark but hours later, Mrs. Connery whispers to anyone that might be awake, "Ship's bouncing."

"Must be gettin' a storm," Ross says as they try to go back to sleep.

In a couple of hours, the ship starts tossing on larger waves. All the passengers are awake, even Brody who says, "Why's the ship creaking?"

"We're getting a little storm," Reverend Stuart says. "Hard to cross the Atlantic without running into a little storm. In the winds and waves, the boards in the ship must bend a little. That's the creaking you hear."

"Waves help rock the bairn hopes he can keep my nipple in his mouth," Myra chuckles. Myra has trouble keeping her milk enlarged breasts in her tight blouse, a sight not missed by any of the male passengers.

Shortly later, a man resting on his straw bed not too far away says, "Dat bairn never suck those tits dry." A woman, probably his wife, reaches over and gives him a shove on the shoulder, "Keeps yer fool mouth shut, ye ole codger, ye've seen bairns fed before!"

Landstuhl Regional Medical Center

Kirchberg-Kaserne, Germany

February 9, 2020

"Captain Stuart . . . Sam . . . I'm your neurologist, Dr. Buxton. Stay awake for me. Your tests are looking good. You must stay awake some. It's not good for your brain to sleep all the time. I'll tell the nurses to get you up tomorrow. Take a few steps . . . be good for you . . ."

"A storm is coming . . . got to keep everybody safe . . . the wind . . . the waves so big," Sam says.

"Captain Stuart! Stay awake for me! Come on now!" Dr. Buxton says, but Sam drifts away.

Gaol!

November 1, 1849

In an oversized hat, William comes down the steps with a cloth covered bucket of biscuits and water dripping from his soaked clothes. O'Brien brings additional biscuit buckets.

"That's quite a hat you have on," Josh says.

"Picked it up in Jamaica on our last port-call there. They use 'em to protect 'em from the sun," William says. "Comes in handy 'dese rainy days."

"Raining hard out there?" Ross asks.

"For hours," William says. "We're all Slippery Johns now. Winds really picking up. I came by when it all started and closed yer hatch," William says, pointing up the steps. "You'll need to keep that closed til we get 'round this storm. Captain steering us slightly northwest trying to get us 'round the worst part. It's a shame, we ahead of schedule, but storms 'bout always happen out here."

Strong winds blow and tall waves hammer the ship all day and into the night.

Hours before dawn, Reverend Stuart says to Samantha in a whisper, "Getting worse out there. Rain like the time of Noah."

"I know," she says as she reaches out and puts her hand on the back of his hand. The darkness hides his hand as he slowly turns his hand so that their palms are together.

"I like that," Samantha says softly.

First light reveals several passengers retching in buckets. Josh says he's feeling sick.

"Everybody turn and look to the front of the ship. That usually help," Ross says.

"Oh my, that was big!" Mrs. Graham says as the ship takes a hit from a large wave.

"This ship been through lots of storms and massive waves before. Nuttin to worry about," Ross says, hoping what he says is true.

Midmorning, a young man and a young woman from the other end of the sleeping quarters make their way over to Reverend Stuart.

The young man says, "My name is Gerald. Most people just call me Jerry. This is Mary Ellen. We heard you're a reverend, and with the storm and all and since we're goin' to get married anyway when we gets to Carolina, we wants to see if you would marry us now. I love her a lot and want to spend the rest of my life with her."

"I loves Jerry, I mean Gerald, too," Mary Ellen says trying to be respectful.

"Well, this is a pleasant surprise. Matrimony on the high seas," Reverend Stuart says, thinking through the unusual request. "We can't go on the deck. It would have to be here."

Mary Ellen feels embarrassed as she says, "We already have a congregation."

"We do. Let's talk a few minutes," Reverend Stuart continues as he asks them some standard questions. How long have you known each other? What do your families think about this? What kind of future do you have planned?

Satisfied this couple is as prepared as most couples who ask him to perform the marriage ceremony, Reverend Stuart says, "How about we do this at the ringing of the next bell?" And then realizes they might not be able to hear the bell with the wind, driving rain, and closed hatch. "Or how 'bout I come get you in a bit?"

"Sure. We really appreciate this. Goin' to be the happiest day of my life, even with this storm," Gerald says while Mary Ellen glows with happiness.

They never hear the bell. So, Reverend Stuart walks across the quarters and talks briefly to the couple. He leads them to the steps where he steps up on the lower step. Word has circulated that all the passengers are invited to witness the ceremony. Reverend Stuart thanks them for their attendance.

During the abbreviated service, Reverend Stuart says, "We have a bit of a Shakespearean scholar with us." Passengers look at each other in amazement.

"Aye, it's true. Samantha is mostly self-taught but knows several sonnets by heart," Reverend Stuart says. Samantha volunteered before the service began.

"Samantha, this is Sonnet 116, correct?" Reverend Stuart asks.

Samantha nods her head slightly, agreeing, and begins.

> *Let me not to the marriage of true minds*
> *Admit impediments. Love is not love*
> *Which alters when it alteration finds,*
> *Or bends with the remover to remove.*
> *O, no! it is an ever-fixed mark,*
> *That looks on tempests and is never shaken;*
> *It is the star to every wandering bark,*
> *Whose worth's unknown, although his height be taken.*
> *Love's not Time's fool, though rosy lips and cheeks*
> *Within his bending sickle's compass come;*
> *Love alters not with his brief hours and weeks,*
> *But bears it out even to the edge of doom.*
> *If this be error and upon me proved,*
> *I never writ, nor no man ever loved.*

Heads turn toward one another in the 'congregation.' Mouths fly open in amazement.

Reverend Stuart continues the ceremony and then says, "Ladies and gentlemen, let me present to you . . ."

But before he can finish Mrs. Graham says, "Wait, they don't have a ring. They can have mine. I don't needs it."

Reverend Stuart must be quick on his feet. "Mrs. Graham, how sweet and thoughtful of you. Gerald take the ring and repeat after me as you place the ring on Mary's left finger."

The ring doesn't fit on the wedding finger. Reverend Stuart says, "Gerald, put it on the little finger and repeat after me, 'I, Gerald Kidd, do take you, Mary Lou McCann, to be my wedded wife.'"

The ring fits. Reverend Stuart says, "The couple may express their love and devotion with the wedding kiss."

A large wave smacks the ship. Several passengers lose their footing but are held upright by other passengers. Still, the couple remains locked in the wedding kiss.

When they finally separate their lips, Reverend Stuart says, "Let not the fury of nature's storms or any other tribulation hinder your love for one another. Ladies and gentlemen, let me present to you, Mr. Gerald Kidd and Mrs. Mary Ellen McCann Kidd."

The crowd roars in delightful approval.

"But we have no wine for celebration!" a man yells.

"No wine but how about rum?" Josh shouts.

"Rum? What rum?" the man asks.

"When we were investigating the knocking on the empty rum barrels a few days ago, we noticed one of the barrels still had some rum in it. They'll just pour that out when they get to the islands for refilling. It could be some powerful stuff," Josh says.

"We can handle that!" a man roars.

"Gives us just a minute to get the top off the barrel. We don't have mugs. So, everyone line up, bride and groom first of course, and we'll have to use the ladles from the water barrel, one at a time," Ross says.

The passengers line up and begin their processional through the line. Some of the men must be reminded they only get one ladle-full the first time through. Reverend Stuart thinks if he just had bread, he would declare it a rite of Holy Communion.

A monster wave hits the ship. Several people fall to the floor. Ross grabs the rum barrel as it almost turns over.

A man still in line points to Ross and shouts, "Best man on 'de ship, saved the rum!" The passengers who should be more afraid now with the monster waves banging the ship toast Ross.

"Let's sing! I know a few 'ole Scottish wedding ballads. I'll sing through one time and then join me," Mrs. Graham invites.

Mrs. Graham tries to teach them several songs, but mostly ends up singing solos. For the finale, she says, "*Let's sing Come Ye Hi, Come Ye Ha, Come Ye A' tae the Waddin.*" And adds, "Traditionally, this ballad was part of a tradition known as 'bedding the bride and groom' used to put the newlyweds to bed for their first wedding night."

A burly fellow, the only burly in the malnourished group, says, "We cans hold up our coats around their straw!"

The groom tells them that will not be necessary as a huge wave hits the ship and seemingly pushes the ship up on its side for a few seconds. "Boom." They are jolted, almost all falling on the floor, as the hull of the ship falls back on the water.

"Whoa, that was close!" a man says.

"Ye best believe it. Waves hitting so hard make ye teeth rattle," another fellow says.

"We're all goin' to drown!" a woman screams.

Ross speaks up. "Everybody calm down. We have a very experienced captain. These ships built to withstand terrible storms. It's going to be uncomfortable for a while, but we'll get through this."

A man feeling his rum shouts, "We'll keep buggering on!"

In a few minutes, a rain-soaked William comes down the steps and makes his way to Reverend Stuart.

"We have some new sailors, some young ones. One of 'em swept overboard. Some want to get baptized now. They really scared. It might do 'em some good. I spoke with the captain, and he says it's fine to do."

"Send 'em on down. We got plenty of water, just needs a little blessing," Reverend Stuart says.

"Make it quick. We need every sailor on deck. Water coming in fast," William says.

Reverend Stuart realizes these frightened young men seek baptism as a comfort. For most their baptisms will mean little or nothing after the storm, but he believes it would be terrible theologically to refuse them. Who is he to decide who is worthy, deserving, and who is not?

In short time, four young sailors come down the steps. Their faces drawn with fear and uncertainty, not sure what they should do or say.

"Welcome. I'm Reverend Stuart. William says you seek baptism."

Two say "aye sir." The other two simply nod their heads.

"Our gracious God welcomes all you who seek baptism," Reverend Stuart says and then announces to all in the quarters. "All are welcome to God's baptism. It's a mark of God's ownership that you will be affirming. God brought you into this world through your parents. God is with you through your lives and beyond. Come forward."

A man starts forward, and another after a shove by his wife. Another couple comes forward and joins the line.

Heads turn as two more men come down the steps. One has skin like charcoal, eyes deep brown, hair black with tight curls. The other slight-of-build man has light brown skin and oily dark hair, probably a descendant of the Moors who controlled southern Spain for centuries. He has a scar from just below his hairline down the left side of his face to the bottom of his jaw, probably the result of a knife or sword fight. Reverend Stuart thinks this might be Jose. They join the rear of the line. The man who was shoved forward by his wife starts back to his wife and straw. His wife meets him.

"I ain't goin' be baptized with no coloreds," he says.

"Get back up there. He needs it as much as you. You might need it more. Somebody goin' kill you. Everybody who knows you wants to kill you. You lazy, you steal, you lie and cheat. You need baptizing, bad!"

And looking to the front, she says, "Reverend, baptize him really good. He might need it twice!"

The man mumbles something and rejoins the line.

One by one, the frightened sailors after their baptisms make their way back up the steps and possibly to their deaths, with waves often sweeping across parts of the deck.

William quick steps down to the quarters, makes his way to Reverend Stuart, and whispers, "Captain wants you to come to his quarters and baptize him."

"Pretty rough out there," Reverend Stuart says with a good deal of apprehension.

"We've thought of that. There's a rope that we use. It's tied out by your hatch and to the next hatch at the storage quarters. Another rope's tied there and to the outside of the captain's quarters. You just hold on to those ropes all the way. If'n a big wave comes across the deck, you holds on for dear life," William says.

"Okay. I guess I must go where the Lord calls," Reverend Stuart says nervously.

He goes to Samantha and the others to explain.

"You stay safe," Mrs. Graham says.

"I wanna go," Brody says.

"You best stay here, Brody. You know, protect the others," Reverend Stuart says.

"All right," Brody says begrudgingly.

Samantha winks at the reverend. His eyes lit up.

Reverend Stuart goes to the steps. William is still at the steps. "I'm goin' with you, Reverend. Maybe, you baptize me if I am worthy? I've been bad at times." And then lowers his voice so no one else can hear, "I quits for a while, but I've been thinking about women a lot lately and wankering almost every day."

"So, what's new?" Reverend Stuart asks.

"There's no deserving to baptism. It's God gift. And all men have their fantasies from time to time. The Lord who created you will be pleased with your baptism," Reverend Stuart says.

William goes up the steps first and immediately grabs the rope. "Just follow me and hold on."

The driving rain soaks Reverend Stuart's clothes in seconds. He feels the wind pushing on his eyeballs. His hair stands straight out. But that's not important. What's vitally important is keeping a firm grasp on the rope. The rain drives against them. The howling wind pushes against them. A wave breaks over the bow of the ship, and water rushes past Reverend Stuart's ankles.

William reaches the hatch of the storage quarters and turns to make sure Reverend Stuart is still holding on. "Halfway!"

When he reaches the captain's quarters, William turns. "Just a little more, reverend!"

About that time a larger wave breaks over the bow. Waist high water surges upon the reverend. His legs go out from under him. Instinctively, he grabs the rope with both hands. And he withstands the watery blast.

Reaching William, Reverend Stuart says, "If that surge of water had been any higher, I don't know if I could have withstood the force."

"And good thing the captain has us steered into the storm. We don't want one of those big waves hitting the port or starboard side. One did earlier. I know you felt the ship go to one side," William says. "Thank God, we made it over here. Dat rope a life saver."

Before they enter the captain's cabin, William said, "There's one more thing I need to tell you. You might not want to baptize me 'cause I messed around with Sweet Jose one night. I didn't do it again."

"William, it happens in circumstances like on a ship or in a prison. It's called experimenting. You will be baptized," Reverend Stuart says.

Safely inside the cabin, Shanks welcomes them. "Reverend Stuart, you want to be a sailor?"

"Much safer being a minister," Reverend Stuart says. A nervous laugh follows.

"I just got word we've lost a couple of our ole shell-backs," the captain says. "Sad for me. Been with me on many voyages."

"Shellbacks are sailors up in the forecastle. They get sprayed with water and hit by waves even in small storms. But they used to it. Water just run off their backs, like they had shells," Shanks says, realizing that Reverend Stuart doesn't know what a shellback is. "Most of these sailors are son-of-bachelors. They have no families. Many abandoned by their mothers. Have no idea who their fathers are. Most grew up on the streets of London or some in other places."

"That's so sad," Reverend Stuart says. "Some people are so unfortunate. No fault of their own. Just dealt a bad hand."

"Reverend, thank you for coming. This is a bad storm. I want you to pray it doesn't get worse," Shanks says.

"And shall I baptize you?" Reverend Stuart asks.

"Aye, what do I have to do?" Shanks asks.

"Nothing at all. Your desire for baptism is all you need. God welcomes you with open arms," Reverend Stuart says.

"But I have never been to church. I've never prayed, but if this storm gets worse, I will," Shanks says.

Reverend Stuart doesn't know if he should laugh, so he doesn't.

"God creates us. God owns us. Submitting to baptism is our recognition of God's grace and presence in our lives," Reverend Stuart says.

Reverend Stuart prays and then baptizes both Shanks and William.

"What do we do now?" Shanks asks.

"Simply live in the love of God and love others as God has loved you. Treat all people as God's children. Realize you are precious in God's eyes and other people are precious in God's eyes," Reverend Stuart says.

A mighty wave strikes the ship. A loud crash comes from the stern. William falls backwards hitting his head on the wall but quickly recovers and helps Shanks to his feet. Reverend Stuart is slower to rise. "Hit my head a little on the post, but I'll be fine."

"William, that sounds like the stern mast might have come down. Go and make sure no one is injured. Take Reverend Stuart with you and get him safely to his quarters," Shanks says and then says to Reverend Stuart, "I don't know what to say except thank you. I'm right with the Lord now."

"You were always right with the Lord. You just know it now," Reverend Stuart says.

William and Reverend Stuart make their way down the rope. Ankle deep water rushes pass them several times, but they make it to the hatch.

"I'll shut the hatch behind you, Reverend. Thank you for what you did," William says.

"The Lord told me to do it, William. I had no choice." They both nod.

Down the steps, Reverend Stuart thinks the place reeks of mildew and despair. The group breathes a sigh of relief upon the reverend's safe return.

"Ye look like a drowned rat," Brody shouts, and they all laugh a little.

Reverend Stuart explains to the other passengers the reason for the loud crashing noise. No one of course is relieved. It's an explanation but makes their situation even worse.

"Captain says we just have to ride it out," Reverend Stuart says.

The passengers, those not retching in the buckets that are beginning to fill, try to rest on the straw. The constant banging of waves makes it difficult. Every few minutes, wind and wave push the ship to the side, and the passengers hold their breaths until they have a minute or two of relative calm.

On the straw, Samantha and Reverend Stuart talk. "I think the only person somewhat enjoying this is Brody. He likes the action, the jolting of the ship. Maybe we should be like him," Samantha says.

"I'm afraid he doesn't know what could easily happen," Reverend Stuart says with a low voice not to be heard by Brody.

"I can swim. How 'bout you?" Samantha says.

"No. And I don't want to have to learn now," Reverend Stuart says.

Hours go by as the ship tosses and bobs over and through the roughest of seas.

A man rises from the straw saying, "I can't take it anymore!" He darts to the steps and out the hatch before anyone is sure what he is doing. The hatch slams down, and the man is never seen again.

"What'd he do?" Mrs. Graham asks.

In a voice low to keep from waking the sleeping Brody, Reverend Stuart says, "He couldn't stand the anxiety and fear anymore. And sought relief, probably over the side. I wish we could have stopped him, but it happened so fast."

"The sailors call it losing yer s h i t," Ross spells out the word trying not to offend the women.

"He cracked," Josh says.

"Oh me God!" Mrs. Connery screams as a monster wave strikes the ship. The ship makes a mighty groan and goes up on its side. Mrs. Connery and all the others in this side of the quarters start sliding with the straw to the other side of the quarters. They hear banging and screams below them.

"Good God!" Ross says. "The other side of the ship is now under water. If they can't get out, they'll drown fast."

"What can we do?" Samantha asks.

"I don't know," Ross says. "There's no way to get to them."

The grim realization of people drowning in what is now below them grips the passengers in this section. And naturally they start to wonder if it will happen to them.

The ship has just enough buoyancy to stay afloat with one side mostly submerged. For the moment at least, the upper side of the ship with their quarters, the captain's cabin, and the sailors' quarters are above water. The waves and wind continue to hammer the ship and also push it. To where? No one knows, probably not even the captain since it would be impossible to use his instruments.

Reverend Stuart wonders if Keltz was swept overboard. Certainly, many of the sailors on deck are now in the water.

Aground!

November 2, 1849

A couple of highly anxious hours pass. Then the ship stops with a sudden thud! Waves and winds continue to pound the ship, but their combined impact causes the ship to upright some.

"We've hit something," Ross says. "Maybe an island? But we'll have to stay here until the storm is over."

"Those poor souls down below," Mrs. Graham says. "I fear the worse."

"Not a sound down there. Just the slushing of water," Josh says.

"Bastard!" A man yells across the quarters. He pushes another man. The man steps back toward the first man and swings his boney fingers made into a fist at his head. He misses and nearly falls forward into the other man. The first man pushes the stumbling man again. When the stumbling man regains his balance, the other man hits the stumbling man in the left jaw. His head jerks violently to the side. The next blow is to the stumbling man's stomach. He's bent over, gasping for air. His eyes wide open and fixed in a stare across the room. Two other men grab the assaulting man. One says, "That's enough. You don't want to kill him. Maybe he deserved that, but that's enough."

"What happened over there?" Mrs. Graham asks.

"I don't know, but everybody pretty tense right now," Ross says.

Strong winds and high waves continue to assault the ship, pushing hard on the port side of the ship.

"Does anyone else get the sense that the ship is not leaning as much as it was?" Josh asks.

"I do," Ross says. "I bet the wind and waves, pushing so hard against the side, up-rights the ship some. And you know the waves are pushing sand up under the boat. So, the ship not going back down as low in the water. That's a good thing. And if the tide comin' in that will help too. In Wilmington, they talk about the blue crabs riding the in-coming tides when the water gets warmer in the spring. Rides the tides up into the rivers where they spend the summer. Sand probably rides the tides, too."

Bam! A massive wave hits the port side of the ship. "Watch out!" Josh screams as the ship's steps come loose from near the hatch and fall toward them. The steps land just a few feet from them. A piece of broken wood hits Ross in the arm. "I'm okay. Just a bruise."

Ross calls Reverend Stuart and Josh over to examine the debris and whispers, "You know, at a certain point, if this ship gets closer to upright, that water in the quarters down below will start coming in here. And now we don't have any steps to get out. We could drown."

"Let's see what we can do," Josh says. "We got all those empty rum barrels. We could build like a pyramid with the top up near the hatch."

"A big wave will hit the ship and knock them over," Reverend Stuart says.

"We wedge them between posts using the boards from the steps to hold them tight," Ross says.

"That might just work," Josh says.

Reverend Stuart goes over and recruits four of the strongest men from among the other passengers and explains the plan. "If ye men will start rolling over some rum barrels, we'll sort through the boards from the steps and see what we can use. It will be dark in a few hours, but we can get a good start. Hopefully finish up in the morning and be ready to get out when this storm is over."

The men help each other get the rum barrels down from the stacks wedged in the corner of the quarters. Then they each roll a barrel across the floor to the steps.

"Bullocks! Watch it! Is that the best you can do?" one man says to the man behind him when he rolls the barrel into the back of his legs.

"Gots away from me," the guilty man says. "Won't happen again."

The project moves along quickly. Barrels stacked with boards make a tight-fitting wedge between the posts and the wall of the quarters.

"Some of the older folks might need a little help, but we can all get out when this storm is past," Ross says.

Darkness comes quickly. They are all hungry but nothing to eat. They do have water. Exhausted, they quickly fall into deep asleep. Loud snoring echoes all around the quarters.

Hours later, Reverend Stuart feels his left eyelid lift slightly. Light starts to peek in around the hatch. He nudges Samantha, and when she stirs a little, he says, "I don't hear any wind. I don't feel any waves." The others still sleep as they look around, but Brody is not on his straw.

"Where's Brody?" Samantha says. Several more people are now awake. They all start looking around and saying, "Where's Brody?"

"Brody? Where are you?" Reverend Stuart says in a loud voice, not worried about waking others up now. Brody must be found.

"I'm up here!" Brody says, sitting on one of the top barrels. "I'm ready to get out of here."

For the first time in what seems like days, they laugh.

"Brody, come on down. We're not quite finished. Have two more rows of barrels to stack," Reverend Stuart says.

"Goin' to be hard getting that last row all the way up there," Josh says as he sits up. "But we have enough strong men to do it."

"Can't get out of here soon enough," Ross says. "Them buckets filled up last night. People having to just go on the floor."

"That water over there is not water from the buckets," Reverend Stuart says.

"That's water from the other quarters. I thought we might get some when the ship got pushed up some. We're still leaning some, but nothing like it was," Ross said.

The men make their way over to their escape structure. "We need more barrels," Josh says. Four men from the other group head over for the barrels.

"Ross, we're going to need more strong men to get those last barrels up to the top. See if you can get a couple more to help," Josh says. "Samantha said she would help, but we probably won't need her. Well, here she comes anyway."

"I can do a lil' lifting," Samantha says. "Put me where you need me."

With lots of groaning, grunting, cussing, and several "Sorry, reverends," the last barrels are in place. About that time, the hatch swings open.

"William! Stop! The steps are gone!" Reverend Stuart shouts.

"Okay. Thanks!" William says as he falls flat on the deck and puts his head, arms, and shoulders through the hatch opening. "Everyone all right down there?"

"We're all alive," Reverend Stuart says. "Before the steps collapsed, we had a man jump overboard."

"Reverend, I think we lost an older man last night. They're trying to wake him up over there, but I don't think they goin' get him woke," one of the men says who has approached the barrel tower.

"I'll go check on him," Samantha says.

"We lost seven sailors, seven souls," William says. "But we lucky not to lose more. Baddest storm I ever been in."

"What about Keltz?" Reverend Stuart asks.

"Wait a minute," William says as he withdraws from the hatch opening.

Another figure has dropped to the deck and his head starts through the opening. A head of black hair lowers through the opening, "Reverend, it's me!"

"Keltz, you're all right! We've been worried," Reverend Stuart says.

"Reverend, you goin' be drinking from that silver cup soon. I knows it!" Keltz says.

'Silver cup?' Reverend Stuart wonders for a second and then realizes Keltz talks about the communion chalice.

"Just glad you're okay, Keltz. You and William. How about Captain Shanks?" Reverend Stuart asks.

"He's fine. Trying to figure where we are now. He thinks the bad, ole storm blew us into the Chesapeake Bay. Not too far from Carolina," William says.

"Nice sand over there, and big pine trees as far as I can sees," Keltz says, pointing over the side of the ship.

"Looks like ye folks really built something there," William says.

"Yep, one of those big waves knock the stairs down. So, we built this . . . uh . . . I don't know what to call it," Josh says.

"It's the Keltz Tower," Samantha says. "We named it after Keltz." Keltz's face glows.

"The man on the other side is dead. Looks like he died in his sleep. Maybe his heart just stopped," Samantha whispers.

"Does he have family?" Reverend Stuart asks.

"All by himself. Kicked off a farm, I bet. Headed to Carolina to find a job, I guess," Samantha says.

"Yep, we almost finished the tower. Just got to secure these last barrels," Ross says to William.

"We'll get some ropes. Just in case," William says.

Josh says, "Let's get the women over here first. Get them out. Then Brody, then the rest of us. And then I guess the dead man."

"Reverend, there could be lots of dead over in the other quarters. You goin' to have a bunch of services," Ross says.

"Seven sailors swept overboard. They're gone. We'll have a reading of their names or something like that on deck when we can. Maybe get you to say something and pray, reverend, but that will be no time soon. We gots so much work to do," William says.

One by one they get the passengers out. Clear, fresh air greets them. Bright sun warms their wet clothes. Debris litters the beach, but the water is brilliant blue. Small white caps come and go.

"I'm sorry for all those folks who drowned, and I am thankful to be alive. Gosh, it's good to be out of that hell hole. I might jump in the water just to rinse dis smell off me," Mrs. Connery says. "But I can't swim."

"Yep, smells worse than ten-year-old fermented mead full of dead rats down there. Thank God to be out of there. Not getting' me on another ship," Mrs. Graham says.

"I'm with you," Mrs. Connery adds.

"Captain wants everybody up in front of the forecastle at the ringing of the next bell. I hope it still rings. Hadn't tried it yet," William says.

In a short time, the bell rings. Tired souls make their way to the forecastle. Warm sunshine, and dry air feels good on their weary bodies. A row of seagulls on the front bow scream at the living.

Captain Shanks nervously clears his throat, "We've endured a terrible gaol. The gaol costs us good sailors and unfortunately over half the passengers."

Gasps rise from the motley gathering.

"As you probably heard already, the starboard side passenger quarters went under water when the ship went up on its side. There was nothing we could do. When we can, we'll get them out, and our plan is to bury them on the shore, just above the sandy beach area. I have not told him this yet, but I'll ask Reverend Stuart to say a few words when we can gets all that done. It will take a few days, but we'll have the ship ready to sail again. We can make it to Wilmington without the stern mast. We'll get that fixed there. They have a very good shipyard. We'll have to takes some strong measures to get this ship off the sandbar. Ship might have been fortunate to wedge against the sandbar as it did. It keeps her from sinking. The wind and waves pushed her in a more upright position."

"Thank God!" a woman yells.

"But here is what we must do to get the Isabelle to float again. My sailors will have to throw all the cargo overboard to make the ship lighter, and unfortunately, we'll have to take all the passengers ashore. Once we're afloat. our rows . . . that's sailor-talk for rowboats . . . will bring you back to the ship. Some of you might choose to stay. I've heard good things about this area. Lots of seafood, crabs, oysters, fish, and farmland. My chart shows a town not far from here. You folks from Scotland can help me pronounce *Kil mare neck*."

"Is that 'bout right Reverend Stuart?"

"Kilmarnock. Beautiful little town in Scotland," Reverend Stuart says.

"We're from Kilmarnock, Scotland!" a man and his wife exclaim. "Bonnie place! I tell you! . . . at least the Kilmarnock in Scotland. But we might stay here. See what it's like. Maybe puts down some roots."

Shanks continues. "We'll start dropping the rows soon. Go back to yer quarters and gather yer belongings. Take your blankets. You probably sleep on the beach a couple of nights. The weather probably stay like this, usually does after a big gaol. The skies usually stay clear for days. When all the passengers are on shore, the rows will come back with food. Now, somes of the food got water, but we hope most of it is okay. I've enjoyed being your captain. We been through rough time and hope to see you soon . . . those of you who come back on board."

Walking back to their quarters to gather their meager belongings, the Campbeltown group talk among themselves.

"I'm getting' off this ship and ner' getting on another one," Mrs. Connery says.

"I feels the same way. I'll go to this Kilmarnock with Mrs. Connery," Mrs. Graham says.

"I'll go with Mrs. Connery!" Brody says. "She been good to me."

"Oh, Brody, you're so sweet!" Mrs. Connery melts with the affection.

"I'll go on to Wilmington," Ross says. "I have a job waiting for me there."

"I have two brothers in Carolina. I'll go on," Josh says.

"Joshua and I will go with Josh," Myra says to no one's surprise. The two have spent a lot of time talking, and the others were guessing they were "getting sweet" on each other.

Feeling a responsibility for Brody and Mrs. Connery, Reverend Stuart says, "I'll go to Kilmarnock, and see what it's like. I like the name, for sure."

That leaves Samantha the only uncommitted one.

"Samantha, go with us. Please! Please!" Brody begs.

Reverend Stuart looks at Samantha. His eyes tell her he wants her with him.

Turning to Brody, Samantha says, "Brody, let's go to Kilmarnock!"

The group collects their belongings from the quarters and gather with other passengers to board the rows. They wait and let all the other passengers reach shore. In the meantime, they hug and say their good-byes to Ross, Myra, Josh, and little Joshua.

"Josh, I'm going to miss you!" Reverend Stuart says.

"We've had some good times together," Josh says to the Reverend. "After I look up my brothers in Carolina, I might head back this way . . . you ner' know."

The Kilmarnock bound board William's row, and his oars take them toward shore.

"William, you've taken great care of us," Reverend Stuart says. "You're a good man."

"And you baptized me!" William says. "I'm Christian now. Feels real good."

Landstuhl Regional Medical Center

Kirchberg-Kaserne, Germany

February 10, 2020

"Captain Stuart! This is Harry, Staff Sergeant Harold Means. I'm your physical therapist. I got orders to get you up today, take a few steps. You got to do it. You got to get your limbs and brain moving. You can't sleep all the time. Captain Samantha Stuart, your chart says to call you Sam. Is that okay?"

"Ah . . . ah . . . yeah, sure. Everybody calls me Sam. Named after my great grandmother Samantha Logan Stuart. She helped slaves escape. I . . . I . . . was just dreaming about her. Weird, I guess?"

"You've been in a deep sleep for days, and I imagine you've had lots of vivid dreams," Harry says.

Samantha blinks her eyes, trying to clear her head.

"All right, let's get started." Harry says.

Ashore!

November 3, 1849

When William runs the row up on the beach, Brody puts one hand on the side of the row and vaults over the side. Reverend Stuart assists Mrs. Connery and Mrs. Graham onto the dry sand. Samantha follows.

The immigrants wish William goodbye. Mrs. Connery says, "All mothers want a son just like you!"

"They do!" Mrs. Graham adds.

"I wish all ye the best, and maybe our paths will cross again," William says as he puts the oars into the water and the row backs away from the shore.

"Where we go now?" Brody asks.

"I see a dock up the beach. There must be a road up there," Reverend Stuart says.

Brody dashes ahead, splashing in ankle deep water. "Look two turtles sunning on that rock!"

"That boy is getting' harder and harder to keep up with," Mrs. Connery moans.

"Yep, there's a road up here. It goes that way. Let's bugger on!" Brody points to the north.

"Brody, you are a great scout," Samantha laughs. "Those turtles might be our welcoming party."

"Along with that gaggle of geese up on the beach," Mrs. Graham says.

The five ship-wreck survivors put their feet on the rain softened road and start their journey to the north. Late blooming flowers bleed with color on each side of the road.

A few miles up the road, Reverend Stuart says, "There's another road to the left, but the road to the north looks more traveled. I bet that's the road to Kilmarnock. I wonder how far our sea-legs will take us. We're not use to a lot of walking."

"I'm goin' to need some water soon," Mrs. Graham says as she sits on a large rock white with lichen.

"Hopefully, we'll come across a spring or a creek," Reverend Stuart says as he strains to see through the dense thickets along the side of the road.

A pair of yellow butterflies swoop in front of them. They chase each other. First one chases and then the other.

"Maybe de butterflies a sign for us. A good sign. Beauty and freedom ahead of us," Mrs. Connery declares. "And look at those dragonflies. One just buzzed right past my ear."

"Massive beech trees," Reverend Stuart says.

"There's a wagon comin' up the road behind us," Samantha says.

"Whoa! Whoa!" the wagon driver commands the horse as he draws alongside the weary walkers.

"I don't think I've seen you folks 'round here before," the driver says who looks to be in his fifties and in dark pants, dark coat, a white shirt, and a well-groomed beard.

"We just got off a ship at the beach back there. A terrible storm ran us aground. We were headed to Carolina, but the captain made us get off the ship . . . to help the ship float off the sandbar. We figure we'll just stay and see what Kilmarnock's like," Reverend Stuart says.

"Well, get in the wagon. I've got a big ole empty house with lots of bedrooms just up the road. My wife died two years ago. I get lonely . . . it'll be good to have some company. Climb in. The ride a lil' rough, but I'll try to take it easy," the man says. "My name is Duffer, William Duffer. Folks just call me Bill."

"Bill, my name is Charles Stuart, Reverend Charles Stuart. This is Samantha, Brody, Mrs. Connery, and Mrs. Graham."

"Tis not often you find a lost Reverend," Bill Duffer chuckles.

"Yer a God-send, Mr. Duffer," Mrs. Graham says. "My knees couldn't go much farther."

"Glad I found you, instead of some of the no-counts around here. They'd want to be paid for a lil' ride," Duffer says. "And just call me Bill."

The wagon goes by a field of dandelions. In a pasture a short distance up the road, grazing goats raise their heads. Bill Duffer pulls the reins to the right, and the horse pulls the wagon down a straight road and into a circular road in front of a large, white wood-board house with red brick chimneys on both sides. White-throated sparrows sit on top of the chimneys. A smaller white house with its own chimney sits to the right behind the big house. They learn later this is the kitchen, set apart from the main house because of the unwanted heat in the hot summers generated by the wood burning cook-stove and the possibility of a grease fire that might otherwise burn down the entire house.

Brody leaps off the wagon. Bill Duffer, the perfect gentlemen, helps each woman off the wagon. Reverend Stuart insists he can get off on his own.

"Who's that?" Brody asks as he points to a large, black man drawing water from a well.

"That's Reuben. You will meet him later. He's a fine man. I love him like a brother," Bill says.

"Let's go inside, and I'll show you your bedrooms," Bill says.

Huge double doors greet them. Bill opens the right door and motions them inside. He shuts the door behind him. A huge chandelier hangs from the lofty ceiling. A wide staircase looms a few steps in front of them.

"Mrs. Connery and . . ." Bill Duffer has forgotten Mrs. Graham's name.

"Mrs. Graham," Reverend Stuart offers.

"Yes, of course, Mrs. Graham. You and Mrs. Connery will stay down here. Your bedroom is to the left. That bedroom has two beds. I think you will like it. Make yourself at home while I show these folks their bedrooms. And that's the dining room on the right," Bill says.

Motioning to Reverend Stuart, Samantha, and Brody, Bill Duffer says, "Follow me up the steps."

At the top of the steps, Bill says, "That's my bedroom on the left."

Looking at Brody and pointing straight ahead, Bill says, "Young man that's your room straight ahead. Perfect for you. Small with one small bed," Brody darts down the hall.

"My own room!" he shouts.

"Reverend and Mrs. Stuart, that be your bedroom to the right."

Charles Stuart and Samantha Logan look at each other. Before they have time to think, let alone say anything, Bill Duffer steps between them, takes them by the arms, and escorts them down the hall.

"Make yourselves at home. I'll tell the cook to put on some extra vittles. She's a fine cook. You'll taste for yourselves in a few hours. But how about a good wash first? I'll tell Reuben to get the water hot. Give him about thirty minutes," Bill says.

Bill quickly makes his way down the steps. The same steps he has used for the fifty-plus years of his life, having grown up in the house.

"Ladies is there anything you might need?" Bill asks after knocking on their bedroom door.

"Oh no. We're so relieved to have real beds. We slept on straw for weeks on the ship," Mrs. Graham says as she feels her cheeks warm with the thought of her head on a soft pillow.

"This wonderful!" Mrs. Connery adds. "There's something about this place that reminds me of my home back in Campbeltown." Tears in her eyes form long lines down her cheeks. "I guess I never see that house again."

"Ladies, I am so sorry for what has happened. All I can do is welcome you into my home and share what I have. Maybe soak in the tub a few minutes would be good for you after that long voyage. I'm on my way to tell Reuben to get the water hot. Give him about an hour. The Reverend and Mrs. Stuart will wash first. So, just relax a bit. Oh, the closet down the hall has Mrs. Duffer's dresses and blouses. Pick out something you like," Bill says.

"Thank you so much, Mr. Duffer," Mrs. Graham says. "I know ye miss yer wife. Will it be hard seeing us in her clothes?"

"It'll be okay. I got some sadness too. Life's just painful at times," Bill says. "I'm goin' show Brody around before dinner." Brody and Bill make their way out back.

After Bill shuts the door, Mrs. Graham listens to make sure she hears Bill going out the back door of the house and then says, "I'd like to be a fly on the wall in that bath house! I don't think those two have ever done anything like bath together."

"I bets the Reverend ner' been kissed," Mrs. Connery snickers and then puts her hand over her mouth in embarrassment.

"It'll be hard to keeps a straight face at dinner," Mrs. Graham says.

Bill and Brody go out the back door where Reuben is chopping wood. A white long-tailed cat rests nearby, apparently used to the sound of the ax striking the huge pieces of wood. A large man, Reuben rises to at least six foot and three inches. Hard work has chiseled his arms into muscles that look like they might make his skin pop. Tight dark curly hair stands on his head, making him look even taller. Charcoal skin and dark brown eyes envelope a warm glance when he sees Bill approach.

"Reuben, you can split more wood in an hour than most men in a day," Bill says.

"Thank you, Mister Duffer," Reuben says.

"Reuben, I've told you to call me Bill."

"Won't be right," Reuben says.

Bill realizes once again that Reuben is a product of slave culture and has a hard time stepping out of that.

"Reuben, we have four, I guess five people, counting Brody, who need a good wash. Can you get the water hot in the bath house?"

"Yes, sir. I does it now," Reuben says.

"What's that pile?" Brody points to large heap of shells.

"Those are oyster shells. Reuben and I have oyster cages down on the river. When they get big enough, we bring the oysters back here and shuck 'em. Oh, some good eatin' inside those shells. In a few days, we'll go down to the river, bring back some oysters, so you can have your first oyster."

"What do they taste like?" Brody asks.

"Taste like the sea, salty," Bill says.

"Like nuttin' you ever had," Reuben adds.

Bill and Brody make their way to the kitchen house where Cora already prepares the evening dinner. He politely knocks on the door.

"Come in. Mr. Duffer, you don'ts have to knock cause this yo house," Cora says. The petite Cora's eyes dance on her face. Her long white dress covers her brown skin. Like Reuben, she prefers barefoot and only wears shoes when the weather is really cold. A red bandana wraps around her hair, giving her a serious-about-work appearance.

Bill suspects they are perhaps an unmarried couple and not brother and sister as they claim. He understands what people in their condition must do to survive, so he has never asked about their relationship. He is happy to provide them a log cabin on his property and pay them for their work on the farm.

"Cora, we have five visitors for dinner. I'm sorry to do this to you at the last minute, but I picked them up on the road. The storm blew their ship into the bay and up on a sandbar last night," Bill says.

"No problem," Cora says. "We havin' ham anyway. I'll just go back to the smokehouse and cuts some more off that big ole hangin' ham. You gots three more hangin' up when you needs them."

"Cora, remembers what I told you. You take back to your cabin the ham and vegetables that you and Reuben need. That potato cellar still over half full of the last digging. So, we got plenty of food," Bill says.

As Bill and Brody leave the kitchen house, smoke from the hickory wood Reuben burns greets his nostrils. He loves the fresh smell of hickory smoke, a fragrance like no other to him.

As Brody and Bill pass by a weathered gray patina outbuilding, Brody points, "Why is that hole in the bottom of the door?"

"Oh, that's the cat-hole. Cat can go into the storage building and take care of the mice. Mice would take over the place if not for our cat," Bill explains.

"That's the biggest I've ever seen!" Brody says as he eyes a saw stretched across the outbuilding and hanging on several nails.

"That's a crosscut saw. Reuben and I use it to cut down trees when we must. I get on one side and Reuben gets on the other, and we pull it back and forth to cut the wood. It's a thing of beauty, watching Reuben work a crosscut saw," Bill explains.

Back in the house, Samantha tries to calm an anxious Reverend Stuart. "Everyone thinks we're married. Captain Shanks assumed we were. Bill assumes we are. But are you going to be comfortable with this?"

"I guess I better be. I don't think we have any choice now. Bill's a very nice man, and it's just better to let him keep believing we're married," Reverend Stuart says.

"Mrs. Graham and Mrs. Connery won't ever say anything. I talked to them on the ship. Our secret is safe with them," Samantha says.

"I don't think Brody even thinks about such things. He's more interested in a place to fish or a tree to climb," Reverend Stuart says.

"You don't think they'll be bothered if we see each other naked in a few minutes?" Samantha laughs but stops abruptly because a flash of "did anyone hear me?" anxiety sweeps through her.

"Knock!" The sound at the door has Samantha holding her breath.

"Your water's hot. Go on down to the bath house any time now. Reuben will take good care of you," Bill says.

"Thanks, we'll go now," Reverend Stuart says as he opens the door.

Bill stands in the doorway with clothes on both arms. "You and I are about the same size. Shirt and pants are clean. I think they will fit you."

"Thank you. I've had these same clothes on far too long," Reverend Stuart chuckles.

"Mrs. Stuart, my wife was much larger than you, but she was about your size when we were first married. And she never got rid of this gown. It was one of her favorites. I think it will fit you," Bill says.

"Bill, that's so thoughtful," Samantha says.

Samantha and Reverend Stuart make their way down the wide steps to the first floor and out the back door.

Reuben takes a steaming bucket of water into the tiny bath house. They hear him pouring the hot water into the tub.

As they approach the bath house, Reuben says, "You'll need one more bucket of hot water. I'll knock on the door and sit it inside, but I won'ts look inside. Then, I'll take a pitcher of cold water to your rooms while you bathe."

"Thanks, Reuben. I'm Reverend Charles Stuart and this is . . . . " He pauses briefly. "This is my wife, Samantha." Reverend Stuart feels relief as he says that. It feels right.

When they enter the bath house, Samantha says, "Charles, they think we're man and wife. I guess we must act like it."

Without hesitation, Samantha starts unbuttoning her blouse. Charles watches her undress for a moment and then realizes he is staring.

"Charles, remember I had older brothers. Not much bothers me. Ye okay?" Samantha asks.

"It's just that I've never watched a woman undress before," Reverend Stuart says.

"I'll need some help with the little hook in the back. You okay with that?" Samantha asks.

"Sure, I mean . . . uh . . . I'm okay," Reverend Stuart says as he approaches Samantha.

"I don't know why they put hooks back there?" Samantha says as Reverend Stuart gently releases the hooks. Reverend Stuart notices a brown birth mark, uneven but almost in the shape of a heart, on her right shoulder.

As Samantha turns around, Reverend Stuart sees her bare breasts, the first female breasts he has ever seen. Her large perfectly formed breasts lunge toward him as she turns, and large rosy nipples greet his eyes.

"Ye're . . . uh . . . beautiful," Reverend Stuart says as he realizes his face has turned as red as her nipples.

"Don't be embarrassed. What do ye preachers say . . . 'It's God's Will' or something like that . . . I mean here we are . . . We didn't plan this," Samantha says.

"I didn't know if I would ever get married," Reverend Stuart says.

"I think God's goin' to will this water cold if we don't get in," Samantha says as she slips off the remainder of her clothes and twists her long red hair into two strands that she ties together on the back of her head.

As she steps into the tub, Reverend Stuarts admires her backside, well-formed shoulders that taper down to a slim waist, and perfectly round buttocks that could have been designed by Michelangelo, he thinks.

A knock at the door and Reuben says, "I goin' open the door a little and sits your other bucket of hot water inside. It's just right for pourin'."

"Thank you, Reuben," Reverend Stuart says as he gets his last foot out of his pants. He crosses the tiny room and lifts the bucket by the handle.

As he sits the bucket by the tub, he sticks his hand in the water and says, "It's just right. I'll pour half of it over you, and if you would please, you can pour the other half over me when I get in," Reverend Stuart says.

"Sounds perfect," Samantha says.

As Charles pours the water over Samantha, she closes her eyes and moans, "Are we in heaven? This feels so good."

After a few minutes of the warm water pleasure, Samantha says, "I best get out before the water cools. I want you to enjoy this too."

As Samantha steps out, Charles sees for the first time where her legs come together reddish pubic hair, a perfect match to the hair on her head. Water beads on her breasts as streaks of water go down her long legs.

"Here, dry with this. I think Bill left these for us," Reverend Stuart says as he hands her a large cotton piece of cloth that has been torn in half, the other half meant, he assumes, for his drying.

Reverend Stuart watches as Samantha dries herself with long even strokes up and down her body. Her breasts push up as she dries underneath them.

"You gettin' in?" Samantha says.

Now realizing he is staring, Reverend Stuart says, "Oh, of course, of course."

"A bath! It's been so long!" Reverend Stuart says.

"Enjoy for a few minutes. Then I'll give you your baptism," Samantha says, and they both chuckle.

As Samantha pours his half of the water over his head, a knock at the door jolts them slightly, but they quickly hear the voice of Mrs. Graham. "We're sorry. We didn't know if you were still in there."

"Give us just a few minutes, and we'll be out," Reverend Stuart says.

Back in their room, Samantha and Reverend Stuart try on their new clothes.

"Can you tie this in the back for me?" Samantha asks.

"Of course," Reverend Stuart says. "I'll tie a bow, but I'll have to hold your hair to the side." Samantha's striking, red locks almost reach her waistline. "There you go . . . all tied up."

"Everything fits perfectly. And my, ye look handsome, Reverend Stuart. And I gets to sleep with you tonight," Samantha says.

"Samantha, you like to tease me, but I think you like my innocence. I just don't know how much longer I'll be innocent," Reverend Stuart says. Samantha winks at him.

Ding! Ding! Ding! "I bet that's Reuben ringing the dinner bell," Reverend Stuart says.

Reverend Stuart extends his right arm and says, "Mrs. Stuart, shall we dine?" Samantha glows and winks again.

As they step outside the bedroom door, Brody's already headed down the steps. "Brody, you hungry?" Reverend Stuart asks.

"I coulds eat anything . . . and lots of it," Brody says.

Mrs. Connery and Mrs. Graham, already downstairs, stand in the foyer, so they all enter the dining room at the same time.

"Welcome, my friends. Looks like Mrs. Duffer's clothes have been put to fine use. You ladies look so lovely," Bill says. "And this is Hudson." He points to his large, long-haired, English Cream Golden Retriever resting lordly on the hearth.

"He's beautiful," Samantha says.

"Have a seat please. Cora and Reuben have prepared us a fine meal. They always do," Bill says.

They all assume the chair at the head of the table belongs to Mr. Duffer, so they avoid that seat, everyone except Brody.

"Brody, that's Mr. Duffer's chair. Come sit beside me," Mrs. Connery says. "You can see the fire in the fireplace better from here." Indeed, behind the chair at the head of the table, the fireplace roars.

"Smell that hickory burning, folks?" Bill says. "Hickory's very hard, dense, so it burns slow, and gives off that sweet smoke."

"Yes, that's wonderful, so sweet," Mrs. Graham says. Reverend Stuart notices how quickly Mrs. Graham always responds to Mr. Duffer. He wonders if she is trying to charm Bill.

"Young man, you have a glass of water, but the adults have a glass of local blueberry wine. Ernest McBride, on the other side of Kilmarnock, has a lovely vineyard, and the blueberry wine is one of his best," Bill says. "I have promised Brody his first oyster soon. Reuben and I will go down in a few days and get some out of the Rappahannock."

Cora and Reuben enter the room. In front of her, Cora holds a large platter of sliced ham. In one of his massive hands, Reuben has a large bowl of boiled potatoes, and in the other hand, a bowl of corn on the cob.

Brody eyes grow as big as the dinner plates. "So much food!" he says.

"You deserve some good meals, folks. You've had such a hard journey," Bill says.

"You are so kind and say the kindest things," Mrs. Graham says.

"I'll pray," Bill says. Everyone bows their heads, except Brody, who keeps looking at the food.

Reverend Stuart quietly sighs relief that he was not asked to pray, as he is usually asked to pray almost everywhere he goes.

"Brody! You should wait until after the blessing," Mrs. Graham says. During Mr. Duffer's prayer, Brody has reached into the bowl closest to him and now has an ear of corn on his plate.

"The lad is hungry. Let's all eat," Bill says. "And, you know, I've not had a crowded table in a long time. You folks are such a blessing to me. It gets lonely around here."

Brody attacks the food, barely taking breaths between bites. "Brody, slow down, you gets all you want, you don't have to eat so fast," Bill says.

"It's all so good!" Samantha says.

"I'm so lucky to have Cora and Reuben," Bill says.

"Are they slaves?" Brody asks impulsively. All the guests hold their breaths, not knowing what the reaction might be to Brody's question, but they have all wondered the same thing.

"No, they're not slaves. They're free. I bought their freedom from the owner of a plantation in Charles City. I told them that if they wanted to come here and work as free people, I would give them a cabin to live in and pay them fair wages," Bill says.

"That's wonderful! You're wonderful!" Mrs. Graham says.

"It ain't right to make slaves out of other men and women. I don't care what color their skin is or where they're from. We have some preachers in the area who say it's all right to have slaves because they had slaves in the Bible, but I don't agree. They quote the Apostle Paul in the Bible where he says, 'slaves be obedient to your masters,'" Bill says.

"And they probably use the 'mark of Cain' excuse from the Bible. But that's a misuse of the Bible as well. Or they might use the 'curse of Ham' as another twisted justification for slavery," Reverend Stuart explains.

"So can Cora and Reuben go into town and other places?" Samantha asks.

"Yes, but they best be very careful," Bill says. "They'll get snatched and taken down south and sold as slaves. They stay here almost all the time. They might go into Kilmarnock with me from time to time, but that's all. They know the risks."

"When I get older, I'm goin' set all the slaves free!" Brody declares.

"Brody, I like the way you think. You eat your dinner, so you grow up big and strong and make that happen," Bill says.

"Why don't the plantation owners set the slaves free?" Mrs. Connery asks.

"Most plantation owners say they can't afford to free their slaves. They say it's economic self-preservation. But one fine man did free his slaves. In 1791, Robert 'King' Carter, who owned thousands of acres just north of here and owned over five-hundred slaves, walked into Northumberland County Courthouse with a deed of gift giving freedom to all his slaves. Carter said that slavery was contrary to the principles of religion. In the deed of gift, he declared the freed slaves could name themselves, and buy or lease land. The other plantation owners in this area threatened to burn his house down. Thomas Jefferson and George Washington questioned the right for one person to own another person, but they argued that they could not afford to free their slaves. So, King Carter stands alone as one who freed his slaves. Some of us here are very proud of what he did. Others despise the man."

Minutes go by, and no one says a word. Attention focuses on the ham, potatoes, and corn. Brody eats a large piece of ham, several boiled potatoes, and devours corn on the cob. Three cobs, then four, pile on his plate.

"Brody, ye put many more cobs on your plate, and we won't be able to see you!" Samantha jokes.

"Reverend Stuart, what was your church like in England? Did you say the name of the town? Sorry, if I have forgotten," Bill says.

"The town was Campbeltown, Scotland. We're part of England now, but most of the Scots don't like it," Reverend Stuart explains.

"I didn't know that . . . that Scotland is part of England," Bill says.

"Yes, for over one-hundred years now. Ever since the Battle of Culloden in April of 1746, Scotland, begrudgingly, been wed to England," Reverend Stuart says.

"He don't say anything about it, but Reverend Stuart's related to the last king of Scotland," Mrs. Connery says.

"Really?" Bill says.

"Distant relative," Reverend Stuart says. "Bonnie Prince Charlie, he was called, but his real name was Charles Edward Stuart. But my part of the Stuart family was not considered of royal blood. My ancestors were farmers and clergy."

"Let's see . . . 'Bonnie' means . . . I know I've heard . . ." Bill struggles to remember.

"Beautiful," Brody says. "If something is bonnie, it's beautiful."

"The lad is from Scotland and knows his Scottish sayings," Bill says. "What kind of place is Campbeltown?"

"It's a small town with a harbor," Mrs. Graham says. "Good people for the most part. Most of those people still resent the English though. They made life hard on our ancestors and tried to take away most of our traditions. They wanted us to be English, but we've hung onto many of our traditions."

"Ten years ago, Campbeltown had the most distilleries in the world of any one place. Twenty-nine," Samantha says. "My family has a pub, so we know those kinds of things. But many of those distilleries are closed now."

"Campbeltown, like most of Scotland, been hit hard by the potato famine and crop failures. Many people starve to death. The English haven't helped. They take our grains grown on Scottish soil and give it to their soldiers. And that's why there are so many Scots in this country now. Stay in Scotland and they'll starve," Reverend Stuart adds.

"I know. This town was settled by Scots, and I guess some were from Kilmarnock . . . so they named it Kilmarnock. Lots of Scottish settlements in the big valley, the Shenandoah Valley, in the mountains, and even more Scots settled in North Carolina," Bill says.

Cora steps through the door with pride in her face. In her extended hands, she holds a steaming apple pie. Behind her, Reuben holds a second hot apple pie.

"Now you're in for a real treat," Bill says.

"Apple pie!" Brody exclaims.

"Young man, I gives you the first piece!" Cora says.

"Brody, you wait until everybody is served before you start eating. Okay?" Mrs. Connery says.

"All right," Brody says, not happy.

The slices of pie don't last long on anyone's plate.

"That's better than my pie," Mrs. Connery says.

"No, it's not!" Brody insists.

"Brody, you're so sweet," Mrs. Connery says.

"Well, I know you folks are tired. You've been on quite a trip, and I must go to Warsaw tomorrow and it's a long trip, there and back in one day," Bill says.

"What will you do in Warsaw?" Mrs. Graham asks.

"I'm a timber broker. I'll look at some timber on a farm, and if its ready for harvesting I'll get the landowner a good price from a timber company," Bill says. "I get a small percentage of the price, that's how I make my living. But wait . . . tomorrow is Sunday, not Monday. I go to Warsaw on Monday. My days run together sometimes. Part of gettin' older, I guess," Bill says as he rubs the top of his head.

"Go to church with me tomorrow?" Bill asks.

"See-ins how we don't have anything else to do, let's go to church with Bill," Mrs. Graham says as she looks at the others.

"Church will be a good place to spread the news about the shipwreck. I expect a lot of people will want to go down and help if they can," Bill says.

"A lot of cargo was thrown overboard to take some weight off the ship. I don't know if they'll try to get it back on when they get off the sandbar?" Reverend Stuart says. "If not, they'll be a lot of supplies in the river."

"Bill, thank you so much for the dinner and all the hospitality," Mrs. Graham says.

"It's my Christian duty," Bill says. "Jesus says 'we are blessed even if we just give a person a cup of cold water.'"

"Well, this was certainly much more than a cup of cold water," Mrs. Graham says.

"Indeed, delicious meal, and I want to thank Cora and Reuben," Reverend Stuart says. "Maybe, I'll step out back to the kitchen house and speak to them."

The ship survivors make their way out back and to the kitchen house where they thank Cora and Reuben for their dinner.

"You gots breakfast coming in the morning," Cora says. "We gets sausage from Mr. Barnham. He knows how to make sausage. We'll have eggs and grits, too."

"What's grits?" Brody asks.

"Reuben and I were on a plantation in Georgia before we were sold to the family in Charles City. Folks in Georgia loves their grits," Cora says.

"How do you make grits?" Mrs. Connery asks.

"We takes stone ground corn and mix it with butter and milk and then boils it until it is just right. I thinks you'll like it," Cora says. Reuben nods his head and lifts his thick eyebrows in agreement.

Making their way back inside, Mrs. Connery says, "We gets to sleep in a bed. Praise God on high! I thought we were goin' perish on the ship."

"We have a lot to be thankful for. Let's get a good sleep, and be ready for tomorrow," Reverend Stuart says.

In their bedroom with door shut, Samantha says, "Well, Mr. Stuart, we're sleeping together. And I must tell you I always sleep without clothes on. Clothes rubbing on my skin keeps me awake. You okay with that?"

"Come to think of it, Bill didn't offer us any night-clothes," Reverend Stuart says.

"Maybe he doesn't wear night-clothes either," Samantha chuckles.

"Heavens, the people of Campbeltown would have a massive row if they knew about this. The pastor and Samantha sleeping together with no clothes on," Reverend Stuart says.

"We don't have to worry about what those people think anymore," Samantha says as she starts to undress. Charles looks away.

"Charles, you have to get over this," Samantha says. "Will I have to teach you how to kiss?"

"Just give me a little time. It's just me. I'm not ready. It's not you. I think you're beautiful, kind, everything I could want in a wife. But I took ordination vows not to . . . you know . . . outside marriage. So, let's get married. Okay?" Reverend Stuart says.

Samantha doesn't respond since it sounds like an off-handed remark.

"Samantha Logan, will you marry me?" Reverend Stuart says.

"Charles Rory Stuart, I will marry you," Samantha says.

"Tomorrow night, we will exchange vows," Reverend Stuart says.

"I like that. Tomorrow, we wed!" Samantha says.

Samantha lifts the gown over her head. Her perfect breasts offer themselves to an embarrassed Charles.

"It's okay," Samantha says. "This night would you just hold me?"

"Of course," Charles says as he slips into the bed and holds out his hand for Samantha to join him.

As her skin touches him, he realizes he has never felt anything this soft. His arm goes around her back and her arm around his waist.

"You're warm," he says.

"I like your touch," she says. The weary travelers soon have trouble holding their eyes open and drift into deep sleep.

Without curtains or shades, first light moves across their faces. Eyelids open. Minds calculate quickly where they are. They turn and look at each other. Warm expressions are exchanged. Her arm goes across his body.

"Cora has a great breakfast planned," Charles says, feeling a bit uncomfortable having shared a bed with a woman for the first time.

"Let's get dressed," Samantha says.

Mrs. Connery and Mrs. Graham have already stirred Brody, and all three are standing in the dining room.

"I hope you two slept well?" Mrs. Graham asks, trying to hold back a big grin.

"Wonderful sleep. How 'bout you folks?" Samantha asks.

"Never slept better," Mrs. Graham says. Mrs. Connery nods her head in agreement and adds, "And we had to wake Brody. He was still in a deep sleep."

"Good morning!" Bill offers as he enters the dining room. "I hope your beds were comfortable?"

"Wonderful!" Mrs. Graham declares. The others add their agreement and thanks.

"Well, let's have a seat. I went by the kitchen, and Cora will have breakfast on the table in minutes."

Before they have time to start a new conversation, Cora steps through the doorway, balancing three bowls. "Sausage, eggs, and grits!" she announces. "I'll be right back with maple syrup."

"Cora knows I like maple syrup on my sausage," Bill says. "I have a friend in Highland County, high in the Virginia mountains. Every year, he brings me maple syrup he harvests from his maple trees. Delicious!"

They pass the bowls. Brody takes four pieces of sausage. "Brody don't take more than you can eats," Mrs. Connery says. "You can always have more but lets everybody get some first."

"Brody, maple syrup for your sausage?" Bill offers and passes to Brody a white jug dotted with black specks.

"I'm so glad we came to Carolina! I loves this syrup!" Brody says.

"Brody, this is Virginia. We were supposed to go to Carolina, but we got off the ship in Virginia," Mrs. Connery responds.

"I love Virginia," Brody says.

"Folks, Reuben has the wagon hitched and ready to go," Bill says. "You'll like our church."

"Do slaves go to church?" Brody asks. The room grows quiet.

"Yes, they go to church," Bill says.

"Do they have their own churches?" Samantha asks.

"There a few who do, but most of the plantation owners want their slaves to go to church with them. They have a special section for the slaves, maybe even balcony seating," Bill says.

"I get it," Reverend Stuart says. "The plantation owners want to control what the slaves hear. The owners probably won't let the preachers read from Exodus where God set the slaves free from Egyptian captivity. That's clever and a way to keep the slaves under control."

"That's what it is," Bill says.

Church

November 4, 1849

After breakfast, they gather outside. A red-headed hawk circles overhead. A rooster chases a hen in the side-yard. Reuben holds the snorting horse steady as they climb into the wagon.

"This day could not be any more beautiful!" Samantha declares. "The air is cool and fresh. Hardly a cloud in the sky. The breeze is just right."

"How far is Kilmarnock?" Reverend Stuart asks.

"Not far. We're not a big town. Good people for the most part," Bill says as he clicks his tongue in the roof of his mouth, the signal to the horse to start the slow trot up the road.

Farmland spreads from each side of the road. Large white houses with barns and sheds behind them sit in the middle of the massive fields. Mules chew grass pulled from the ground. Cows stand in a creek. Most fields lay barren having given up their crops recently. Stubs, looking like rows of tiny soldiers, remain where cornstalks once stood. Rocks white with lichen dot the areas around the fields.

Beyond the main houses, small shacks sit on four corner foundations of piled stones. Smoke curls skyward from leaning rock chimneys. People with dark skin sit and stand on slanted, uneven porches.

"Are they slaves?" Brody asks.

"Yes, Brody. I think they are," Reverend Stuart says.

"They look sad," Brody adds.

"Probably have a hard life," Reverend Stuart says.

In a few miles, Bill says, "That's Kilmarnock up ahead. Church is on the other side of town. It's on Church Street. Several churches on the street. That's how it got its name."

The wagon passes several large residences as they enter town, large white colonial style homes with columns across wide front porches. Rows of windows line across the fronts of the two-story houses.

"That's John McAndrew's house," Bills says as he points to the left. "He owns the hardware store. He'll be at church."

The horse and wagon with driver and five thankful to be alive passengers pass along Main Street. A few stores line each side of the street. Recent rains leave the street soft, and each passing wagon and horse leaves imprints in the street. Bill pulls the right rein so that the wagon avoids a pile of horse dung in the street. "Some people don't do what they supposed to. Everybody supposed to clean up after their animals."

Bill takes a right on Church Street. On the left a sign says, "Kilmarnock Presbyterian Church." Several obedient horses stand quietly hitched to their wagons and seem unbothered by Bill's horse and wagon as they pull alongside.

"Hold on. There's a bucket by the tree. I'll get it so you ladies have an easier step down off the wagon," Bill says.

Brody jumps off the wagon. Reverend Stuart swings his legs over the side and drops to the ground. Samantha exits with equal ease. Bill holds the hands of Mrs. Connery and Mrs. Graham as they step off. Both women impressed with this church-going man.

"Just follow me. We be a few minutes late, but that's all right, probably just making the announcements," Bill says.

They take the three wooden steps into the entrance of the church. The front door covered by a tiny porch roof.

Bill leads the way to the unoccupied second pew from the front and on the right. He stands in the aisle and motions for his guests to file down the pew. Mrs. Connery, Mrs. Graham, Brody, Samantha, and finally Reverend Stuart make their way down the pew. Bill sits on the end near the center aisle.

A lot of grey heads dot the pews, along with several young couples with small children.

A short, stout man stands behind the pulpit. The little man has a round face and a round bald head. A scruff of brown hair remains above each ear. Almost as wide as he is tall, suspenders looping up and over his white shirt and broad shoulders hold up his brown trousers. He pauses while Bill and his guests file in. As soon as they are seated, Bill whispers to Reverend Stuart, "That's Ted Jenkins. He fills in since we don't have a pastor. He doesn't try to preach. He reads some scripture and reads from a devotional book. We sing a lot of hymns."

Mr. Jenkins turns toward Bill and says, "Bill, you bring guests."

Bill stands and says, "These folks were walking up the road from the Rappahannock River yesterday and spent the night at my house. Their ship was pushed into the bay by the big storm. The Isabelle now stuck on a sandbar waiting for high tide. The passengers had to get off the ship to help the ship float off the sandbar. These folks decided they wanted to come to Kilmarnock rather than continuing to Wilmington."

Mr. Jenkins says, "Why don't you people stand and tell us your names?"

One by one the visitors stand and tell the congregation their names. Mrs. Connery and Mrs. Graham go first. Then Brody says, "I'm Brody." And sits back down immediately. No one seems to mind that he doesn't give a last name.

Not knowing how to identify herself, Samantha simply says, "Samantha" and sits back down.

"I'm Reverend Charles Stuart, a Presbyterian minister." He sits down, but a stir sweeps across the congregation. Wives elbow husbands. Friends turn and look at each other with anticipation on their faces.

The little man in the pulpit clears his throat and, ignoring the other guests, stares at Reverend Stuart. "Our minister dropped dead over a year ago. We've prayed for the Lord to send us another minister. We thought the Lord was ignoring our prayers, but here you are!"

No one is more surprised than Reverend Stuart.

The little man continues, "I can't speak for the entire congregation, but we have a splendid house for you and your lovely wife. We were left the house in Mrs. Tatum's will, one of the finest homes in Kilmarnock. There are lots of bedrooms for your friends."

The little man is not just impulsive, but he is weary of being the church spokesperson. He wants desperately for Reverend Stuart to take over his responsibilities.

"Reverend Stuart, come up here and speak to your congregation. And then we'll have a congregational meeting and vote on you being our new pastor!" the little man proclaims.

Bill turns his head to the right and with raised eyebrows looks at a stunned Reverend Stuart.

"I guess you better let me out," Reverend Stuart says. Bill steps out into the aisle. Reverend Stuart slides his legs between the pews and steps into the aisle. There are three small steps up to the pulpit. The little man has already exited to his right as Reverend Stuart comes up from the other side.

Behind the pulpit, Reverend Stuart pauses and taking a deep breath scans the sanctuary. Stained glass windows show scenes from the life of Jesus. With an unfinished ceiling, he looks through the rafters at the underside of the roof. He's reminded immediately that all the people in the pews and himself are unfinished as well, all survivors of life's storms and traumas. No doubt all the folks seated before him have lost family members and probably had close encounters with death themselves. They are here clinging to hope, hope that life has meaning, and that death when it comes is not the final word for them.

"Good folks of Kilmarnock and the Kilmarnock Presbyterian Church, I'm so sorry to hear about the loss of your pastor. I was the pastor of Campbeltown Presbyterian Church in Campbeltown, Scotland, for a little over three years. A series of events had us on a ship to Wilmington, North Carolina. A terrible storm, that I understand you felt here as well, pushed us into your Chesapeake Bay and onto a sandbar. We were told to disembark the ship to help the vessel float off the sandbar with a high tide. A few of us decided to come to Kilmarnock rather than re-boarding the ship for Wilmington. I can't explain why. It just felt like the thing to do. You know, just a hunch, that this is where we needed to be. We would be honored to be a part of your community and church. And if you think I should fill this pulpit and serve as your pastor, I would be honored."

Reverend Stuart heads back to his pew while the little man goes back to the pulpit.

"Friends, we have an opportunity to call a pastor. I'll ask Reverend Stuart to step outside while we consider this very important and sacred matter. I would remind the visitors here today that you cannot vote in a congregational meeting since you are not a member here."

Reverend Stuart has stood in the aisle while the little man made his announcement. Samantha rises, slides down the pew, past Bill Duffer, and joins Reverend Stuart in the aisle. They walk down the aisle and out the front door.

"Well, Reverend Stuart, doesn't take you long to find a job," Samantha grins.

"Mrs. Stuart, I didn't have time to confer with you, but I . . . uh . . . well, it seems like a good fit," Reverend Stuart confesses.

Samantha lowers her voice. "I like being called Mrs. Stuart. I think we can have a good life here, Reverend Stuart," she says.

"If they'll have me?" Reverend Stuart adds.

"Oh, ye know they will," Samantha says, and as she does, the door opens. Bill Duffer says, "Reverend and Mrs. Stuart, please come back in."

He leads them to the front of the church and asks them to turn and face the congregation. "Reverend Stuart, this congregation has voted unanimously to call you as their next pastor. Do you accept this call?"

"Yes, I enthusiastically accept this call to be pastor of Kilmarnock Presbyterian Church."

The congregation applauds. Mrs. Connery and Mrs. Graham look at each other briefly with stunned and yet happy looks on their faces and then join the applauding. Brody continues to count the nail heads in the floor in front of him, his method of dealing with his boredom.

As the applause fades, a woman five rows back on the right stands.

"Claire, so good to see here. I know you've been on the sick. Glad you're feeling better," the little man says.

"Reverend Stuart, my name is Claire McFadden. My husband and I want to invite you, Mrs. Stuart, and all the others with you to our house for our big Sunday dinner. And Bill Duffer, please join us. We owe you a big debt having found our new pastor."

Reverend Stuart looks at Samantha. She responds immediately. "We would love to join ye. Thanks. And I know a little about cooking. I can help."

"Wonderful!" Claire says.

The little man stands up and says, "Before we leave, we'll celebrate with Holy Communion. This church has not had a pastor for a long time, and without a pastor we can't celebrate the sacrament. I asked Betty to slip down the street to our house . . . and here she is now . . ." Betty comes through the door with a loaf of bread and two bottles of wine.

The little man continues, "Reverend Stuart, there's a *Book of Worship* on the pulpit shelf. Will you lead us in Holy Communion?"

"Of course," Reverend Stuart says.

Reverend Stuart prays for the blessing of the bread and wine. He holds the silver chalice high. The congregants file forward. Reverend Stuart places a blessed piece of blessed bread on each spiritually hungry tongue, and all sip from the cup of God's grace. The congregation sings *A Mighty Fortress Is Our God,* and Reverend Stuart renders the benediction.

Back in the wagon, Bill Duffer heads to Claire McFadden's house. Along the way, Samantha says to Reverend Stuart, "You remember on the ship after the storm when Keltz said 'Reverend, it won't be long until you drink from that silver cup again'?"

"I wonder how he knew?" Reverend Stuart says.

"Maybe Keltz has a high spirituality?" Samantha says.

"Probably," Reverend Stuart says.

Claire McFadden, the first person out of the church door, already prepares the Sunday meal. The people in the wagon see a curl of grey smoke coming out of the McFadden's left chimney, the kitchen side.

"I just had to wring two more chicken necks," she says as the guests enter.

"What can I do to help?" Samantha asks.

"Wash the potatoes and put them in the pot. I have the cookstove good and hot. It didn't go out after breakfast, and I puts three sticks of stove-wood in when I got home," Claire says. "The biscuits are almost done."

While the two women prepare the food, Claire whispers to Samantha. "We don't have a doctor in town right now, but if you need help, there's a woman here who has helped a lot of us. She don't have no education, but she knows what you need. When you go see her, she'll want you to pee in a pan. She smells it, and then she knows what herb or root to give you. If you need her, let me know, and I'll take you to see her," Claire says. Samantha thanks Claire for the information.

As expected, Claire asks Reverend Stuart to say the blessing. Then they pass around the bowls: chicken fried in lard, boiled potatoes smothered in fresh butter, turnip greens with chunks of ham for seasoning, biscuits, and ham seasoned red-eye gravy.

"I'm glad we have gravy for the biscuits," Brody says. "We hads so many biscuits on that ship."

Mrs. Connery explains to Claire about their biscuit-only meals on the ship. "They kept us alive. We should be thankful for that."

"You people went through so much. We're glad you are here. You will love Kilmarnock," Claire says. "And you'll have to come back soon and eat with us. Maybe, we'll have haggis."

"What's haggis?" Bill asks.

"A traditional Scottish meal. We take oats and sheep organs and stuff them into sheep intestines. I season and boil 'em. Was a celebration meal, maybe for a wedding or a birthday, for our ancestors in Scotland," Claire says.

After the meal and cleanup, they gather on the front porch after bringing extra chairs out from the dining room. The house sits on Main Street. They talk and have front row seats for the occasional horse drawn buggy or wagon.

Two white men on horses come down the street. The first man wears a white, brimmed hat, dark brown vest under a black jacket. His long-pointed beard is striking, and his large green eyes glare at the porch observers. His scowling demeanor communicates that he doesn't care what they think. A black brimmed hat sits on the head of the second rider. The right side of his face disfigured by something like a horse kick. He is smaller and doesn't communicate authority like the first rider who rides like a proud general who has just conquered new territory.

"Look!" Brody says. "They're pulling people, black people, with ropes."

"What's that about?" Samantha asks about the man and woman with hands tied and ropes around their necks. The ropes are tied to the saddle horns on the horses, and the two people must walk fast to keep from being pulled to the ground. The woman looks like she fell to the ground at least once. Her dirt-stained clothes are torn, face bruised and bloody.

"They're no doubt runaways from somewhere down south," Claire says. "This is one of the escape routes for runaways. Just to the north, they can cross over into Maryland. But the big plantation owners to the south join together and keep bounty hunters here to capture them."

"What will they do with them?" Samantha asks.

"Well, it depends. They return some to their plantations. But they don't know where to take them if the runaways won't talk. Those hang," Claire says.

"Oh my God!" Samantha says.

"They wouldn't hang that woman, would they?" Samantha asks.

"Oh yeah. If she won't talk, she'll hang soon, yeah, both of them," Claire says.

"I'm goin' follow them. See what I can do," Samantha says.

"Ain't nothing you can do," Claire says. "If they stop at the hanging-tree on the edge of town," she points down the street, "they good as dead."

Ignoring Claire, Samantha steps off the porch, with Reverend Stuart behind her, and into the street.

Turning his head back to the porch, Reverend Stuart says, "Brody, you stay here. We'll be back soon."

"Samantha, you don't know these people and their ways. Watch what you say," Reverend Stuart says.

The horses, riders, and roped slaves start to draw a crowd following behind them.

Teenage boys shout, "Hang 'em!"

The growing crowd of followers enjoy the spectacle. Jeers ring out, "Runaways hang!" "Plantation ain't so bad compared to a rope!" "Ain't no African God goin' save you!"

On the southern edge of town, the riders stop at a huge oak tree with a large, almost perfectly horizontal, limb about twelve feet off the ground.

The rider in the white hat with the male runaway reaches the tree first. He pauses, unties the rope from the saddle horn, and throws the rope over the limb. For a few seconds, the man and the rope are free, but the rider quickly rides under the limb, grabs the rope, ties the rope back to his saddle horn, and says in a frosty voice, "Last chance to tell us where you're from!"

The roped man says nothing. The rider rubs his pointed beard and then puts his heels into the side of the horse. The rope tightens. The man jerks forward, losing his balance, but stays on his feet. In the next instant, his feet leave the ground. The rider pulls the horse to a stop. The roped man kicks his legs. His body moves back and forth. His eyeballs push out. He tries to wiggle his head. He gasps. He gasps again. He hangs motionless.

"Give him a few minutes. Make sure he's dead," the rider in the white hat says.

The roped woman screams, "Josiah!" Josiah is motionless. She cries and says, "Josiah, I be with you soon."

The rider in the white hat says, "Woman, if that's what you want, we'll give it to you. But tell us where you from, and we'll take you back."

The woman's mouth in defiance does not open.

Samantha whispers to Reverend Stuart, "They rather die than go back to their plantation. Must be terrible there."

"They know they'll be treated very brutally if they return, probably whipped until the skin falls off their backs," Reverend Stuart says to Samantha.

"Cut him down," the rider in the white hat says. His limp body thumps on the ground. The woman wails.

The second rider throws his rope over the branch, and for a moment, the rope is limp and unattended.

"Run!" Samantha screams.

It's too late. The experienced rider is on the other side of the limb just as the woman takes her second step and has the rope securely around his saddle horn. The rope jerks. She falls to the ground. In the next instant, the rope tightens as the horse and rider pull ahead. The woman drags on the ground. Now under the limb, the rope pulls her up. When her feet are well off the ground, the rider stops the horse. The woman dangles as a gurgling sound comes out of her mouth. The rider backs the horse up. The woman's feet almost touch the ground. Then the rider's heels touch the horse's side, the woman jerks into the air. Her neck gives off a cracking sound. The horse stops. The woman swings slightly and becomes motionless.

"Did you hear her neck pop?" the rider in the black hat says.

"Music to my ears," the rider in the white hat says. "Bastards won't tell us what planation they're from. Probably know we can't get a reward. But they got their reward."

Glaring at Samantha, the rider in the white hat, his nostrils flared in anger, says, "Lady, I don't know who you are, but if you ever interfere with our hangings again, I'll put a rope around your neck."

"Let's go," Reverend Stuart says as he takes Samantha by the arm.

"Who's that?" a boy asks. "I don't know. Ner' seen that woman before," another boy says. The small crowd disperses in different directions.

Samantha and Reverend Stuart walk quickly toward Claire's house.

"What kind of place have we come to? How can God forgive those men?" Samantha asks.

"That was awful. God rest their souls. Not everyone here's like those men, good people here too," Reverend Stuart says.

"We have to help these people," Samantha says.

"It would be dangerous," Reverend Stuart says.

"I don't care," Samantha says. "I'm goin' do something."

Back at Claire's house, Brody asks, "What happened?"

Samantha and Reverend Stuart look at each other.

"They took those people away," Reverend Stuart says just before he gags, goes to the end of the porch, and vomits.

"Are you okay?" Claire asks. "Hope it won't me cookin'."

"Oh no. Not your cooking. I just a . . . got a weak stomach I guess," Reverend Stuart says.

"Some of those captured slaves they take to Mount Misery. People say it might be better to hang," Claire says. "Some of the stubborn slaves under the whip so long they get struck dumb and never talk again."

"I've heard of Mount Misery. It's a big farm over on the eastern shore of Virginia. Ed Covey is his name. Covey has the reputation of breaking any slave's resistance. He's a brutal man, whips slaves before the sores of their last whippings heal. Plantation owners send slaves to him that won't obey. He hurts 'em so bad, they start obeying or die. The plantation owner pays him a reward. I've read about Frederick Douglass who was a slave there, whipped every day, but escaped to the north. A brilliant man, he wrote a book about it. I think Douglass is a minister now up north," Bill says.

A silent Samantha boils with anger as she hears about the brutality.

"Okay, let's head back to the house," Bill Duffer says, knowing exactly what the pair witnessed.

They thank Claire for the meal and head to the wagon.

"I'm sorry. It's terrible," Bill says to Samantha as they walk toward the wagon. "Some of us here want to do something about slavery. It's awful and against everything Jesus taught us."

Bill directs the horse and wagon down Main Street and takes the second right turn down Irvington Road.

"That's your house over there!" Bill points to a large house with three red-brick chimneys and several outbuildings. "That house left to the church, and that where our pastor and family live. You can move in tomorrow morning."

"Oh, that's a nice house, three stories and a balcony on the second floor. Look at the cathedral windows, the long ones pointed at the top. Dormers even on the sides with porthole shaped windows," Mrs. Graham says.

"Very generous of the church to let us live there," Reverend Stuart says.

"The church was extremely fortunate to receive this house, one of the finest in the area." Bill says.

Landstuhl Regional Medical Center

Kirchberg-Kaserne, Germany

February 12, 2020

"Captain Stuart, good news for you!" the nurse says.

"What's that?" Sam asks.

"You're being flown to Walter Reed tomorrow."

"Walter Reed Hospital, Bethesda, Maryland?"

"Yep. They'll probably put you through all the tests that you've had here. They don't seem to trust us here. So be ready for that. We're supposed to just stabilize the patient and send them on, but we're very thorough."

"I'll be a little closer to home. That feels good!"

"They won't let you sleep as much as you have here."

"I've never slept and dreamed so much. Dreaming about my great-grand-mother. I've heard stories about her my whole life, but my brain has been filling in the blanks. It's weird, but I feel like I know her so much better now."

A Kilmarnock Wedding!

November 5, 1849

Back at Bill Duffer's house, the new residents of Kilmarnock prepare for bed. Everyone returns to their rooms, except Mrs. Connery who stays downstairs for a few minutes.

"I wonder why Mrs. Connery is still downstairs?" Reverend Stuart says.

"I don't have a clue," Samantha says.

"I'm officiating at a wedding tonight, and I am getting married tonight," Reverend Stuart declares with a twinkle in his eye.

"I'm a bride tonight, but I don't have a wedding dress. We could be completely natural, like the Garden of Eden."

"Samantha, you're really challenging this virgin preacher."

"Or we could have an old Scottish wedding. We slit our wrists and tie them together for the night," Samantha says.

"I'm not that much into tradition!" Reverend Stuart chuckles.

"Let's have one candle burning, and over in that windowsill," Reverend Stuart points to the farthest window from the bed.

"The bride can be ready very shortly." Samantha offers.

With their backs to each other, Samantha and Reverend Stuart slip off their clothes. They turn to face each other.

The candlelight glows perfectly on Samantha. Her long red hair, highlighted by the candlelight, falls on each side of her chest.

Reverend Stuart turns around, and although he starts to speak, is stunned at the beauty before him. "I'm a lucky man, but I need to be a preacher for the next few moments."

"Samantha Logan, you and I are gathered here in the presence of God to become husband and wife. Let us pray.

"Almighty God, bless this union. May we continue to live as your people, and may we love and cherish each other all our days. Amen."

"Amen," Samantha says.

"Samantha Logan, do you vow to be my wife both in this life and for all eternity?"

"I do."

"Charles Rory Stuart, do you vow to be my husband both in this life and for all eternity?"

"I do."

Charles steps toward Samantha and puts his arms around her just above her waist. She puts her arms around his shoulders. They look at each other's lips. Heads move forward and lips meet. Her lips, soft, moist, and tender, open against his lips, inviting him to open his lips. They release and take a step back.

"I now pronounce us, husband and wife, in the eyes of God. Amen."

Charles takes Samantha's left hand in his right hand and bids her toward the bed.

"Knock! Knock!"

"Someone's at the door," Samantha says.

"Who is it?" Reverend Stuart asks.

"It's Brody! There's a snake in my room!"

"Okay, I'll be right there," Reverend Stuart says as he slips on trousers and shirt.

"Sorry," he says to Samantha. "This shouldn't take long."

Samantha pulls the sheet over her so that Brody will not see her nude body when Charles opens the door.

Down the hall and into Brody's room, Charles sees a black coil in the corner of Brody's bedroom. A head raises from the coil when they enter the room. A red tongue flicks at them.

"It's a black snake. They're not poisonous. It's probably really scared and doesn't know what to do. I see an extra blanket on that table. I'll throw the blanket over the snake, and hopefully wrap the blanket around the snake. Brody, go down the steps and open the front door."

"Okay."

Reverend Stuart takes the blanket and unfolds it until it is big enough to go around the snake. The snake raises its head even more.

The tossed blanket falls on the snake. Reverend Stuart springs toward the snake, grabs the blanket, wrapping it around the snake. The snake thrashes inside the blanket. Out the bedroom door, Reverend Stuart moves as quickly as he can down the steps. As he approaches the open front door, the snake finds an opening, squirts out of the blanket onto the floor, and in a flash wiggles out the front door. Brody slams the door.

Reverend Stuart laughs. "Brody, you woke up everyone within miles the way you slammed that door."

Bill opens his bedroom door and leans over the railing above. Then Mrs. Graham and Mrs. Connery, with worried faces, step out of their bedroom.

"Everything's okay. Brody had a visitor, a black snake in his room. It's gone now. Black snakes are not poisonous, but they do scare us. Everybody can go back to bed," Reverend Stuart says.

"Sorry folks," Bill says. "That ole' snake been around here for ages. Helps the cat keep the mice at bay, but I do wish he would stay in the barn. I guess he likes to visit over here from time to time."

"That's not funny! I hate snakes," Mrs. Graham says.

"He's gone now. He won't be back for a long time," Reverend Stuart says. "Everyone can go back to sleep. We're moving to a new house tomorrow."

Opening the bedroom door, Charles blows out the candle and tiptoes toward the bed. If Samantha has fallen asleep, he doesn't want to wake her. He carefully raises the sheet and slips into the bed. A hand, then an arm, go around him. Another arm goes behind his head with a hand embracing the back of his head. Warm legs touch his legs. Then Samantha's right leg goes over his legs. She kisses his neck, then his cheek. Their lips meet.

Samantha whispers, "I talk a lot, but I'm a virgin, too. Be gentle."

"Of course, my love," Charles says.

"I'm all yours," she says.

"I love you," Charles whispers.

"I love you."

Time seems to stand still. Fifteen minutes later, they are exhausted, and sleep comes quickly.

When light comes through the windows, eyelids slowly raise.

Samantha speaks first. "Last night was perfect. The only thing that could have been better is if we had Mrs. Graham to sing."

Charles' hand goes over his mouth but a laugh squirts out. "Samantha, you make life so good."

"Life was really good last night," Charles says as her right hand rubs his chest.

Samantha says, "I could stay in bed all day."

"I wish we could, but we go to our new house today!" Charles says.

"I'm dreaming, life's not this good," Samantha offers.

"I guess we best head down for breakfast soon. I hear some stirring down there," Charles says.

Cora serves the household another wonderful meal with eggs scrambled with ham bits, large warm biscuits, baked to a golden brown on top of a white body, and to anoint the biscuits: grape preserves. On each plate, Cora places a patty.

"I call Cora's biscuits 'cat-head biscuits.' Big as a cat's head and oh so soft," Bill says.

"So good," Mrs. Graham says.

Brody shakes his head up and down, making a mumbling sound since he can't speak with a full mouth.

"I think Brody's enjoying this breakfast. He's attacking it like it owes him money," Samantha says.

"What's this patty?" Mrs. Graham ask.

"Scrapple. It's also called pannhass by the Pennsylvania Dutch. Cora puts pork pieces, chopped organ pieces, into a bowl with cornmeal, buckwheat flour, a little lard, and, of course, spices. She makes these little patties and pan-fries them. When we have a hog killing, we try not to waste anything," Bill says.

With breakfast over, Bill says, "I have an announcement to make. Actually, we have an announcement to make. Mrs. Connery join me for this special moment."

Mrs. Connery pushes her chair back, rises, and joins Bill at the head of the table.

"I've asked Mrs. Connery to marry me," Bill says.

"I have accepted," she says.

"We plan to ask Reverend Stuart to perform the ceremony in due time." And as he looks at Reverend Stuart, Bill says, "He might be a little rusty, but I'm sure he'll brush up on it."

Reverend Stuart nods his head while thinking what if they knew about last night.

Out of the corner of her eye, Samantha sees a speechless Mrs. Graham, obviously as surprised as anyone. Her face turns pale as she takes a deep breath and slowly lets it out.

"Of course, Mrs. Graham can stay with us. We'll have plenty of space," Bill says.

"I want to stay here too," Brody says.

"The court in Scotland gave custody of Brody to Mrs. Connery. That court's ruling is not binding here of course, but if that's what Brody wants to do, he could learn a lot here on the farm," Reverend Stuart says.

"Yeh, I wanna stay here," Brody insists.

"That would be great," Bill says. "I have a couple of things to do, and then I'll take Reverend and Mrs. Stuart to their new home. So why don't we meet on the porch in about an hour?"

"That works for us," Reverend Stuart says.

Back in their room, Samantha puts her arms around Charles and says, "Let's spend some more time together before we go downstairs."

Down on the porch, Mrs. Connery and Brody come out to say goodbye to Reverend and Mrs. Stuart.

"Has anyone seen Mrs. Graham?" Mrs. Connery asks. "After breakfast, she told me to go on up to our bedroom, and she would be up soon. But she never came. I looked throughout the house, but she is not in there."

"I'll go ask Cora if she has seen her," Bill says. "You folks wait here."

Several minutes go by before Bill comes around the corner of the house. His hat is off, and his face looks like he has seen a monster.

"I'm . . . I might get sick . . . Cora had not seen Mrs. Graham . . . so, I thought, oh dear God, I can't believe this . . . I thought I would look in the barn. I opened the door and saw her hanging there . . . ."

"What!" Mrs. Connery screams. "Oh, dear God. She losts her daughter and her mind!"

"She took one of the ropes in the barn . . . I can't talk about it anymore," Bill says.

"Bill, her daughter hung herself on the ship. Jumped overboard with a rope tied to the ship around her neck," Reverend Stuart says.

Bill sits down on the edge of the porch. He puts his face in his hands and lowers his head to his legs. Mrs. Connery gently rubs his back. "I liked her a lot. I don't understand this."

Bill raises his head and says, "I'll get Reuben to cut her down . . ." Crying, Bill stops talking for a few minutes . . . "I'll get him to dig her a grave unless you folks have a different plan for her."

"No, I don't think we do," Reverend Stuart says after looking at Mrs. Connery and Samantha.

"Will you say a few words over her, Reverend?" Bill asks.

"Of course, of course," Reverend Stuart says.

"Why don't you and Mrs. Stuart stay one more night here. I don't feel like going back into Kilmarnock today," Bill says.

"Yes, we'll stay here," Samantha says.

Walter Reed Hospital

Bethesda, Maryland

February 16, 2020

"Captain Stuart sounds like you had quite an experience in Afghanistan," Dr. Thurmond Tate says. "What do the soldiers call that? A 'dirt nap'?"

"Yes, and I thought I was going to die. The Taliban gave me a little air-hole to keep me alive for a while and to die slowly. I think they wanted my body to be found. A way to terrify our soldiers and how they might slowly die in the ground," Sam says.

"I hear a goat herder found you," Dr. Tate says. "He noticed where new soil was on the ground. He thought something had gone on and alerted the military base. You are a lucky woman."

"I know," Sam says. "I'd given up hope. I was so weak. The next thing I knew I was in Germany. They took good care of me there."

"You've been sleeping a lot." Dr. Tate says. "Extreme dehydration will do that. Plus, when your potassium gets low your brain can start doing strange things. Your brain shuts down. Your brain wants your body to repair and recover, so it secretes its own sleeping chemical. The human body is amazing. I've been doing this for over thirty years and continue to be amazed by the human body and the will to live."

"Thank God for friendly goat herders. I'll have to send him a Christmas present for the rest of his life," Sam says.

Dr. Tate chuckles. "Tomorrow, we'll start running some tests just to make sure everything is working properly. I think you're fine, but we need to cover ourselves, you know, liability and all, these days. I know you had a lot of testing at Landstuhl, but we have our protocols here."

"I understand," Sam says.

"I bet our food is better," Dr. Tate says. "Soldiers coming from there almost always complain about their food."

"Their food was not bad. A lot better than the rations we had out on patrol."

"We'll do an MRI of your brain first thing. Takes about twenty minutes."

"I was in a burial pit for days. That will be nothing."

"We'll have to do labs, CT scan, EKG, chest x-ray, and since you were in the ground so long, we'll have to keep scanning you for fungus."

"Okay. Dr. Tate, is there a psychiatrist or psychologist here I could talk to? These dreams have been so vivid and real. Maybe if I just talk through them a bit that would help. I'm a psychologist, so I know talk-therapy can really help put things in perspective."

"Oh sure, I'll make that referral. Dr. Franco is wonderful."

A House!

Kilmarnock, Virginia

November 6, 1849

Bill, the soon to be Mrs. Duffer, and Brody drop Samantha and Reverend Stuart off at their new home.

"Look at the furnishings!" an excited Samantha says as the walk through the first floor of the house that seems to have everything they need.

"Someone has left us two boxes of clothes in the bedroom. I guess they know we don't have anything," Reverend Stuart says.

Calling out from the kitchen, Samantha says, "There's food in the shelves, even spices."

"I'll go out and look in the cellar Bill told us about," Reverend Stuart says. Moments later he is back in the kitchen telling Samantha about the white potatoes, sweet potatoes, onions, and the purple-top turnips in the cool cellar. "The potatoes and onions are huge. They must have very fertile soil here."

"Charles, they are really happy to have ye here," Samantha says.

"Us. Happy to have us here," Reverend Stuart says. "We're a package deal."

After touring upstairs, Reverend Stuart says, "I don't think we'll even use the two upper floors. Maybe we'll go up and sit out on the balcony some."

Samantha and Charles love their new home. The congregation of Kilmarnock Presbyterian Church love them. New people join the church in the months and years to follow. The clergy couple enjoy the rituals of the little town: Christmas, Easter, and Fall Harvest celebrations, and the Burning Socks ritual every May. Townspeople gather and throw a pair of winter socks into a roaring fire in the middle of town to celebrate the coming of Spring.

Samantha strikes up a deep friendship with Hilda and Bernard Eckhard, German immigrants. The Eckhards attend the Lutheran church in Kilmarnock and have been secretly assisting the Underground Railroad for several years.

Hilda invites Samantha for afternoon tea.

"We saw a terrible hanging the first day we were in Kilmarnock, and I hear there have been more in Westmoreland lately," Samantha says. "I so want to help the runaways."

"You can," Hilda bravely offers.

"How?"

"You could get us arrested if you tell anyone what I am about to tell you. We are part of what some people call the Underground Railroad. There's no railroad of course, but Bernard and I are 'conductors.' We guide 'passengers' from the Rappahannock River to 'stations' or what some call 'safe houses.' A station is safe if a lantern glows in a window. Another conductor will take the passengers to the banks of the Potomac and to safe passage into Maryland or sometimes they'll board a friendly ship that will take them through the Bay and to Boston or New Bedford."

"I wanna help," Samantha says. "This slavery stuff makes me so angry. How dare these people think they can enslave another human being. And I've seen how they treat them."

"We're not as healthy as we've been. Bernard has trouble breathing. My knees hurt almost all the time. We can still be involved, but you could become a conductor," Hilda says.

"I'm on board!" Samantha says. "Tell me more."

"Members of a Quaker community in North Carolina guide the passengers to the south side of the Rappahannock River. The passengers stay in an old storage building near a wharf up Meachim Creek in Topping. A tide mill grinds grains there, and the owner likes what we're doing. We meet the runaways there and get them across the river. Once on this side of the river, we put them underneath hay in a wagon and take them to a station outside

Lancaster Courthouse. Someone else, we don't know who and don't want to know, takes them from there. What we need the most help with right now is getting them across the Rappahannock. That's hard on Bernard's lungs and on my knees."

"We'll do it," Samantha offers. "But we don't have a boat."

"You can use ours. We don't need it anymore. Our deadrise skiff is tied up down by the river in a little creek. You must watch the weather. The waves can get big out there in a storm, and it's two miles across. You and your husband are young, and you both look strong. Rowing shouldn't be too hard for you. And there will be four of you to row. Two men in town help us, but I can't tell you their names. They have a wagon to take you to the river. If the weather is bad for days and the river too choppy, a family in Urbanna on the other side of the river have a safe house where the runaways can stay a few days before they cross The River Jordan, that's what the runaways call our river."

"I'll have to talk to Charles about this. But I know he'll want to help."

"It's very dangerous. If we get caught, there's no telling what they would do to us. So be careful."

Charles agrees to be a conductor. They practice rowing across the Rappahannock in the dark. When they bring the passengers across, it cannot be a full moon, and the water must be calm.

In the first five years, they bring over five-hundred passengers across the river and take them to their first station. From there, other conductors get the passengers to the banks of the Potomac.

In the next five years, tensions increase over slavery in the area and the conductors face even more danger. Locals talk of a civil war. Most of them sons of plantation, young hotheads organize rallies in Kilmarnock and surrounding towns condemning Yankee sympathizers and "slave-lovers."

Rumors circulate in Kilmarnock that Reverend Stuart and his wife are involved in helping the runaways. At a fundamentalist church on the northern outskirts of town, a pastor says in a sermon that the liberal preacher and his "Jezebel wife" at the Presbyterian church are helping runaways.

Festus Johnson hears the sermon. The next Sunday morning, March 17, 1861, Festus attends Kilmarnock Presbyterian Church. He enters the sanctuary just after Reverend Stuart begins the service and sits quietly on the last pew near the entrance door. As is his custom after the benediction,

Reverend Stuart walks down the aisle of the sanctuary, opens the double entrance doors, and stands on the little porch to speak to each attendee as they leave.

Festus follows the pastor out the door. Reverend Stuart extends his hand for a traditional handshake. Festus reaches inside his jacket and from a pocket pulls out a fourteen-inch hunting knife. He screams "slave lover!" plunging the knife into the chest of Reverend Stuart.

Festus apprehended that afternoon in his father's barn spends a few weeks in the county jail but is released in April 1861 when the Civil War begins with the confederate attack on Fort Sumter. Festus promises the sheriff he will join General Lee's army and "kill lots of Yankees."

A shocked Samantha spends nearly a week in bed, grieving her fallen husband. With even more resolve, she resumes her conductor duties. Slaves, emboldened by the war, want to "go north and join the Union army." Samantha and Brody, who is now in his early twenties and has refused to join the Confederate Army, transport the runaways across the Rappahannock River.

The runaways come faster than they can get them across the river. Samantha and Brody take chances. With an almost full moon and calm water on April 6, 1865, Samantha and Brody row across the Rappahannock and bring back four men and two women. On the other side of the river, a man in a brimmed white hat, a pointed beard, and intense green eyes waits for them. Samantha immediately recognizes him as the runaway catcher and hangman. He takes them to the sheriff's office who reluctantly places the two in a cell. Three days later, General Robert E. Lee surrenders at McClean House in Appomattox, Virginia. The sheriff unlocks their cell door. "Go home. General Lee surrendered. War's over."

Before his death, The Reverend Charles Rory Stuart and Samantha Logan Stuart created two human beings. Charles Rory Stuart, II and Gregory Logan Stuart resided in Kilmarnock having children of their own. Samantha Stuart died in 1921. She was ninety-two. The State of Virginia erected historical signs on Route 33 on the Kilmarnock side of the Robert O. Norris Bridge commemorating the passage of the escapees from human bondage who crossed the Rappahannock River with the aid of freedom lovers like Samantha Stuart.

Walter Reed Hospital, Bethesda, Maryland

February 21, 2020

"And that's the story of my great-grandmother and great-grandfather. I identify a lot with my great-grandmother," Sam says to her therapist, Dr. Franco.

"That's quite a story, and those were incredible dreams. I don't think you've been psychotic. And, you know from your studies and work, there's so much we don't know about our dreamlife. Freud had some theories about the unconscious and our dreams. And I suspect genetic scientists will someday discover why we dream about what we do, maybe something encoded in our inherited DNA. I think it is safe to say that your great-grandmother is with you, even a part of you," Dr. Franco says.

"Carl Jung said our dreams tap into universal archetypes, which contain clues to help us find happiness," Sam adds.

"That's interesting and goes with what I read just the other day. Paul McCartney found himself 'in a time of trouble,' but his deceased mother, Mary, said to him in a dream, 'Let it be.' McCartney wrote a song about it," Dr. Franco says.

"I certainly had a time of trouble," Sam chuckles.

"Well, you go home now and rest up from your time of trouble. You can monitor yourself for symptoms of PTSD, like flashbacks, nightmares, depression, anxiety, excessive alcohol use, and those kinds of things. Enjoy civilian life and enjoy your career as a psychotherapist. You'll do well in your career," Dr. Franco says.

Union Station

March 15, 2020

Sam steps from a Walter Reed Hospital military van at Union Station in DC. Walking through the station, she admires the classical architecture with ancient Greek and Roman inspirations. Every ethnic group and nationality seem represented in the crowded station.

A cold and windy day, Sam walks up the tracks to her coach. She'll go to the lounge car when it opens. For now, she sits in her assigned coach seat. The train struggles out of Union Station. After picking up speed, the passenger-car rocks back and forth on the tracks. A few passengers get off and a few get on when the train stops in Alexandria, and from there the train crosses the bridge of the upper Potomac River. After a brief stop in Fredericksburg, Virginia, with even fewer passenger changes, the train rolls toward Richmond. Sam sees brown fields and an occasional field colored green by winter rye, a cover crop that is plowed under before spring corn or soybean planting.

Brakes hiss and screech as the train pulls into the Amtrak station on Staples Mill Road, Richmond. Sam grabs her shoulder bag from the overhead storage bin and joins the line to exit down the coach steps.

Outside the rear of the station, family and friends watch for their favorite passengers to walk toward the station. Rory Stuart, Sam's brother, eyes the passengers. A massive grin appears on his face when he sees Sam. Sam waves. Rory waves. They meet and hug in the cheek biting cold.

"Let me take your bag," Rory says.

"It's nothing," Sam says.

"You look great for what you've been through," Rory says.

"Thanks. You don't look bad yourself," Sam adds.

"Your sis has moved to Cape Charles over on the eastern shore, but she'll be in Kilmarnock to see you today."

"Why Cape Charles?" Sam asks.

"Tom got a good job, manager or administrator of something. They'll tell you all about it when we get to Kilmarnock," Rory says.

"What about you? How's the waterman?" Sam asks.

"Slow year. The oyster crop was good in the fall, but crab numbers are still low. They lowered our bushels per day. They want to protect the females, but I don't know why they limit the males we can harvest. We get over two-hundred dollars per bushel. So that helps," Rory says.

Rory's 2013 white Toyota Tundra roars past most of the traffic on I-64 as they leave Richmond behind on their way to Kilmarnock. Past the exit onto Route 33, Sam sees familiar landscapes as they pass through the little towns of West Point and Saluda.

As they approach the Rappahannock River and the two-mile Norris Bridge, Sam views the Chesapeake Bay to the right of the bridge. White flakes hit the Tundra windshield.

"It's starting to snow. I love it when it snows on the river. I didn't get this in Afghanistan," Sam says.

"Forecast says snow. It won't amount to much, just a little slippery slush," Rory says.

Weathered docks with boats on lifts and riverfront houses in whites and light blues dot the shoreline.

"I've really missed this place," Sam says. "Work hard and retire on the coast. Many have made their dreams come true."

"I heard the other day that one of the President's cabinet members just bought a house down here. The guy that manages the seafood market says that many of the CIA and FBI officials have houses down here. It's a quick trip from DC," Rory adds. "We went to the new restaurant on Windmill Point. In the summer, it's like being in the Florida Keys."

On the other side of the river, Sam says, "Look, those signs about the runaways who crossed the river here. When I was in the hospital, I dreamed a lot about our great-grandmother who helped a lot of those poor people."

"Your namesake was quite a woman," Rory says.

The Tundra pushes on toward Kilmarnock. At the outskirts, a huge sign stretches above and across the road. "WELCOME HOME 3"

"Oh, my gosh. They still remember me as '3.' I'd forgotten all about that nickname!" Sam says.

"Well, not many people are three sport stars in high school. I don't know how you did it, tennis, volleyball, and soccer, and still made straight A's," Rory says.

"Yeah, but that was way back when," Sam says.

"There's a ceremony at the high school gym tonight. Everybody will be there," Rory says. "People want to thank you for your service and welcome you home."

Sam laughs. "I mean. I just served my county. Not a big deal."

Charlottesville

March 28, 2020

"This will be your office," Abby Bowen says.

"Nice," Sam responds.

"We are so happy you chose to join our practice."

In her mid-forties, Abby, recently divorced, dresses stylishly in tight dresses showing her curvy figure. Her ancestors were Native Americans and Africans. Her skin is smooth and light brown. Her black hair falls just below her ears. Stylish brown glasses sit on her nose, giving her a smart-professional appearance. Abby was a year ahead of Sam in the Ph.D. program at the university, so she is very familiar with Sam and her diagnostic-therapeutic acumen.

"I've always loved Charlottesville, and there's not a lot of demand for psychologists in Kilmarnock. Those watermen are tough people. They just grin and bear it. My mother wanted me to stay closer, but I can go see her on a lot of weekends. Plus, I'll eat oysters and crabs right out of the river."

"Yum! The Rivah's famous for oysters and crabs," Abby says.

"I'll bring back a few dozen oysters and a half-bushel of crabs next trip," Sam says.

"Your timing's good for your start here. We're having a social tomorrow afternoon with the area clergy association. They're a great source of referrals. I don't see how they do what they do with the preaching, weddings, funerals, meetings, praying over new construction. That's a big thing here in the Charlottesville area, got to bless those new buildings. And they do a lot of counseling, but that's where we come in. I suggest they limit their counseling sessions to a couple of sessions and then if needed refer either to local community mental health or to us, depending on the issues," Abby says.

Counseling center staff kept their calendars clear for the next afternoon. Area clergy start filing in a few minutes before 3:00 p.m. Folding chairs form a large circle.

Abby checks her watch. "Let's get started. How about we go around the room and introduce ourselves. I'll go last and say a few things about the center. I'll try not to bore you. If I do just start looking at your cell phones. I'll get the hint. Then we'll head over to the adjoining room for refreshments.

"Let's start on my right," Abby looks at Sam.

"I'm Samantha Stuart, the new therapist here. Folks just call me Sam. My brother and sister grew tired of saying Samantha, and Sam stuck. Born in Kilmarnock, I'm from a family of watermen. They go out into the Chesapeake Bay and bring in all the things you see on the menus around here: crabs, oysters, rockfish, flounder, and cobia.

"I just returned from Afghanistan. I was in Army Intelligence. The first year I did a lot of post-combat testing, PTSD evaluations, and therapy. Then, I volunteered for reconnaissance mission training and eventually led patrols looking for signs of Taliban. My father eventually died from a wound he suffered in Vietnam, so I wanted to keep soldiers from being killed. I thought if our patrols could warn of Taliban presence, we might keep them from killing each other. A lot of people thought I was crazy for volunteering, but there was the dad thing in my psyche. And as a secondary gain, the Army paid off all my student loans for college and grad school. So, plenty of self-interest as well. My great-grandfather was a Scottish Presbyterian minister . . .."

"Well, here comes one now, a Presbyterian pastor anyway," Abby interrupts.

"Sorry folks, the Queen of Sheba, the matriarch of our church, dropped by just as I was leaving. She's demanding and hard to get away from. The other pastors here know about those church dynamics." All the pastors shake their heads in agreement.

"Maybe you need a secret escape hatch," Sam jokes.

The Presbyterian pastor nods his head and chuckles.

"I was just telling the group that my great-grandfather was a Scottish Presbyterian pastor who was exiled to Virginia for being too progressive. He and my grandmother were heavily involved in the Underground Railroad in the mid-1800s." Sam continues and tells the group about how she thought about attending Union Presbyterian Seminary in Richmond to be a pastor but decided to become a psychotherapist instead. "I don't like working weekends." The group laughs.

Sam thanks the pastors for their hard work. "You are on the front lines. Studies show emotionally hurting people often first turn to their pastors and spiritual leaders for help. You play a critical role in our society."

Attendees introduce themselves one after another, and the late arriving pastor introduces himself.

"I started to become a psychotherapist but decided to become a pastor. I guess I like matriarchs and working weekends. I'm Eli Hemings, pastor of Winterford Presbyterian Church. Eli is short for Elijah, sort of like Sam, I guess. I grew up just outside Charlottesville, played college football in North Carolina, and went to seminary in Richmond. I'm related to Thomas Jefferson, but we don't look much alike. I'm single, like to jog, lift weights, hike, travel, cook, read, and attend clergy gatherings. This is my first church, and it's a baptism by fire. Many of the members are progressive, but we have some highly opinionated groups in Bade County. Winterford is, of course, the gateway to one of Virginia's finest ski resorts. So, we have quite a mix of old Virginia families and ski resort people. One other thing about me. I work part-time at the Charlottesville Center for Pastoral Counseling. I'm a licensed professional counselor in Virginia."

Abby gives a quick overview of the therapy practice and invites the attendees to the adjoining room for refreshments.

Sam works her way around the room, intending to speak to each pastor, and thank them for attending. Eli chats with Abby on the other end of the room.

"Sam, come on over. I want you to meet Eli," Abby says. Abby makes the introduction. "You two get acquainted. I need to speak to a couple more people." Abby floats around the room with welcoming words for each pastor.

"Eli sounds like you have an interesting professional life, pastor and therapist," Sam says.

"Yeah, it keeps me in the two worlds I find most fascinating, theology and psychology."

"That's interesting, my two favorite fields as well. One of the most difficult decisions I ever made was between seminary and the Ph.D. program. I decided I like one on one interactions more than public speaking."

"You volunteered for Afghanistan. That's incredible! What an experience that must have been."

"It was quite the experience. I'll tell you about it some time. Maybe over lunch? Abby wants us to spend some time with each pastor today. I've got a couple more pastors to chat with. Here's my card with my cell phone number on it."

"I'll give you my card as well," Eli searches his pockets. "I don't have any with me. I'm not a good organizer."

"Well, call me sometime. Soon, I hope."

"Okay. I will."

A few conversations continue as most of the pastors leave. The last pastor to leave, Eli waves to the staff as he exits the front door.

"Folks, if you would help me put these chairs up and set up two tables in the middle with eight chairs, I would really appreciate it. Tomorrow morning, I've loaned the room to a committee of the Charlottesville Arts Council. They'll be in here from 10:00 a.m. until about noon or so." Abby, Sam, and the other therapists fold up the chairs and stack them neatly in the corner.

"That's what you got your Ph.D.'s for . . . chair stacking," Abby and the others chuckle.

Sam sees her first two clients in the afternoon. At the two o'clock hour, she sees a woman referred by the court. The woman was caught embezzling small amounts of money from a dental office where she worked as a bookkeeper. The court, with the dentist's approval, gave her two years' probation and mandatory psychotherapy.

"Are you here for yourself or because of the court mandate?" Sam asks.

The woman hesitates.

"Your motivation will make all the difference. If you are here for the court, we'll go through the motions. You might consider using this time for you. What was the embezzling about for you? What about you or your past caused you to get in trouble? How do you want to change, grow? Something to think about," Sam says and then schedules her for the same time and date next week.

For the three o'clock hour, a married couple with their marriage on the rocks sit in her office. She accuses him of an affair. He denies it. Sam helps them get in touch with their anger for each other. He feels neglected, saying she spends more time with her friends than with him, and is always tired around him. The woman says the husband never shares his deepest feelings with her and that he just wants sex.

Before the couple leaves, Sam gives them sensate awareness homework. Every evening after dinner, they are to sit facing each other. "The first time you do this no words are to be spoken for twenty minutes. You just observe and appreciate each other. Look at each other's hands, arms, chin, nose, eyes, observe any part of the body. But don't say anything. The next day take five to ten minutes to observe and appreciate each other and say nothing. Then take five or ten minutes each to share what you observe and what you appreciate about each other. Come back in on Friday, and we'll talk about it." They agree. Sam's goal is to get them to slow down and get back to relationship basics. Sam chuckles as she remembers the last time she asked a couple to do this exercise before she went to Afghanistan. The couple came in a few days later and confessed they observed and appreciated each other for several minutes and then made love.

Sam spends the next hour on paperwork and heads out the door. Soon, she'll start seeing clients one evening a week and take the morning off. She's been trying to decide what evening to work. She thinks it might be Monday, might make the weekend a little longer.

Sam spots her silver Miata in the parking lot. She presses the remote and the headlights flash on. She tosses her briefcase into the passenger seat. Since it's an unseasonably warm day in March with bright sunshine, she pushes a button on the dash and down goes the top.

Abby located the psychotherapy office close to the University of Virginia to make the office convenient to students. The house Sam rented in the Belmont section of Charlottesville is only a few minutes from campus, but to enjoy the ride she takes 10th Street which makes her drive a little longer.

At home, she wants to enjoy this warm day. She quickly changes into blue jogging shorts, a white t-shirt with matching blue collar, and Brooks Adrenaline running shoes.

Thirty-five minutes later, she's back at the house and retrieves a green bottle of Pellegrino from the refrigerator. Sitting in a white rocker on the front porch, she enjoys the quiet neighborhood. Hunched over the handlebars, a biker pedals his way down the street. A woman and her two small children enjoy a stroll down the sidewalk.

Her cellphone rings.

"Hello."

"Hello, Sam. This is Eli. I enjoyed meeting you today, and I'll be in Charlottesville tomorrow and wondering if we could do lunch?"

"I'd love to, but we have a staff luncheon tomorrow. Abby has a psychiatrist from the university hospital coming. She's good at connecting to referral sources and says she hasn't done enough of it lately. She wants me to meet all these folks."

"Well, shucks," Eli says.

"I'm disappointed, too."

"Hey, I'm still in Charlottesville. How about dinner?"

"Tonight?"

"Yeah. Why not?"

"Okay. I've not even thought about dinner. Just sitting on the porch and enjoying the neighborhood."

"What's your neighborhood?"

"Belmont."

"Oh, wow. Some of the best restaurants in Charlottesville are in Belmont. I'll get us a reservation. Pick you up at seven? We can be at a restaurant in minutes."

"Sure. See you then."

"Oh, your address."

Sam gives Eli her address and glances at her watch. She has time to enjoy the porch a few more minutes.

"Hello," a voice from the right side of the house says.

"Hi."

"I just thought I would step through the hedges and introduce myself. I'm your neighbor, Aili. I saw the moving truck a few days ago. Welcome to the neighborhood."

Sam introduces herself. The two talk a few minutes, and Sam explains she must get ready for a dinner engagement. Sam has a good feeling about Aili, should be a nice neighbor.

In the bathroom, Sam slips off the top, shorts, and panties. With the water temperature just right, she steps in the shower and enjoys the moist, steamy warmth. After drying with an oversized bath towel, Sam slips on fancy-faded jeans, white blouse, and a green sweater.

At seven, Sam steps outside, locking the door behind her. Her face glows as Eli drives up in a black Nissan 370Z sports car. He comes up the steps from the street, crosses the street sidewalk, and walks up her sidewalk. Eli wears casual grey slacks, a white no-button collar shirt, a dark blue blazer, and lace up brown shoes. Quite handsome, Sam thinks, with his dark closely cropped hair in tight curls, light brown skin tone, and dark brown eyes.

"If it's okay with you, we'll just walk to dinner. The restaurant can't be much more than five minutes."

"Sure. I'm used to walking. Did a lot in Afghanistan."

"That green is your color, with your red hair," Eli says.

"Thank you. You look very distinguished."

They walk down the street and take a right turn onto Belmont Street.

"There's our restaurant, fabulous Italian food. But all the restaurants on this corner are very good and quite a selection. Italian, Mexican, Spanish, and hip-American with sushi. We just need a Greek restaurant."

"Never heard of hip-American?" Sam says.

"I know. Just made that up, but they have twists on classic American dishes. Very good. Hey, it's warm enough tonight to sit outside with a heater. Would you mind sitting up there?" Eli points to the second story porch with tables overlooking the street. "There's another couple sitting up there. Maybe we can sit on the opposite end."

"Sure. I love alfresco dining. Well, this is kind of . . . but with a view," Sam says.

"Can I start you off with a cocktail or a glass of wine?" the server asks in a husky voice.

"Well, first, let me ask. Could I grab one of those heaters over there? It could get a little chilly up here later," Eli asks.

"Sure, but I'll bring it over," the broad-shouldered young server says.

"What would you like?" Eli asks.

"I'm a red wine lover," Sam says.

"Dry or fruity?"

"Fruity, just a little sweet," Sam says.

"Full-bodied?"

"Oh, yes."

"There we go," the server says as the hooded gas heater comes to life with tiny flames extending in all directions under the hood. "How about drinks?'

"Do you have a bottle of the cab-franc they bottle over at Whitson Vineyards?"

"We do. I'll bring it right out."

"Where is Whitson Vineyards?" Sam asks

"It's tucked away in a little valley on the other side of Winterford. The vineyard has southern exposure, and the soil is so rich. It's the topsoil that has eroded off the mountains over the eons. I'm goin' to learn all about soils, geography, wildlife. I'm goin' to become a Virginia Master Naturalist," Eli says.

The server returns with the bottle. He pours a small amount in a glass. But Eli says, "We'll skip the taste test. I know how good this is."

"Whatever your pleasure," the server says as he pours two generous glasses and says, "I'll be back shortly to take your order."

Sam and Eli raise their glasses. "To Charlottesville," Sam says. Eli repeats the toast.

"Wow! This is good!" Sam says.

"Glad you like it. It's my favorite of the local offerings, of any offerings . . . I mean just can't get any better," Eli says. "I guess we better look at these menus. I've ordered just about everything on the menu, everything that doesn't have meat. I stopped eating meat recently. You know, healthier."

"I'm a pescetarian. I eat fish, shellfish, and, of course, lots of vegetables," Sam says.

"Yeah, that's me," Eli says.

The young server approaches the table. "Any questions about the menu before I tell you about the specials?"

Sam and Eli shake their heads.

"Okay, you're in luck this evening. Great specials. We have steaks from Argentina, lamb from New Zealand, and fresh rockfish from the Rappahannock River right here in Virginia."

Sam and Eli look at each other and hold back giggles.

"I'll have to get the rockfish. My brother might have caught it. He's a waterman in that area."

"It's very good. I had it during my break between lunch and dinner seatings," the server says. "We sprinkle it with Rappahannock crab meat and just a touch of bearnaise sauce."

"Sold!" Eli says.

"Okay, two rockfish specials. And that comes with smashed potatoes, French-style green beans, and a small Greek salad, Caesar salad, or house salad," the server says.

"Does the Greek salad have lettuce?" Sam asks.

"It does not. The owner's wife is from Greece. She insists that true Greek salads do not have lettuce, just tomatoes, cukes, big slices of sweet white onion, feta cheese, and of course olives."

"She's correct, but she would know better than me. I've spent some time in Greece," Sam says. "I'll have the Greek salad."

"House salad with no onions," Eli says, thinking that he doesn't want to have onion breath.

"I'll be right out with those salads."

"Wait," Eli looks at Sam. "What about oysters for appetizers?"

"Sure, if they are out of the Rappahannock," Sam laughs.

"Yes, we do. We have Rapps, we have Ole Salts from the Bay, and Rochambeaus from the York River."

Eli looks at Sam. "How about a dozen to share? Three, I mean four of each. Math is not my strong suit."

"Let's do it," Sam says.

"When were you in Greece?" Eli asks.

"Military leave between some training exercises before Afghanistan."

"I've always wanted to go," Eli says.

Athens is very busy, crowded, young people on motorcycles weaving their way through thick traffic. Cars blowing their horns. But, the history, the Acropolis, the Parthenon, so fascinating. The festive tavernas at night are loads of fun. Most of them don't open until ten or eleven at night. Greeks take long naps during the afternoon and hit the tavernas later. They say, 'the Germans to our north like to work . . . we like to enjoy life.' The food is so good, right out of the Mediterranean. Squid, sardines, octopus fixed all sorts of ways. I love Santorini but was there only one day. Took a hydrofoil. I'm going back some day and stay a couple of weeks."

"Santorini? That's an island?"

"One of many beautiful islands. You can't go wrong with any of them."

"Your salads. I'll be right back with some fresh bread. The owner's wife loves to bake. The bread is her specialty."

"Eli, tell me about Winterford."

The server sits a plate of bread on the table. Eli pushes it toward Sam for the first piece. "I think that's their yummy garlic butter."

"I'll try it."

The server returns quickly with a tray of oysters. "The small ones on that side are the Ole Salts, next, the Rapps, and these are the Rochambeaus. Cocktail sauce and our special oyster sauce for your enjoyment on the side. Anything else?"

"I think you thought of everything, thanks!" Eli says.

"I get it about the Ole Salts, probably have a salty taste, and the Rapps . . . of course out of the Rappahannock, but why do they call these Rochambeaus?"

"You can thank George Washington for that . . . ," Sam says. "The French General Roshambeau and his army helped General Washington defeat the British at Yorktown, essentially ending the Revolutionary War. Washington named the oysters in the York River after the French General or so the locals say."

"Fascinating. I don't know if Winterford is as interesting but since you asked. Lots of tourists pass through Winterford on their way to the resort. A lot of vacation homes and a lot of retired folks live in the surrounding area, moving out of the big cities, like DC, wanting a quieter more relaxed lifestyle. So, we have it all. We have some very conservative people living out in the small communities and valleys. They want things to be like they use to be, back in the 1950s, Ozzie and Harriet days. We have one group, led by a local businessman, which is very vocal and active in local politics. They call themselves the Sons of Freedom."

"Your Rappahannock rockfish. The chef sears it, and then bakes it in the oven. So, the plates are hot," the server says as he sits steaming plates in front of Sam and then Eli.

As the server walks away, Sam with her raised hands, palms up, says to the sky, "Alhamdulillah."

"Alhamdulillah. Thanks be to God. You know Arabic." Eli says.

"Sounds like you do too," Sam says.

"Comparative religion courses. Never been in an Arabic country but want to go some day," Eli says. "Those people in the little communities around Winterford I told you about . . . they might get very upset if they hear anyone say anything like Alhamdulillah for a prayer of thanksgiving."

"I bet so," Sam says. "We camped with Bedouins a few times outside Kandahar. They taught me 'Alhamdulillah' or 'Thanks be to God!' I was touched by their simple reverence."

"It's a shame." Eli says. "Allah is simply a name for God in another language, the name for God for the Arabic people. Yahweh for Jewish people. In English, we say 'God' but that's just our language, our word for the divine."

Eli picks up the bottle of wine and his face with raised eyebrows asks Sam if she wants more.

"One more glass but that's my limit," Sam says. Eli pours Sam and himself a glass, finishing off the bottle.

Eli says, "I have a friend who is a minister and an archaeologist. He went to Jordan to excavate. The Arabic guide and his two sons got down on their knees five times a day to pray. My friend said he just stood there in the desert while these people prayed. He said where he was from in Tennessee people said the Arab people were 'all heathens.' He said standing there in the desert while these people prayed, he wondered who the heathen really was."

"That's a powerful story. Fundamentalists in any religion can give that religion a bad name. Moslems have their Jihadists. Christians have their own extremists, like the white supremacists," Sam says.

"Dessert?" the server asks.

"Not for me. Thanks," Sam says.

"I'll pass as well. But everything was so good. Thank you," Eli says.

The couple walk down Belmont Street, take a left, and soon stand in front of Sam's house.

"It's been a wonderful evening. Thanks so much for suggesting dinner, and I love the restaurant. Let's do it again sometime," Sam says.

"Absolutely! Well, we both work tomorrow. So, I better get going. Sermon writing for me in the morning," Eli says.

"I have an early staff meeting and several clients after that. So, better get some rest," Sam says.

"Well, good night and talk to you soon." Eli says as he turns toward his car.

"Good night."

Spinning around, Eli says, "I just thought of something. On Saturday, I'm going to hike The Priest. Want to go?"

"The Priest . . . that's on the Appalachian Trail?"

"Yes, and not far from here. Real close to Winterford. It's the steepest hike on the Appalachian Trail, over three-thousand feet of vertical gain, about eight and a half miles roundtrip."

"What time?"

"Meet at my place in Winterford? Is nine o'clock too early?"

"I can do that. Sounds like fun!"

"I'll text my address."

They say 'good night' again. Sam pulls her front door shut behind her as she wonders, 'Such a nice guy, we have a lot in common, will we be just friends, or something else?'

In the kitchen, Sam pushes a button, water squirts out of the refrigerator water dispenser into her glass. She takes a sip and takes it upstairs to her bedroom. Clean sheets welcome her nude body. She sleeps better with all her skin against the sheets. The alarm wakes her at seven. What good sleep, she thinks.

By Friday afternoon, she's convinced she made a good decision to join the psychotherapy practice. She likes her colleagues, loves Charlottesville, and now there's Eli. 'Intriguing,' she thinks.

Friday after work, she talks to Aili again on the sidewalk. Aili says, "I'm calling Door Dash, get some hot pho delivered from the Thai restaurant on Main. Want to come over?"

"Sure, I picked up a bottle of wine today. You like red?"

"Red, white. I drink it all. Bring your wine and come over about seven. I'll order the pho."

"Can you make mine vegetarian or shrimp? I don't eat meat."

"Of course. I usually get shrimp anyway. With all those noodles and vegetables, I don't need anything else. How about you?"

"Just pho," Sam says.

At seven, Sam slips between the hedge row with a bottle of wine under her arm and two glasses in her hand. In faded jeans, a red turtle-neck sweater, and black vest, Aili welcomes her into her home. The doorbell rings, and Door Dash delivers. Aili pulls two large bowls from the cabinet. "Let's don't eat out of their containers."

Sam pours the wine. "A friend told me about this wine. It's a cab-franc from Whitson Vineyards."

"I've heard about that vineyard. Supposed to be a great place. They have small plates and nice shaded seating in the summer. We'll have to go sometime."

"Sure. I love vineyards . . . especially what they produce." They both giggle.

"This is excellent pho. I like the bean sprouts, and so many flavors . . . I can taste ginger, basil, cinnamon, coriander, green onions, and these are rice noodles, right?" Sam asks.

"Yes, but I probably should have told you . . . I think this is a beef broth . . . sorry."

"No worries. That kind of thing happens from time to time."

"This is quay." Aili says, holding up a bread stick with her spray-tanned left arm. "Special flavoring in this, but I'm not sure what it is."

They sip pho and wine. Sam finds out Aili is recently divorced and teaches economics at the university.

After her second glass of wine, Sam says, "I better get to bed soon. I'm hiking The Priest tomorrow."

"You are! Wow! You better get lots of rest. I hear it's quite the challenge."

"I just realized. I don't have an address. I'm supposed to meet a new friend in Winterford. He hasn't sent me his address. Maybe, this is a good excuse, I mean reason, to call him. I like him." Sam, embarrassed, realizes she probably would not be saying this if not for the wine and certainly wouldn't be thinking about calling him.

"You want to hear his voice . . . I can tell," Aili says.

"Hello."

"Eli?"

"Yes, can I help you?"

"It's Sam. Sorry to bother you, but I don't have your address. I'm having pho with Aili, my neighbor, and realized I better get the address," Sam rolls her eyes. Aili puts her hand over her mouth to hold back her laugh.

"Oh, my gosh, I did forget to send it to you. I'm glad you called. I told you I'm not a well-organized person, at least not right now. And today we had a bad car wreck up here. Not members of the church, but I spent most of the day with the family. So sad, their daughter was killed. I'm working on my sermon tonight."

"Hey, if you need to cancel the hike tomorrow, I understand."

"Oh no, I need to hike. Let me give you the address."

"Do you need something to write on?" Aili asks.

"No thanks, I have a good memory."

"How's the pho?" Eli asks.

"Really flavorful," Sam says.

"I'll have to try it soon."

Eli shares his address, and they remind each other of the nine o'clock meet-up before they say goodbye.

"I like his voice," Aili says and then apologizes. "I wasn't trying to listen in."

"No problem."

"Is he a preacher?"

"Yes, but he's not an ordinary kind of preacher. He's very progressive and a very inclusive kind of person."

"Some of these conservative preachers make me gag," Aili says.

"Eli says they're White Christian Nationalists. You know, Christian is the adjective and not the noun. Misplaced priorities. They believe the Christian nation must defend itself, even if it means violence, against outsiders. And the outsiders might be U.S. citizens, Blacks, Hispanics, citizens of Middle Eastern descent, and liberals. Oh, they hate liberals. And they hate Jews, although they use a lot of Old Testament imagery to help justify their cause. They think our government has 'turned away from God.' They forget about separation of church and state. Eli says they use biblical literalism to justify some of their actions but ignore literal interpretations of the Bible in other places," Sam says.

"These ultra-conservative people say they want to be a Christian nation like we were in the beginning. I want to ask them to explain how people can murder Native Americans, steal their land, and then make their wealth on the backs of human slaves and call themselves a Christian nation. Is that what they want to go back to?" Aili says.

"It blows the mind," Sam says as she shakes her head. "The evangelicals claim the founding fathers who wrote the constitution were born-again Christians, but they were Unitarians, Anglicans, Roman Catholics, Quakers and maybe even one atheist. Thomas Jefferson, Eli's ancestor, was a deist."

"I'd almost rather go to jail than to some of these right-wing Christian churches. These preachers act like they have it all together, want to tell us how to live, and what we can and cannot do with our bodies, and then the next thing you know, they get caught in a motel room with another woman or a bathroom with a young teenage boy," Aili says.

Sam roars with laughter.

"I hear people say all the time they must vote for the right-wing conservatives because they're better for the economy. They don't look at economic data. Since I teach economics, I look at the data all the time. Some people are just gaslighted by right wing media. If they looked at the economic data, they would see that conservative presidents have been the largest deficit spenders. George W. Bush was the largest deficit spender in history, and it looks like President Trump will come in as the second largest deficit spender of all time."

"You know what the GDP is?" Aili asks.

"Aili, I'm a psychologist, not an economist, but it has something to do with the economy," Sam says.

"Correct. GDP stands for Gross Domestic Product and measures how much the economy is growing. Bill Clinton had his personal issues, but he had one of the best GDPs of all time at 3.8% and a balanced budget. President Trump has a GDP around 1% and that's after he promised during his presidential campaign to have a GDP over 6%. Conservative presidents don't have great GDPs," Aili says.

"This's all very interesting, but I better get going. The Priest awaits me," Sam says.

"And Eli!" Aili adds. "Eli's comin', hide your heart girl . . . heard that song?"

"Yes. The local radio station in White Stone plays all oldies."

"Listen, we've only had two glasses of wine and should not be this silly," Aili says.

"I know, but girls will be girls! Goodnight. Hope to see you soon," Sam says.

The Priest!

May 1, 2020

"I love the Blue Ridge Parkway," Sam says. "One minute I'm looking at wild, untamed, soaring mountains, then I see flowery meadows below, and look, sheer rock cliffs. Amazing!"

"In a few weeks, trees will start to bud at this elevation. Then, we'll get the first green leaves and flowers up here," Eli says.

"Winter is dying, giving way to spring," Sam adds.

Eli exits the parkway and takes a left on Highway 56 toward Montebello. A sign says, "Crabtree Falls Ahead."

"I remember seeing Crabtree Falls when I was a kid. School field trip," Sam says.

"We can hike Crabtree Falls trail some time. Oops, I guess I'm getting ahead of myself. Sorry," Eli apologizes.

"I like the way you think," Sam affirms.

"Crabtree Falls is the longest cascading waterfall east of the Rockies. Not many people know that. We'll be close to the headwaters when we get to the top of the Priest," Eli says.

"Okay. That's the trailhead on the right. The small parking lot is full. So, I'll pull on the other side of the road. The AT crosses the road here and continues up that mountain over there as the Three Ridges Trail, not as difficult as The Priest. Maybe we should do that this time?" Eli says.

"Let's do The Priest," Sam says. "You okay with that?"

"All right. I brought lots of water and energy drinks. Need some?"

"Eli, remember . . ."

"Oh yes, Afghanistan. Silly me," Eli says.

"I have on too many layers," Sam slips off a long-sleeved sweatshirt revealing an athletic tank top. Eli glances at her perfectly formed breasts but quickly looks away. When she takes off her jogging pants, Eli eyes very short jean-shorts revealing every inch of her long, shapely, tan legs.

"You get that tan in Afghanistan?" Eli asks.

"I figure I'm goin' get plenty warm hiking up that monster," Sam says as she points at the trail.

"That's an interesting birthmark on your right shoulder. It kind of looks like a heart," Eli says.

"Runs in the family. They tell me," Sam says.

They start up the steep trail. Five hours later, they return to Eli's car.

"Thanks so much for inviting me. That was awesome, and such a good work-out! A little hard on the knees coming down, but nothing a warm soaking bath won't fix," Sam says.

"Let's go down the trail to the river. I want to show you something," Eli says.

"A footbridge!" Sam says as they approach the river.

"In the mountains, they call them 'swinging bridges.' This one's a recent con-struction. In the old days, instead of steel cables, they were made of ropes."

"Like the one in the 'Indiana Jones' movie?" Sam asks.

"Exactly. I watched all those as a kid. Hey, I just felt a rain drop. And an-other. We better head to the car."

Rain starts to pound the leaves on the trees.

"We're gonna get drenched!" Sam says.

Soaked and laughing, they reach the car. Swinging doors open, they jump into the seats, still laughing. At first, rain taps the windshield, but then pelts the entire car, each drop sounding like a firecracker exploding.

"That's the mountains. Rain seems to come out of nowhere. Some of these mountains get rain just about every day. Keeps the rivers flowing, I guess," Eli says.

"I love listening to the rain. My porch is a great place to listen to the rain. You'll have to join me on the porch when the next rain comes," Sam invites.

Driving back to Winterford, Eli says, "We're goin' back a different way. This stretch of road is called the valley of howling dogs."

"Why's that?"

"If you drive through here with windows down after dark, you can almost always hear howling. There are lots of bear hunters living along here with hunting dogs. One pen of dogs will start howling, and a little way up the road another will start howling until the whole valley is a howling dog show."

"That's crazy," Sam says.

"You have dinner plans?"

"I hope I do now," Sam ventures.

"We have a fantastic French restaurant in Winterford. The wonderful woman who owns it lived in France for over twenty years. Her recipes are out of this world. It's small, not many tables, but she always makes room for me."

"I have to go home, get a shower, and I'll head back," Sam says.

"I'll come get you. I can think about my sermon as I drive. It will be time well spent."

Dressed in a light blue sweater and short white skirt revealing her long, shapely legs, Sam sits on the porch when Eli pulls up. In a few minutes, they speed up I-64.

"On the drive down, I saw an incredible rainbow. Sometimes, I think you stepped out of a rainbow," Eli says.

"That's sweet."

"When I am near you, the world is so far away." Eli says.

"Eli, you're getting really close to my heart."

After a few minutes of silence, Sam says, "So, we're leaving these great restaurants in Charlottesville and headed to a little restaurant in a little town most people have never heard about,"

"That's it. I'll make a bet with you. If it's not one of the best meals you've ever had, I'll piggyback you home."

"This is it?" Sam asks as they pull into the parking lot.

"It's not very big, I told you. And part of it is a wine shop with imported cheeses and specialty foods. Oh, the menu will have only five or six entrees but trust me."

"Okay."

The hostess-cashier recognizes Eli. "Two for dinner?"

"Indeed, this is my friend Sam. She's new to the area. I told her you had the best hot dogs and fries in the area."

Sam gives Eli a little swat of the hand on his arm. "Stop it."

They follow the hostess to the dining area.

"The dulcimer player coming tonight?" Eli asks.

"Yes, she is."

"We'll have a front row seat then," Eli says.

"Eli, I think they're all front row," Sam says.

"Waters for both of you?"

"Yes, thanks."

"You're right, six entrees on the menu, but the descriptions are incredible," Sam says.

"I know I had fish last night, but I must get the European Sea Bass Provencal with tomatoes, onions, garlic, capers, and black cured olives. It's so good," Eli says.

"Eli, wine tonight?" the server asks.

"Just a glass for me. Got to preach tomorrow," Eli says. "My regular."

"The cab-franc?"

"Please."

"Same for me, and I think we are ready to order," Sam says, thinking to herself it doesn't take long to study this menu.

"Let's order," Eli says.

"French Countryside Tart, please," Sam says.

"I'll have the European Sea Bass Provençal," Eli says.

"Tell me about your dinner salad?" Sam asks.

"Arugula, slivered cucumbers, toasted pepitas, and shaved parmesan with olive oil and balsamic glaze," the server says.

"Sounds wonderful," Sam says.

"That's good for me, too," Eli says. "And I'll have the Gouda and Red Pepper Soup."

"How about you, ma'am?"

"No thanks on soup."

As the server walks away, Sam says to Eli, "Are you like me and drink red wine with everything?"

"Yes, I guess that's rather unsophisticated, but it's what I like," Eli says.

"Yea. And I think we are hopeless foodies." Sam says. "While we wait, tell me about the Virginia Master Naturalist program you mentioned yesterday."

"It's a one-year part-time program. Classes on geology, botany, local wild-life, ecology, climate, and much more. It's going to be my little way of helping to save the planet."

"Interesting. I'll have to investigate that. You have a lot of history here, and we have a lot of history in Kilmarnock. When we go down there, I'll take you to Sting Ray Point. Captain John Smith when he was exploring the Rappahannock River and the Chesapeake Bay was stung by a sting ray. So, they named it Sting Ray Point."

The server returns with Eli's soup and sits another bowl on their table. With a surprised look, Eli says, "That must be for another table. We didn't order that."

"The owner said to bring that to you. It's Leek and Potato Vichyssoise. She wanted both of you to have something."

The dulcimer player arrives just as the salads come out.

"I think you'll like the concert," Eli says.

The entrees come out. "What's in the tart?" Eli asks.

"Zucchinis, baby squash, baby tomatoes, red onion, goat cheese, and the menu said fresh herbs and carrot parsley jewels. It's heavenly. This's like Paris in the mountains."

"So, I don't have to piggyback you home?"

"Not this time. And the dulcimer player is so talented."

"I'll introduce you before we leave. She's a retired Presbyterian minister."

At the conclusion of dinner, Eli says to Sam. "I need to tell you something."

"What's that?"

"I'm in Charlottesville a lot," Eli pauses. "It's to see a team of doctors. I have lymphoma. But they think they've caught it early, and I feel fine. Lymphoma didn't hold me back going up The Priest."

"I was impressed. And you look great. I would have never known. Is it Hodgkin's?"

"Yes, Hodgkin's. Doctors tell me that's more curable. It was strange and sudden. I noticed some swelling under my arm and a little knot on my leg. Went to my local doctor. He sent me to Charlottesville. Treatment started immediately. One day, I'm the healthiest man in the world, and the next day, I'm a cancer patient. Incredible."

"Your hospital has a great reputation. A teaching and research hospital. I'm sure you'll get the latest treatments."

"Yes, I'm very fortunate. Such high-tech chemistry, they might eventually even tell me whether my cancer came from Thomas' or Sally's DNA." They chuckle. "But of course, a lot of other DNA in the mix during all those years."

"We'll go back to Charlottesville a little different way," Eli says as the 370Z engine explodes to life.

He takes a left on Highway 151 that he would usually follow to the right until it intersects with I-64. Instead, in a few miles, he turns on Beech Grove Road.

"I'm glad you know where you're going. I don't. This is a very curvy road and nearly straight up. I think you like driving these mountain roads, don't you?"

"Yes, this is fun, going through the gears."

At the top of the mountain, Eli takes a right.

"Back on the Blue Ridge Parkway," Sam says.

"Yes, I want to show you something."

In a few miles, Eli turns left into an overlook parking lot as the moon glows over the mountains.

"Wow! That's some view!" Sam says.

"That's the Shenandoah Valley, you're looking down from about 4000 feet."

"The screeching?"

"Cicadas. Some people call them locusts. Crawl out of the ground every seventeen years or something like that. They live as nymphs underground, and then emerge in such massive numbers that predators can't eat them all. It's the way they survive as a species. I'm learning some interesting things in the naturalist program."

"I see the little towns and communities down there with their lights on," Sam says. She looks up at the sky. "And so many stars. It's like they're winking at us as the clouds pass over. Eli, you know how to romanticize a girl."

Later, the Nissan 370Z pulls up in front of Sam's house. Streetlamps provide a dim light, making sidewalks and bushes visible.

"That's Aili's house. I want you to meet her soon. She lots of fun. Can you come in for a few minutes? I know you have church in the morning, but I want to give you something."

"Okay."

Inside, Sam asks, "Can I get you anything? Water or a sparkling water? A cup of coffee or tea? Something for the road?"

"No, thanks. I'm fine. Drank a lot of water at the restaurant."

"I'll be right back," Sam goes up the stairs and into her bedroom.

Internally, Eli scratches his mind. 'What's she doing? Slipping into something more comfortable? I don't think so. We haven't known each other that long.'

With quick steps, Sam comes down the stairs. She has something in her right hand. She holds out a set of keys.

"You come to Charlottesville a lot. If you don't feel like driving back, after a treatment or just a long day, let yourself in. Take a nap, whatever. The bedroom on this floor is yours whenever you need it."

"Wow. That's so thoughtful and generous of you. You don't know me . . . ," Eli starts to say.

Sam interrupts, "Just remember the Army taught me to kill with my bare hands." They laugh.

"Three keys. This one is for the front door, this for the back door, and this for the basement," Sam takes Eli's left hand, turns it over, pulls his fingers back, and drops the set of keys in his palm. She leans forward and places a quick kiss on his lips. "You gotta work tomorrow, you best get going."

"Wow. I don't know what to say."

"You don't have to say anything. Just drive safely and take good care of yourself. Can you come back after church tomorrow? I'll have lunch ready. Two o'clock?"

"Fine. Thanks."

Strange Visitor and Interesting Client

December 15, 2020

Over the next few months, Eli continues his treatments. The couple dines at all the highly rated restaurants in Charlottesville. As the weather warms, they visit the vineyards and tasting rooms that have proliferated in the valleys and rich soiled areas of the Virginia mountains.

Sam's case load grows until she has a full client load. The Charlottesville newspaper runs a story about her, how her father was in Vietnam, and how she volunteered for Afghanistan.

Tuesday after work while Sam changes into jogging clothes, the front doorbell rings. Sam bounces down the steps. She can see who is at the door through a window in the dining room. A black pickup truck, the driver, a large man in a plaid shirt with sleeves rolled up his massive arms and wearing a red baseball hat, sits in front of her house. The man pulls a pack of smokes out his shirt pocket, indicating he might be sitting there awhile. A man, probably in his early seventies, in khaki pants, light blue button-down collar shirt, and dark zip-up jacket, stands at her door. A black cap with ear flaps, not pulled down over his ears, covers the top of his head. Grey bushy eyebrows stick out from his face. Sam opens the door.

"Samantha Stuart?"

"Yes, that's me."

"Can we talk a few minutes? Out here on the porch is fine."

"Sure, have a seat," Sam says pointing at a white rocker. "Can I get you something to drink?"

"No thanks. The city tap water tastes like nuclear waste."

"How about a bottle of water or tea?"

They pause the conversation as an inbound jet for the Charlottesville airport roars overhead.

"No thanks. We had coffee at a little diner earlier."

The man sits, cracks his knuckles, and says, "I knew your father."

"Really?"

"Yes, we were in Vietnam together."

"Hmm . . ." Sam mutters. "How did you find me?"

As the man leans back in the rocker and puts his hands together behind his head locking his sausage-like fingers, Sam gets a good look at his dark, cold, dead eyes, like a shark's eyes, she thinks. "I read the newspaper article about you, and how your father served in Vietnam. My grandson is a computer whiz . . . so I asked him to find you. He can do just about anything with a computer.

"That was a brave thing your father did. He was the youngest soldier in our platoon, maybe in our battalion, but he saved a lot of lives. I know it eventually cost him his life."

"What exactly did he do? No one ever told me."

"We were at our base just north of Saigon. The war was essentially over. We were withdrawing, goin' let the lil' bastards from the north have the whole country. I didn't like that decision. I thought we ought to carpet bomb the whole north, kill all the lil' communists. But that's another story.

"We're just in our barracks, waiting our turn to evacuate. We had a big poker game going in the middle of the room, drinking bourbon out of the bottle. The potheads were smoking on the other side of the room. A few guys were reading on their beds. Your dad was reading. One of those pajama-wearing Viet Cong slipped through security, and somehow gets his hands on a grenade, and throws it through our window. It lands right beside your father's bed. He didn't run. He gets up, turns his bed over on the grenade, and falls on top of the bed, I guess, to hold it down. The blast hurt him bad, but no one else even had a scratch. I'd probably be dead if it won't for your daddy," the bushy eyebrowed man says.

Sam sits stunned for a long moment. "Mother said a tiny piece of shrapnel killed him. Been in his chest since the war, and one day found its way to his heart."

The man cracks his knuckles again. "Your father saved us. I want to welcome you to Charlottesville. I don't live here. I'm up near Winterford," the man says.

Sam thinks she'll just keep her relationship with Eli to herself at this point.

"Lot of liberals here in Charlottesville. Flashy European cars in about every driveway. A lot of real Americans up where I live. We drive American made cars. We're goin' change this country to the way it's supposed to be. We got a president who'll fix this country. We must keep him in there."

"I thank you for coming. I'm sorry. I'm a little distracted by the new information you gave me about my father. But I'm glad you told me."

Back inside her house, Sam falls into a leather armchair, still absorbing the news about her father. So, that's why he had the bronze star, the purple heart, and the other medals, she thinks.

She pulls her cell phone from her jogging shorts pocket and presses "Mom."

"Hello."

"Mom, it's Sam. I just had an interesting visitor."

"Oh?"

"A man in his seventies says he lives near Winterford. He said he was in Vietnam with Dad. He told me how Dad saved his life, and the lives of many others by turning a bed over on a grenade."

"Your father was a good man, a brave man. I miss him so. And I think I know who that man is."

"Really?"

"He came down here to see your father one time. Wanted him to join a new political party, the reformed party, or something like that. He didn't think the conservatives in Washington were conservative enough. Your father thought he was an extremist."

"Wow!" Sam pauses, takes a deep breath, absorbing the new information. "I'm thinking about coming home this weekend."

"Wonderful."

"I might bring a new friend with me."

"Okay."

"Is it . . .?"

"Yes, it's a man. He's a pastor, a Presbyterian."

"I'll check with Rory. Maybe, he'll have extra shrimp and crabs. We'll have a seafood boil Saturday evening."

"Sounds lovely. We'll probably stop at *Merroir* on Friday night. I've told him so much about the restaurant, the oysters right out of the water. And you know, *People Magazine's* most popular restaurant in Virginia and all that. It'll be late. I don't leave the office until four or so."

"I would love to see you and your new friend. *Adrift* is a new restaurant with a wonderful chef. *The Vine* is a great place to eat. Several good choices."

Sam and her mother say their goodbyes. A few minutes later, the doorbell rings again. It's Aili.

"Hey, Aili, you want to come in?"

"Oh no, I just thought I would check on you."

"Have a seat," Sam says pointing at a rocker. Two young men silently fly by on their fancy racing bikes.

"The Elmer Fudd looking guy that got out of the pickup truck earlier and came up on your porch. Something about him. I recognized him. He was in the news a few years ago. You were probably in Afghanistan. He helped organize the Charlottesville Unite the Right rally, attended by lots of Nazis. People organized to protest them. A woman was killed when one of them drove a car into her."

"I read about that. What did you say? Elmer Fudd looking guy? From the Bugs Bunny cartoons?"

"Yeah. Short, stumpy little man with a big head and a round face. I was off today, and I saw the truck drive by your house several times. They sat in the street a little while before you got home. He was in the passenger seat. Some super-sized guy with huge ears wearing a red hat was driving."

"He saw the article in the newspaper about me. He was in Vietnam with my father. He just wanted to introduce himself."

"Well, sorry to bother. We do need to look out for each other."

"Thanks. I like having a guardian angel."

At ten o'clock the next morning, Sam has a new client, Betty, who sits in the waiting room while nervously flipping through magazines. A few minutes before ten, Sam takes a clip board out to the waiting room. She introduces herself to Betty and asks her to fill out a couple of forms, one is general information, and the other is for her insurance and policy number.

Betty apologizes. "I'm sorry I had to bring the baby. My sitter called sick. I started to cancel, but she's really good. I can just put a blanket in the floor, and she'll be fine."

"Okay, I'll be back for you, both of you, in a few minutes."

They go into Sam's office. Betty spreads the blanket down on the floor and lowers the baby on to the blanket.

"What's her name?"

"Cynthia,"

"Cynthia's beautiful," Sam says.

"Thanks."

"So, what brings you here?"

"I'm having a lot of anxiety and having trouble sleeping."

"How long's this been going on?"

"Several months."

"How did it start?"

"I don't know how much I should tell you. I know some things I'm not supposed to know."

"Everything you tell me is confidential. You know, doctor and patient confidentiality thing. There are a couple of exceptions according to state law, and that's if you are a danger to yourself or if others are in danger."

"My husband is not supposed to tell me things, but he does. His father is one of the leading businessmen in the Winterford area. They have this group called The Sons of Freedom. I don't know if I should be telling you this."

The baby rolls over on the blanket.

"She's really a good baby," Sam says. "You don't have to tell me everything today. I'm more interested in you than your father-in-law. Tell me about you."

Betty shares her story. She grew up near Lynchburg. Her father and mother both worked at an electrical parts plant there. After high school, Betty got a server job in a brewery near Winterford. Her future husband was a customer and asked her out on a date. Betty and Rock were married three years ago and live on a small farm owned by her father-in-law near Winterford.

"We've had a good marriage. Rock works for his father and does things with him after work. I've been seeing less and less of him lately. I'm worried he might get into some big trouble."

"Have you talked to Rock about that?" Sam asks.

"Yes, and his nickname is Rock. Long story but a nickname his father gave him. He's so devoted to his father. His father has a lot of control over him and over a lot of people in our area. A lot of the people work for him. His father even built a baseball field for the kids in the area. His father is a local hero. He volunteered for three tours of duty in Vietnam. He was a sniper and tells stories of piling up bodies, Vietnamese, he shot. And stories of cruelty too, putting tires around prisoners' heads and setting them on fire."

"Are you a little angry with your husband?"

"Yeah, I guess so, but mostly scared."

"Angry and scared. That's a tough situation. Must feel like you're pulled in two different directions. We only have a little bit of time left today, and we want to get you sleeping better. So, I'm going to ask you some questions about your lifestyle and see what we can tweak that might help. Then next time we'll get into the relationship stuff. Okay?"

Betty agrees, and Sam talks to her about her caffeine consumption, diet, and exercise. Sam teaches her some relaxation and breathing exercises to help her get to sleep.

"You know there are some medications that would help you sleep, but let's don't go there until you try some of these lifestyle changes and talk some about your feelings about your marriage and in-laws," Sam says.

"Give me just a minute to look over your paperwork you filled out in the waiting room and see if I have any questions," Sam says.

Everything looks in order, but Sam notices one thing. Her last name, her married name, is the same as the man who came to her house. The man who served with her father in Vietnam. And Betty said he was a Vietnam war hero. 'Interesting,' Sam thinks.

Sam rises from her chair, walks to the door, and puts her hand on the door-knob when Betty says, "I don't think it's a good idea for my husband to know I come here."

"I understand. Again, this is a confidential setting," Sam starts to tell Betty that some couple sessions might be helpful in the future but decides not to mention it now.

The Patriot

December 21, 2020

A converted lumber warehouse, the Sons of Freedom meeting place sits on the Patriot's property. The silver metal building seats almost three hundred in folding chairs. The stage is a large wooden structure about thirty feet by thirty feet. Two chairs sit on the stage. American flags and confederate flags decorate each side of the stage along with large pictures of the President of the United States. A banner across the bottom of the stage reads: SONS OF FREEDOM: Jesus and Country.

Cigar smoke fills the air. The Patriot gives each attendee a cigar, and most have lit up. Built-in fans in the walls hum but struggle to pull out the smoke.

The mostly male audience consists of employees of the Patriot and other interested individuals. Several young men with mullets dot the seated crowd.

Tiny Jenkins stands six foot and six inches and always wears a red baseball hat, self-conscious of his large ears that stick out like silver-dollar pancakes. Tiny's hands are so big he can make a fist like a bowling ball, and his friends say, "he can hit you so hard, you'll shit your eyeballs." As the supervisor of the lumber mill, he could also be called the Patriot's bodyguard since he accompanies him most everywhere he goes.

With teeth like a horse, Onion drives a forklift at the lumber yard. Onion's hair is reddish yellow, his head round, and his voice high-pitched.

Blonde-haired Noodle, as thin as a pasta-noodle from a bowl of soup, drives a lumber delivery truck. With his almost white hair and pale blue eyes, Noodle has a ghostly appearance.

Looking like he spends his life in a house's crawl space, Hunch is a lumber inspector who has spent his adult life hunched over a conveyor belt grading lumber boards in the Patriot's lumber mill. He almost always wears a Hard Rock Cafe t-shirt. These men and the others in the building think the Patriot could stop the tides if he wanted to because he gives them an identity, a purpose, a place, a family. They are loyal to their deaths.

Rock and Roll sit on the front row. They are the nicknames for Patriot's sons. He didn't like his sons listening to rock music when they were teenagers and told them if he caught them listening again, he would tell everyone to call them Rock and Roll. The nicknames stuck. Roll with his spiked black hair almost always wears a black Metallica t-shirt, in a half-hearted sign of rebellion.

Most of the men in attendance have nicknames they've given each other. They have not given a nickname to the Patriot's younger brother, half his face missing due to oral cancer surgery. Not even this uneducated and crude group of men want to call attention to his deformity.

Farmers, factory workers, retirees, and other small business owners make up the remainder of the audience. Some drive in from neighboring counties. A mechanic from an auto repair shop walks in and takes a seat. A greasy rag hangs from his back pocket. Grease spots dot his shirt and pants. With black grease packed under his fingernails, he reaches out to shake the hand of a businessperson in a fine suit sitting beside him, who gets an up-close view of the mechanic's bad teeth.

The Patriot walks to the microphone. "Boys, I got a great joke for you. Why do they bury liberals twenty feet underground?" They wait for an answer. "Because down deep they're really nice guys!"

The audience roars with laughter.

Showing no respect for his audience, the Patriot scratches his ass and says, "I got us a great speaker tonight. Dr. C.S.A. Johanson is from the *American Institute* just down the road in Lynchburg. He knows more about our government than all those representatives and senators in Washington put together. Tonight, he's going to tell us what's wrong with our country and how to fix it."

The men cheer and whistle. Dr. Johanson thanks them. The Patriot pulls up his pants as he walks away and reaches in his pocket for a stick of gum, unwraps it with his fat fingers, and sticks it in his mouth before sitting down.

Pointing to the Patriot, Dr. Johanson says, "First, I want to thank this man. There's a reason we call him the Patriot. He's the kind of man who loves

America and will let America be America. These liberals in and out of government won't let America be America. Let's give this man a big round of applause."

The audience stands and applauds. Rock puts a finger in each corner of his mouth and lets out a shrilling whistle. The Patriot tells them to be seated.

Dr. Johanson continues. "I've been studying history and governments my whole life. And I'm going to walk you through history and tell you why governments fail . . . Governments and nations that fail have one thing in common. If you look at the governments of the countries we're going to talk about, you'll see why they failed. They got liberal."

The men cheer in agreement.

"The Greeks, the Romans, they got liberal. They let their people govern themselves. What happens when you let people govern themselves? People do whatever they want to do. They get lazy and just live off the government. The government eventually collapses. And that's where this country is headed if we don't do something about it. You have a leader here," pointing to the Patriot, "who will do something about it. The election was stolen. You know it. Everybody knows it. And who stole it? The liberals!

"Look at the history of the world. Egypt had a great empire for thousands of years as long as they were ruled by one Pharoah. China was ruled by a single emperor for hundreds of years. It was a great empire. More recently, Russia was ruled by the czars, and Russia was powerful. China and Russia tried communism. It failed. Communism is just another form of liberalism. The people trying to rule themselves. It always fails.

"Look at Europe. When were the countries of Europe the strongest? When they had kings to rule them . . . that's when they discovered and colonized the rest of the world because the rest of the world was weak!

"And the kingdom of God doesn't have a whole bunch of kings. Just one! Jesus Christ is King! God is no fool. One King . . . King Jesus!"

The men roar, cheer, and whistle in approval.

"The liberalism in this country cannot stand. Our country is too precious to let liberals ruin it. Liberals are as trustworthy as a bag of snakes! This country was founded by men like us, not by a Great Harlot like the one who ran for President. God worked a miracle to keep her from getting elected. We must get the liberals out of government, out of our schools, and get liberal books out of libraries. They're like thankless children, wanting more and more handouts. Liberal teachers are infecting the minds of our young people. Just down the road in Charlottesville, we have that compost pile of liberalism. This man, the Patriot, is working with other great Americans around the country, and they'll take our country back. Whatever they ask you to do, you need to do it. And let the liberals pound their highchairs!"

One man stands, then another, until all are standing and applauding. A woman in the back yells, "Thank you Jesus!"

The Patriot comes back to the microphone and thanks the professor. "And now our good friend Reverend Joney will dismiss us with prayer. And next month, we'll gather again to hear a speaker from the Russian embassy in Washington. You know what we say, we'd rather live with Russians than liberals!"

The men applaud. Reverend Joney prays.

"Almighty and merciful God, we know you seek liberty and freedom for all pure Americans. And we know you will bring justice down upon those who corrupt our land with liberal laws and perverted lifestyles. The ungodly. Women loving women. Men loving men. Bi-racial babies born on this earth that you don't want born. Thank you loving God for raising up these men of faith and freedom to be your winnowing forks who will someday go forth and remove the ungodly chaff from our land. Amen."

Such is the nature of the monthly gatherings of the Patriot's men, The Sons of Freedom, who leave the meetings with their emotions swollen like the raging waters of a flood swollen river.

The Patriot's ancestors were some of the first settlers of what later became Bade County, Virginia. In the mid-1700s after the Monacan tribes were driven to the west, Thomas T. Bidall received massive land grants, thousands of acres. The Patriot inherited most of the land, along with a sawmill and lumber industry. He built a small motel, a service station, a convenience store, a funeral home, and several other small enterprises. He owns farms, where he raises turkeys and chickens in cramped fowl houses, long buildings with screen wire keeping the birds from flying away. Outside of the mountaintop resort and a few other businesses, the Patriot controls much of what goes on in Bade County. He refuses to employ anyone except white Americans, although he does have a young, immigrant housekeeper who lives in his house. Rumors are that she not only has to keep his house but must keep his sexual desires satisfied.

The Patriot 'employed' the housekeeper after his wife of many years left him. Sally Bidall married the much older Mr. Bidall when she was just out of high school. Winfried Bidall insisted everyone call him Mr. Bidall, even his wife. Over the years, she found ways to educate herself, not always telling her husband the truth about her activities. She took courses at the University of Virginia. Joining a women's support group in Charlottesville, she started to realize how oppressive her marriage was. She avoided him, faked illnesses, and begged him to let her get a job. He refused, but she slipped into Charlottesville when he was at work or at his rallies.

In Charlottesville, she meets an Episcopal priest. They have lunch together, talk on the phone, meet when possible, and dare plan a life together. A few years later in the middle of the night, the two women move to New York City where the priest takes a job at a counseling agency and Sally Bidall enrolls in a small college.

Stinging with hurt, the Patriot was humiliated and murderously angry. His two sons, employed in the family businesses, sided with their father. The Patriot became even more right winged and politically active. He blamed his situation and the country problems on liberals and lesbian preachers. Not only was he plotting revenge on his ex-wife but on all liberal politicians as well.

His internalized anger leads to health issues. He takes Advil by the handful for his headaches. Four big glasses of bourbon are required to get him to sleep at night. He finds the whole world disgusting. He says his sons are as "lazy as old dog turds." He doesn't address his employees by name but calls the ones he respects "hoss" and the others "mental midgets." His hero is General Nathan Bedford Forrest, the first Grand Wizard of the Klu Klux Klan.

Pictures of Robert E. Lee, Lee Harvey Oswald, John Birch, Strom Thurmond, and several presidents of the United States decorate the walls of his office. Mounted deer heads sit between the pictures. Although the man is most likely worth millions, he heats his office with a wood-burning pot-bellied stove. In the summer, two window mounted air-conditioner units hum all day long. He makes sexist remarks toward his two secretaries, but they laugh it off, although they secretly despise the man. He tells his male employees that he'll never give a job with much responsibility to anyone who has "a period."

When he starts reading the novels of Frank Peretti, the Patriot believes there has to be a necessary spiritual war. After he reads *This Present Darkness*, the

Patriot is convinced that conservatives are the children of light while liberals are the children of darkness. He sees a coming holy battle between these forces of good and evil. He thinks all the publicity about climate change is simply a way to distract from the fact that liberals are turning a Christian nation into a secular nation. Not knowing his thinking is along the lines of primitive dualism, he admonishes his followers to read *This Present Darkness*, "the greatest book written since the Bible."

The Patriot's one redeeming quality is his devotion to his English Setter who sleeps beside his bed and by his desk every day. Named after conservative talk-show host Rush Limbaugh, 'Rush' has black specks all over his white, short-haired, body, and with long white hair falling from behind his tail, belly, and the back of his legs. The Patriot threatened to rename him when he accused Rush Limbaugh of not being conservative enough. Rush almost died when The Patriot, so frustrated with him when he refused "to point" quail on a hunting trip, shot him. Fortunately, Rush was far enough away from the gun that the shotgun pellets barely penetrated his skin.

Revenge against his ex-wife takes a backseat after the election of November 2020. He cannot stand the thoughts of another liberal in the White House. He contacts other right-wing political groups around the country, The Proud Boys, and The Oathkeepers. Plans are made for January 6, 2021.

Plans Revealed

January 4, 2021

Betty likes Sam and trusts her. In the counseling sessions, she talks openly.

Sam shuts the office door and offers Betty a cup of tea. "Earl Grey? I have honey."

"No thanks."

"Let me know if you change your mind."

They both sit. Betty's eyes dart about the room.

Anxious, Betty talks immediately, "My husband tells me they are going to the Capitol on January 6. He says the President wants them to come. They're taking weapons. It's scary. They have a preacher telling them it is God's will for them to go and prevent a new president from taking office. My husband says there will be a lot of people there, coming from all over the United States. He says someone in the government will take down the metal detectors so weapons can get in the Capitol."

"This is shocking!" Sam says.

"Either way, it's going to be bad for me. If they fail to stop the inauguration, my husband will go to jail. If they stop it, I fear we might have a civil war. People will get killed."

"You're carrying a heavy load with all this inside information," Sam says.

"I've thought about going to the sheriff's office, but he's a good friend of my father-in-law."

"What if I contact some people I know in the military?" Sam asks and regrets in the next moment what she said.

"Would you?"

"I can try, but you can't tell anyone. Okay?"

"Okay."

"They're having an initiation tonight."

"An initiation?" Sam asks.

"The Sons of Freedom is by invitation only. The person must be recommended by a member of the group who has been a member for five years. That's the way they hope to keep out undercover agents. They'll gather at the tunnel after dark. They carry torches as they march the new guy into the tunnel. Rock says they make the guys kneel and repeat a bunch of oaths. I think they shave the guy's head and a bunch of silly stuff. Of course, they're drinking beer most of the time and hammering donuts."

"What's the tunnel?"

"Near Afton but not the Crozet Tunnel that's owned by the county. The old tunnel they use was supposed to be a railroad tunnel from the Shenandoah Valley through the mountain and into this side of Virginia, but they ran into very hard rock back in the early 1900's. They stopped digging that tunnel and dug the Crozet Tunnel instead that they got to go all the way through the mountain."

That evening, Sam tells Eli what she knows.

"You can't get involved. You could get hurt, even killed," he says.

"My great-grandmother, Samantha Stuart, was a brave woman. She risked her life to help runaway slaves cross the Rappahannock River. She continued even when her husband, my great-grandfather, was murdered by a racist on his church steps. I must be as brave as she was."

"So, you're named after her."

"Yep. And I need to be brave like her and stand up for what's right."

"I'll do everything I can to help you. Just keep me informed."

"I found out something else. My client's father-in-law, this guy they call the Patriot, was in my father's platoon in Vietnam. He came to see me a few days ago. We sat on the porch. He saw the article about me in the newspaper and how my father was in Vietnam. His grandson tracked down my address.

"My father saved his life. Fell on a hand grenade thrown into their barracks . . . well, he turned a bed over on the hand grenade. He took shrapnel, but no one else in the room was injured. My father saved the life of the man who wants to destroy democracy in this country. And my father died years later from a piece of shrapnel that made its way to his heart. I'm having a hard time with that."

"Holy cow!" Eli says. "Doesn't seem fair. I don't blame you for being upset."

"I'm going to contact a colonel I know, at the Joint Expeditionary Military Base in Virginia Beach tomorrow and tell him about this plan to attack the Capitol. I hope he's still there," Sam says. "I think he knows some people in the FBI."

The Day After

January 7, 2021

"Betty, before we start, I want you to know I contacted a Colonel at a military base and told him what you told me. Wow, you were right about the riot. It didn't look like they were prepared. Maybe they didn't believe me. Did your family make it home okay? I know you were worried," Sam asks.

"Well, they didn't go." Betty says.

"What?"

"Yeah. They were told not to come, to stay back because they are part of a backup plan. They had big screens set up at the meeting house and watched it unfold. I didn't go to the meeting house, but my husband was there."

"I guess you were relieved your husband didn't go to DC."

"Yes, but there's going to be more."

"What do you mean?"

"My father-in-law has been working on a backup plan with some politicians in Texas."

"Really?"

"Rock has told me parts of it, but he has stopped talking to me. He's upset about something. His father has never liked me, and I think his father has finally turned him against me. If his father finds out I am coming here, I am in big trouble. He hates therapists since his wife ran away with one.

"Rock says there are three power-grids in the United States. One for the east coast and another for the western states. Texas has always insisted on having their own power-grid. We might be moving to Texas. I don't know when, but I might not be part of their plans anymore.

My father-in-law's grandson, Rock's nephew, works for the energy department in a branch that controls the east coast and west coast power grids. Just got the job recently, but he's a computer genius. Rock says Derek's seen some of the coding and security for the grids, and it's sloppy, probably went to the lowest bidder. He thinks he can easily get in, but says it will take some time, maybe a couple of years, to get full security clearance. His grandfather been buying him every computer gadget that has come on the market since he was four years old. He can do anything with a computer. So, Rock says the plan is for Derek to work himself into a position where he can sabotage the east and west power grids. The eastern and the western parts of the country will be without power, but Texas will have power. Then the politicians from Texas will have the east coast and west coast at their mercy. 'Do what we say if you want us to turn your power back on.' Is what Rock says. They'll rejoice in other peoples' misery and their glory."

"Oh, my God," Sam says. "Maybe the brass at the military base in Virginia Beach will listen to me this time."

That evening Sam and Eli meet for dinner at a Mexican restaurant near Sam's house. Eli orders pan seared whole cauliflower topped with local farm eggs and mole verde. Sam orders a split avocado filled with zucchini, tomatoes, corn, onions, chipotle mole, and queso fresco on a bed of Spanish rice.

"These dishes are based on the regional cuisine of Oxaca, Mexico. I don't know where else you could find this kind of menu," Eli says.

"Oh, so good," Sam says.

As they walk back to Sam's house, Sam tells Eli about her client's story today but is careful not to reveal the client's identity.

"I waited until we finished dinner to tell you what I heard today. Didn't want to upset you," Sam says as she puts the key in the door.

Sitting on the brown leather sofa inside, Sam continues, "If their plan works to turn off the power grids on the east and west coasts, the country will be in chaos. Generators won't last long when propane tanks are emptied. No electricity means no refrigeration. Food will spoil. If it happens in winter, there will be no heat in cities, and in summer, no air conditioning. People will try to flee cities, but gas stations will be without electricity. Gas pumps won't work. Highways will be blocked by cars. It could be Armageddon like."

Hearing what Sam has described, Eli feels like a knife is twisting inside his belly. "That's scary. Lots of upsetting news today. A woman was seriously in-jured outside Winterford. An empty logging truck, for seemingly no reason at all, slammed on brakes in front of a woman's car. Her car went under the logging truck."

"That's awful. Does she have a family?" Sam asks.

"Yes, but fortunately neither her daughter nor her husband was with her. She's in intensive care here in Charlottesville."

"Were they members of your church?"

"Oh no, they wouldn't come to my church. Her father-in-law is that guy they call the 'Patriot' and ironically it was his company's logging truck that slammed on brakes. How crazy is that?"

Sam feels a cold chill sweep over her.

"What's wrong?" Eli asks.

"You can't tell anyone this, but that woman is my client. She's the one who's been telling me about the January 6 plans."

Both stunned and motionless, Eli steps forward and put his arms around Sam. He holds Sam for what seems like an eternity. They both search for words.

"Most people don't realize we face a very uncertain future in this country," Sam says.

"Sam, we have each other whatever happens."

"We do. Why don't you spend the night?"

"If not, I'll just go home and think about you all night . . . your hair, your skin, your eyes."

Change of Plans

May 8, 2021

Dogs bawl on the other side of the vineyard.

"You have dogs in the vineyard?" Eli asks.

"We sure do. That's how we keep deer, bear, and other animals out of the vineyard," the server says. "Sounds like they just chased something away."

"That's interesting," Sam says.

"Yeah, it's the best way the owner has found to protect the grapes. Dogs do a great job protecting their territory," the server says. "What would you like to go with your wine?"

"How about the cheese plate?" Sam says. "Want anything else, Eli?"

"Let's get the fruit as well."

"Cheese plate and fruit plate coming right out."

Sam and Eli sit at an outside table at a vineyard south of Harrisonburg, Virginia, and just off the Blue Ridge Parkway.

"This is one of my favorite vineyards," Eli says. "We can see thirty miles in almost any direction."

"A sitting on top of the world feeling, I love it," Sam gushes.

The server arrives with the cheese and fruit. "I'll keep an eye on you in case you need another bottle of wine."

Sam and Eli munch on the cheese and fruit and sip on the 2015 Cab Franc.

Eli takes Sam hand. "I've got a couple of things to tell you, and it's the good news and bad news kind of things."

"Oh?"

"Yeah, first the good news and the bad news is not so terribly bad. I saw my doctors this morning, and I am cancer free!"

Sam cries. Warm tears run down her cheeks. "That's wonderful and such a relief. I don't want to hear anything else, but I guess I must."

"I'm healthy, but my church is not."

"Is that the bad news?"

"Yes, I think I'll have to resign for the good of the congregation."

"I guess I sound callous, but I don't care. If you are cancer free, that's all that matters right now."

"Well, I care about those people, but that's why I am resigning. I was careful not to say anything political in the church because we have people all over the political spectrum, but some in the church who have never been crazy about me anyway found out that I spoke at the political forum in Charlottesville last month. I don't think this group of people has ever been happy with my skin color anyway, but this seems to be the final straw for them. I'll find another church. That should not be a problem."

"What did you say at the forum that got back to them? Too bad I was seeing clients that evening. I would have gone with you."

"The panel was several local government leaders and three clergy including myself. I just said what we are facing now is not 'political.' When we talk 'politics,' we're talking about issues and which politicians we like best because of how they feel about the issues. You know, higher taxes or lower taxes, or increased military spending or less? Those are political issues. But what we are facing now in this country is much more serious. People on the far right are pushing for major structural change in government. Changes that are not allowed in our constitution. We have some who want to move away from democracy and toward autocracy. Instead of our leaders being elected by the popular vote, they want state legislators to have the power to nullify election results and declare the winners. It is a fundamental change to how we govern ourselves and the potential loss of our democracy. And if they get their way, a few people will stay in power. What I said got back to some of the more conservative members of the congregation, and they're not happy."

"Maybe, they'll just leave the church?"

"I don't want the church to split up over me. If I resign, things will calm down, and they'll call another minister. It's something I should do, resign."

"Eli, I'm so sorry. I know you're hurting over this church stuff. But if you want me to, I'll go where you go. I can get a job anywhere with my degree and Army specialized trauma training. Heck, I've got a waiting list now."

"Of course, I would love you to go, but I hate upsetting your life too."

"It will be fine. I've been all over the place with the Army for training and assignments. Moving has become second nature, it seems. Wherever we end up, I want to do something like my great-grandmother did. She helped free slaves in this country. I'm thinking I might get involved in refugee re-settlement. Syrian or Ukrainian refugees, it doesn't matter."

"I want to be with you, Sam. I'm a lucky man."

"There are a few things I want to do first."

"What's that?"

"I want to make sure my contacts in the military understand the threat to our country with this power grid plot. And the soldiers on the mission with me that were never found. I want to go see their families. They are all on the east coast. That won't take long. And then I want to go to Scotland. I want to go to Campbeltown where my great-grandparents lived before they came to Virginia. And I would like for you to go with me."

"Oh wow, I'm in. Let's do it."

A New Future

August 12, 2021

United Airlines flight 974 nestles down on the runway at Edinburgh's Turn-house Terminal at three minutes after ten in the morning.

"This is probably not the best time to visit Scotland with the summer tourist crowds and all the baggage problems airlines are having, but I like your idea of not checking a bag," Eli says.

"I learned to pack simple in the Army. A couple of carry-on bags and I'm good. No more waiting for luggage," Sam says.

The couple make their way through the terminal.

"Rental cars are this way," Eli points to the right. "I'm glad you've had experience driving on the left side of the road. I'm afraid I'd forget and end up on the wrong side of the road."

"I rented a car when I was in Southampton for training. I drove to London and didn't have any problems. It's a concentration thing," Sam says.

"I'm glad you're driving," Eli says.

"I think we have time to see Edinburgh Castle today," Sam says.

"Sounds like fun," Eli says.

After the castle tour, Sam and Eli check in at Cheval Old Town Chambers, a historic hotel in Edinburgh Old Town.

"A bed. Feels so good," Eli sprawls across the king size bed.

"Don't get too comfortable . . . we have dinner reservations at Makers Gourmet Mash Bar," Sam says.

"I read the reviews. I can't do the traditional haggis with the sheep organs, but they have a vegetarian haggis with fresh vegetables," Eli says. "And Scottish whisky! They won't serve whisky here unless it is at least twelve years old."

"I'm looking forward to the Scottish cheddar cheese and chive mash as a side," Sam says.

After dinner, whisky, and a deep sleep, Eli splashes water on his face at the sink and tiredness slowly retreats from his face. Sam slips on a yellow poke-a-dot sundress that falls several inches above her knees. Eli wears tan pants and a light brown polo shirt. They head for their first stop on the way to Campbeltown, Lock Lomond, and Trossach's National Park.

After a couple of hours at the park, Sam says, "There's a lot more to see here, but we should get on the road to Campbeltown. We still have about two and one-half hours of driving. And I want to go by the Linda McCartney Memorial Garden. It's on Hall Street in Campbeltown."

Later that afternoon, Sam pulls the black Audi A3 Sportback into the parking lot of the Craigard House Hotel in Campbeltown, Scotland.

"Looks like a castle!" Sam says.

"And you can't beat the view! The water is so blue, and the hills on the other side as green as green gets. Maybe we should change our plans and stay longer than one night," Eli says.

That evening they enjoy dinner at Craigard House Hotel's own restaurant Lochside.

"Wow, this is not your regular fish and chips," Eli says. "This might be the best branzino I've ever had! The gournay cheese sauce with garlic just puts it over the top!"

"You must try my prawns. I think they're sauteed in the finest white wine and butter in Scotland! Heavenly good!" Sam says. "The menu says the prawns are from Sterlingshire. We'll have to go there!"

They both laugh.

At the hotel, they find a glass of fine scotch whiskey on each bedside table.

"Wow, that's a nice touch and very smooth whiskey," Eli says as he sips.

"You know, whisky makes me frisky," Sam teases.

"You can't be frisky with your clothes on," Eli counters with his face starting to heat.

"I can fix that!" Sam says.

Sam skin tingles as Eli kisses her neck.

The next morning, they enjoy the Scottish breakfast at Lochside.

"What time is church?" Eli asks.

"Eleven," Sam says. "I don't get anxious very often, but I'm a little nervous about visiting my great-grandfather's church."

The members of Campbeltown Kirk took good care of their church building over the years. The sanctuary now sits on a fortified foundation. The roof and siding were replaced numerous times over the decades. Modern plumbing and HVAC were added last century. An educational building and a church office now sit to the right of the sanctuary.

"Look at that!" Sam says as she points toward the educational building. "Refugee Relocation Center!"

Sam and Eli take the two steps that lead up to the sanctuary's tiny porch. Sam thinks about how many times her great-grandfather took those steps. Certificates of Presbytery and local church organization memberships hang on the walls. Clergy headshots line one wall. Sam looks hopeful to find her great-grandfather's picture, but the earliest headshot is from the 1930's.

A framed list of "Previous Pastors" catches her eye. She rapidly looks down the list. Several pastors down the list, she sees "Charles Rory Stuart, Pastor, 1847–1849."

"Well, we have visitors!" Sam and Eli turn to see Ross Ainsley behind them.

"Yes, we are visiting from the United States. I'm Samantha Stuart and this is my husband to be, Eli Hemings."

"Welcome to our little church!"

"I just found my great-grandfather's name on your list of previous pastors. Charles Rory Stuart, 1847–1849. In 1849, he went to Kilmarnock, Virginia, and became a pastor there. That's where I was born."

And turning to something that was really intriguing her, Sam says, "I see you have a refugee relocation center. I'm impressed!"

"Yes, we help find new homes for refugees from Ukraine, Syria, and other places. Some will be in the congregation this morning. We are looking for a new director, maybe someone with a background in trauma recovery. We can talk about that later. I can't wait to introduce you. Come on in the sanctuary. Sit up front if you will. It will make it easier for the congregation to see you when I introduce. By the way, my great-grandfather was a judge for this area about the same time your great-grandfather was here. I've done a lot of genealogical research on our family. Archibald Ainsley was his name. They called him the Sleeping Judge. Often, he couldn't stay awake during court."

Sam and Eli follow Ross Ainsley down the center aisle, and he directs them to sit on the right on the first pew.

Members of the congregation chatter. Hands shake. Warm glances exchanged. When Ross Ainsley ascends to the pulpit, conversations quickly conclude.

Ross Ainsley clears his throat. A baby continues to cry softly on the back pew. Another couple comes into the sanctuary and find seats near the back.

"Welcome to Campbeltown Kirk. A warm welcome to members and visitors. John Smith, I see your sister, Anne, is with us again. So good to have you.

Did I get a surprise a few minutes ago in the foyer! This young woman is a descendant of one of our pastors. Samantha, would you introduce yourself?"

"Of course. My great-grandfather, Charles Rory Stuart, was the pastor of this church from 1847 until 1849. He moved to Virginia where he was pastor of Kilmarnock Presbyterian Church until his untimely death in 1863. My great-grandmother, Samantha Logan, was from here as well. Her family had a tavern, Logan's Tavern. It must be gone . . . we could not find it when we drove around town. My great-grandmother was very instrumental in Virginia's part in the Underground Railroad that helped escaped slaves cross through Virginia to freedom in the north. I'm touched this church is still here. I still have chills running up and down my back after seeing my great-grandfather's name on that list. This is a very special day for me," Samantha sits.

"Samantha's husband-to-be is with her. I'm sorry I don't remember your name. Would you introduce yourself to the congregation?"

Eli stands and turns to face the congregation.

"I'm the Reverend Elijah Hemings. I'm a Presbyterian pastor and between churches. When we return to Virginia, I'll be looking for a new 'call.' That's what we call an invitation to become a pastor, 'a call.' So, you might say I'm between jobs."

Members of the congregation turn to look at each other. Eyebrows raise. Some nod their heads at each other as if to say, 'this is interesting!'

"Well, Reverend Hemings, this congregation is a member of the Gloucester Presbytery. So, we are Presbyterians as well. Our pastor died of a heart attack over a year ago, and we've been unsuccessfully looking for a pastor."

Ross Ainsley pauses for a moment, seemingly to make sure he should say this.

He looks first at Eli, then at Sam, and carefully says,

"Could the Lord have sent both of you to us?"

CPSIA information can be obtained
at www.ICGtesting.com
Printed in the USA
JSHW010739210623
43510JS00001B/3